THE
Second
MRS. BENNET

A Pride & Prejudice Variation

CATHERINE BILSON

Copyright © 2024 Shenanigans Press. All Rights Reserved.

This book and all its contents are protected by copyright law. No part of this publication may be reproduced, distributed, or transmitted in any form or by any means, including photocopying, recording, or other electronic or mechanical methods, without the prior written permission of the publisher, except in the case of brief quotations used in reviews or other non-commercial uses permitted by copyright law.

For permission requests, please contact:

Shenanigans Press

PO Box 323, MORAYFIELD QLD 4506 AUSTRALIA

Email: admin@shenaniganspress.com

Contents

1. Chapter One — 1
2. Chapter Two — 12
3. Chapter Three — 22
4. Chapter Four — 41
5. Chapter Five — 55
6. Chapter Six — 71
7. Chapter Seven — 83
8. Chapter Eight — 97
9. Chapter Nine — 113
10. Chapter Ten — 126
11. Chapter Eleven — 141
12. Chapter Twelve — 151

13.	Chapter Thirteen	165
14.	Chapter Fourteen	181
15.	Chapter Fifteen	198
16.	Chapter Sixteen	209
17.	Chapter Seventeen	220
18.	Chapter Eighteen	231
19.	Chapter Nineteen	246
20.	Chapter Twenty	257
21.	Chapter Twenty-One	271
22.	Chapter Twenty-Two	279
23.	Epilogue	288
24.	A Loss at Longbourn - sample chapter	293
	Also By Catherine Bilson	302

Chapter One

As a tranquil sunrise spread golden hues across the sky, the house of Longbourn awoke to a morning far removed from the chaos that had once been its daily custom. The song of birds served as a gentle reveille, replacing the shrill exhortations of Mrs. Bennet which had so often disturbed the peace. Indeed, a remarkable sense of harmony now reigned at Longbourn, and it owed much to the calm and capable presence of its new mistress, the second Mrs. Bennet; the former Charlotte Lucas.

"Good morning, Mrs. Hill," Charlotte greeted the housekeeper as she descended the stairs, her words accompanied by an encouraging smile. "I trust all is well?"

"Indeed, ma'am," replied Mrs. Hill, her eyes reflecting her gratitude for the orderliness that now characterised the household. "The staff have already begun their tasks, and the girls are preparing themselves for breakfast."

"Thank you, Mrs. Hill," said Charlotte, pleased with the report. She moved gracefully through the halls of Longbourn, observing the smooth functioning of the house with a quiet satisfaction. Gone were the days of uncertainty and disarray, replaced now by a sense of purpose and direction that could only be attributed to Charlotte's steady hand.

As she entered the dining room, Charlotte found herself immersed in the comforting sights and sounds of a family meal. Elizabeth and Jane shared a light-hearted exchange, while Kitty and Lydia engaged in animated chatter about their recent letters from friends. The absence of Mary, who was currently under the tutelage of the Gardiners in London, left a notable void at the table, yet the overall atmosphere remained congenial and amicable.

As she surveyed the scene before her, Charlotte felt a deep sense of purpose and fulfilment. The delicate balance between duty and desire had long been the subject of her contemplation, ever since she had agreed to marry Mr. Bennet after the passing of his first wife in childbed. Assuming the role of stepmother to his five daughters, Charlotte knew that her decision had been born from a genuine love for her new family, as well as from a keen sense of responsibility towards the welfare of Longbourn. And in this quiet moment of reflection, Charlotte could not help but feel that she was indeed fulfilling her destiny.

"Good morning, Stepmother," Elizabeth exclaimed, looking up with a warm smile. "You entered so quietly, I did not hear you! Come, have some of the toast before Lydia eats it all."

Lydia squawked indignantly, plucking a strawberry from her plate and flinging it at her sister. Elizabeth caught it deftly, but it was Charlotte who immediately stepped in.

"Lydia Bennet, we do not throw food in this house, and nor do we squawk like a chicken. Have you finished your breakfast? Then be off upstairs with you, and finish your packing. Your father wishes to leave within the hour to escort you and Kitty back to school after your holiday."

Lydia sighed, but she obediently murmured an apology to Elizabeth for throwing the strawberry – one which was immediately followed by an apology from Elizabeth for teasing her – and left the room, trailed by Kitty.

"I love them dearly, but there is no denying Longbourn will be a good deal quieter once they are gone back to school," Jane murmured, picking up her teacup for a sip.

"How pleasant it will be to be just us grown-up ladies here," Elizabeth agreed, with a warm smile at Charlotte.

Charlotte did not say anything, never liking to speak ill of any of her stepdaughters, but privately she agreed with Elizabeth. She loved Kitty and Lydia too, but the pair could be silly at times, especially when they got together with Charlotte's younger sister Maria. Certainly Charlotte thought it for the best that Kitty and Lydia would be safely away at school if the rumour Charlotte had heard just the previous day came to pass – that a militia regiment might quarter for the winter in Meryton. Keeping silly young girls away from redcoats was not particularly how Charlotte would like to spend the next few months.

It was a little past the appointed hour when the Bennet carriage departed, Kitty and Lydia hanging from the windows to wave their handkerchiefs until Longbourn was out of sight, while their father sighed and rolled his eyes with impatience at their silliness. He would spend a night or two in Oxford visiting old friends before returning, knowing Longbourn was safe in Charlotte's capable hands until then.

Elizabeth linked arms with Charlotte as they turned from waving their farewells to go back inside the house. "I am planning a long walk this morning, Stepmother. Shall you accompany me?"

"Thank you for the offer, Lizzy dear, but undoubtedly Kitty and Lydia will have left a dreadful mess in their room to sort out, and I will not leave it all to poor Hill." Charlotte kissed her cheek. "If you should happen to come home past Lucas Lodge, would you drop this receipt off for Mama?"

Elizabeth took the folded paper with a laugh. "Of course! Are there any other errands I may make myself useful about?"

"Not today. Enjoy your walk, dearest!" Charlotte watched as Elizabeth set off at a determined pace, heedless of the rising wind that whipped her dark curls about.

Jane was in the stillroom, Charlotte saw as she passed. The eldest Bennet daughter was fond of flowers and herbs, and liked to make soaps and lavender-water as well as a few simple herbal remedies. Charlotte encouraged Jane in the hobby; it was a useful skill for the mistress of a house and flowers unfortunately tended to make Charlotte sneeze if she spent too much time in close proximity to them.

Lydia and Kitty had indeed left a disastrous mess, with discarded clothes, ribands and knick-knacks strewn all around their room. With a fond sigh and a shake of her head, Charlotte set about bringing order to the room, much as she had spend the last ten years bringing order to Longbourn as a whole.

The first Mrs. Bennet's sad departure, even as she tried so desperately to give her husband a long-desired son, had thrown the household into utter disarray. Jane, at twelve, and Elizabeth at ten had tried as bravely as they might to pull the family together, but it was clear to all his acquaintance that Mr. Bennet needed a wife to give his daughters a mother, and soon. Lady Lucas and Mrs. Phillips had been in complete agreement on the matter, and when Lady Lucas' eye fell on her daughter Charlotte, just eighteen but so sensible, and so plain it was very possible she might never attract a suitor at all, it seemed an advantageous match indeed to promote.

Charlotte, for her part, had been quite happy to be placed before Thomas Bennet as a potential wife. Yes, he was almost twenty years her senior, but he was an intelligent, kindly gentleman – despite his occasional acerbic witticisms – and being mistress of a house such as Longbourn was far more than she ever might have dared dream for herself. She was not romantic, but Thomas was patient and gentle with her, and over the last few years she had come to love him deeply.

Her one regret was that she had never managed to give him a son either – had never conceived at all – but she would not permit that lack to blight her joy in her home and her family. Completing her self-appointed task, she looked about the now-tidy room with a satisfied smile.

On his return from Oxford two days later, Mr. Bennet stepped down from his carriage and into an immaculate Longbourn, blissfully quiet, his wife and two eldest daughters quietly occupied in the parlour. Elizabeth as usual had a book in her hand, and Charlotte and Jane both plied their needles industriously.

"What a charming scene to come home to," Thomas Bennet declared, and all three ladies looked up with welcoming smiles.

Charlotte has truly brought order to this estate, Mr. Bennet mused, his thoughts returning to his wife's passing and the chaos that had once reigned at Longbourn. The memory of Mrs. Bennet's shrill voice and incessant fretting seemed like a distant echo, replaced by the calm, organized demeanour of his new wife. Marrying for good looks was all very well – at least Fanny had given him daughters of remarkable beauty – but marrying a woman of good sense had been a far better decision.

Charlotte rose and came to his side, threading her arm through his and reaching up to kiss his cheek. "Welcome home, husband," she said warmly. "You are in good time for dinner."

"And it smells excellent," Thomas said, sniffing appreciatively. Roast lamb, unless his nose was much mistaken, and doubtless there would be mint sauce and roasted potatoes to go with it.

As mistress of his house, Charlotte was quite peerless in laying an excellent table, though how she managed to do it on less than half the money Fanny had always spent every month he could not fathom. His wife's frugal habits stood Longbourn in good stead, however; he had even been able to set a little more by for his daughters' dowries in the last few years, and though they would never be called well-dowered, he believed he would be able to manage a thousand pounds for each of them when the time came.

"Some letters came in the post for you this morning, Papa," Jane remarked, laying aside her needlework. "I placed them on your desk."

"Thank you, my dear. Well, I had best go wash this travel dirt off me. I would not want to delay our dinner. Not when it smells so good!"

After dinner, Thomas felt so comfortable and at ease with his wife and eldest daughters that he did not retire to his study, instead collecting his letters and sitting with them in the parlour, enjoying listening to the gentle flow of sensible female conversation. Recognising the handwriting on one letter, he sighed and left it until last, finally cracking the seal when he had no more excuse to delay.

"Hmph," he muttered, reading the ornately curlicued handwriting with some difficulty. "Still an idiot, then."

"Of whom do you speak, Papa?" Elizabeth asked, with a laugh in her voice.

"Our cousin, my dear." Thomas glanced across at Charlotte. It had been her idea, a few years ago, for Thomas to reach out to his cousin and heir and try to mend the breach between them. As in many other matters, she had been quite right. The fear that his wife and daughters would be turned out of Longbourn had eased considerably once Thomas began correspondence with William Collins. The man was silly, but not vicious, and he would not hold the old grudge of his father against Thomas and his daughters.

"Collins has taken his orders finally, and is lucky enough to be the recipient of a living already. In Kent, apparently, some place called Hunsford." Thomas read the letter again. "He sings the praises of the lady who awarded him the living, a Lady Catherine de Bourgh."

"I cannot think much of her," Charlotte murmured, plying her needle. "For what woman of sense would award a man of Mr. Collins' abilities a valuable living?"

All of them laughed, though kind-hearted Jane shook her head. Neither she nor Elizabeth had actually met Mr. Collins; both had been spending the winter in London with their Gardiner relations two years prior when Mr. Collins had paid his one and only visit to Longbourn. They had heard quite enough of his silliness and obsequious manner to believe the lack of his acquaintance no particular loss, however.

The following morning brought visitors to Longbourn, regular ones. Charlotte's mother Lady Lucas had made it her habit to call in at least twice a week, usually accompanied by her younger daughter, Maria. Over the years the visits had changed from Lady Lucas poking about and offering her advice, to the ladies sitting in the parlour, drinking tea, and indulging in a little gentle gossip, while the younger girls giggled abovestairs.

With Kitty and Lydia absent, Maria was perforce obliged to sit down in the parlour with the others. She sighed and looked bored, sitting by the window to look out. Jane took pity on her and went to sit beside her, talking quietly to her while the older ladies gossiped.

Today, Lady Lucas had a particularly interesting piece of gossip to impart. "What do you think I heard yesterday!" she exclaimed once she was settled in a comfortable chair with tea in hand and a plate of delicate cakes at her elbow. "Mrs. Phillips heard it first from the grocer, and then the butcher confirmed he had an order too!"

"An order for what, Lady Lucas?" Elizabeth asked curiously.

"Why, for Netherfield Park! It is let again, at last!"

"Goodness," Charlotte said mildly, giving her tea a delicate stir before setting down her spoon. "Another party of gentlemen coming to use it as a hunting box? What has it been, four years? But since we did not see hide nor hair of them in society last time, I cannot think it will matter this time either."

"This time will be different," Lady Lucas said smugly, obviously pleased to be imparting new information. "The house has been let by a gentleman, name of Bingley, and his sister is coming with him to keep house, and they are bringing a large party of guests, so I am told. They have certainly sent down enough baggage! Five carts passed Lucas Lodge this morning on the lane to Netherfield!"

"A gentleman and his sister," Charlotte mused, interest obviously piqued. "Not a wife? I wonder how old he is?"

"Hopefully of an age to be of interest. Quite wealthy, I suspect. He must be, to be letting Netherfield." Lady Lucas offered a knowing smile. "Could be a good thing for one of your girls, Charlotte."

"How so?" Elizabeth asked with a laugh.

"To marry one of you, of course." Charlotte placidly sipped her tea.

"Stepmother!" Elizabeth stared at her, plainly shocked.

"Elizabeth. Dearest. This is our home, and we all love it dearly, but even you must admit there is a tragic dearth of eligible young men in this neighbourhood. Your father and I were only persuaded to part with you and Jane to stay with your Gardiner relatives in London in the hopes of widening your social circle and perhaps finding some eligible suitors." Charlotte shook her head. "And despite both of you being admired everywhere you go, and that one young man writing Jane some very pretty poetry, not one suitor has ever come up to scratch."

Elizabeth opened her mouth, seeming about to deny Charlotte's words, but then she hesitated, glancing across to where Jane sat beside Maria at the window.

"Jane is two and twenty," Charlotte said gently. "More than of an age to be wed and have a family of her own. While neither your father nor I would ever press any of you to accept a gentlemen we did not feel was worthy of you, nor one that you did not whole-heartedly wish to marry, we would like to see at least some of you well-settled, now that you are of age."

"And the mistress of Netherfield would certainly be well-settled!" Lady Lucas trilled, reaching for the plate of cakes. "I shall have Sir William call as soon as I hear the new tenants are arrived, and you must encourage Mr. Bennet to do likewise, my dear. For as everyone knows, a gentleman in possession of a good fortune must be in want of a wife, and who better than one of your girls?"

Chapter Two

A FEW DAYS LATER Mr. Bennet was sitting in his study, a half-read book open in his lap, when Charlotte entered. Her keen eyes took in his relaxed posture and the empty teacup on the side table.

"Enjoying your solitude as always, I see," she said, laughter lending a lilt to her voice as she joined him by the hearth.

Mr. Bennet's eyes crinkled with amusement. "You know me too well, my dear."

Charlotte's expression grew thoughtful. "Have you had occasion to call on our new neighbours at Netherfield Park yet?"

"Call upon them?" A teasing light entered Mr. Bennet's eyes. "Whyever should I do that?"

"Ah, come, Thomas!" She tapped him on the knee reprovingly. "You must know I am thinking of Jane and Lizzy. If Mr. Bingley is indeed as young and handsome - and rich - as Mama has told me, he would be a fine match for one of them."

"Ah, but he might like you best, if he should chance to meet you, for you are as handsome as any of my girls."

Charlotte's expression softened. She knew that was not in the least true - she did not compare even to Mary, the plainest of the sisters - but she loved her husband for saying it, just the same.

"As it happens, I paid a visit to Netherfield just this morning," Mr. Bennet remarked, marking his place in the book with a ribbon.

Charlotte leaned forward eagerly. "And what did you make of the party? Any gentlemen of merit?"

"I had the pleasure of Mr. Bingley's acquaintance today. He seems a fine young man - amiable, genteel, and clearly able to support a wife in comfort."

Charlotte nodded approvingly. "High praise coming from you. Do you think he might suit one of the girls?"

Mr. Bennet stroked his chin. "Perhaps. Though he struck me as rather too obliging. Our Lizzy would walk all over such a man, I daresay, but sweet tempered Jane may be just the thing for him."

"We must wait until we meet him at the assembly to know for certain," Charlotte concluded sensibly. "But I am glad to hear you approve of the gentleman so far."

Mr. Bennet chuckled. "My dear Charlotte, you missed your calling. You would have made an excellent matchmaker."

Charlotte smiled archly. "I only want what is best for our family."

"I know you do."

"And what of Mr. Bingley's party?" Charlotte pressed. "His sisters? Any other gentlemen we should take note of?"

Mr. Bennet waved a hand dismissively. "I'm afraid I didn't have the pleasure. Bingley was alone when I called."

Charlotte's face fell slightly. She had hoped to gather as much intelligence as possible about the Netherfield party before their introduction at the assembly. Their fortunes and characters were still a mystery.

"Well," she mused, "I suppose we shall have to reserve judgement until we meet them in person."

"Quite right, my dear," Mr. Bennet agreed. "And I daresay they will be reserving their judgements about us as well."

Charlotte nodded. "Then we must be on our very best behaviour. I will make sure the girls understand how important it is that we make a good impression."

Mr. Bennet chuckled. "What a good thing we sent Kitty and Lydia off to school, eh? Else they should doubtless be making a spectacle of themselves."

Charlotte sighed. Mr. Bennet was unfortunately right about that. But she was determined to do all she could to secure prosperous futures for as many of the Bennet daughters as possible. The assembly ball would be a good beginning, and getting at least one of the girls advantageously married could secure the futures of all the rest. There was time yet for Kitty and Lydia to grow up and learn some sense.

"Jane and Lizzy will be admired by all," she said resolutely. "Now, I must go speak with Hill about the girls' gowns."

The Assembly Rooms in Meryton were abuzz with anticipation as the Bennet sisters entered on the evening of the assembly. Charlotte had ensured their gowns were freshly pressed, their slippers polished, and their hair styled in the latest fashions. Jane and Elizabeth were undoubtedly the most handsome young ladies in the room, and certainly did not lack for partners, even if none of the young men who asked were what Charlotte would consider eligible.

When the Netherfield party arrived, Charlotte noted Mr. Bingley's immediate attraction to Jane. His eyes lit up as they were introduced and he quickly secured her hand for the next two dances. Jane's cheeks were prettily flushed as she gracefully moved through the steps with Mr. Bingley, the two stealing admiring glances when they came together.

Mr. Bingley's friend Mr. Darcy stood aloof, his countenance severe as his gaze swept disdainfully over the room. Mr. Bingley's sisters, Miss Bingley and Mrs. Hurst, appeared just as displeased with the company, though more socially adept, entering into conversations and dancing with great technical skill, if little flair.

Charlotte kept a watchful eye on Jane and Mr. Bingley as they danced a second time, noting how he leaned in intently whenever Jane spoke. It was clear he was utterly captivated by Jane's beauty and sweet nature.

When the dance ended, Charlotte gently steered Jane to a quiet corner of the room, handing her a glass of lemonade.

"He seems quite taken with you," Charlotte said in a low voice.

Jane blushed. "Oh, he is just being friendly, I am sure."

"My dear, he has hardly taken his eyes off you all evening," Charlotte pressed.

Jane bit her lip, a shy smile spreading across her face. "He is very amiable. And quite handsome."

"Indeed," said Charlotte. "But take care, we know little of him yet. Do not set your heart too firmly until we are sure of his character."

Jane nodded seriously. "Of course. It is too soon to know what his intentions are."

Charlotte squeezed her hand. "Enjoy it, but cautiously, my dear. Now, you may not dance with him again tonight, lest you tempt gossip to circulate, but if he should care to take a turn with

THE SECOND MRS. BENNET

you about the room, and indeed accompany you to supper, that would be quite acceptable."

"Yes, Stepmother," Jane said with an obedient nod. Her eyes were bright as she turned her head, and Charlotte observed at once that Mr. Bingley, even though ostensibly engaged in conversation with his friend Mr. Darcy, had never taken his eyes from Jane.

Elizabeth stood near Bingley and his friend, speaking to Charlotte's mother, and Charlotte wondered what had happened when she saw Elizabeth stiffen, and turn first pale, then flush pink. Elizabeth then put her hand to her lips and began to giggle, and Lady Lucas looked about her in consternation.

Charlotte made her way across the room quickly, catching Elizabeth's elbow. "What happened?" she asked in a low voice, but Elizabeth was giggling too hard to answer her. It was Lady Lucas who spoke.

"Well, I hardly know how to tell you, Charlotte. Mr. Bingley's tall friend, Mr. Darcy, seems to think himself very above the company. Dear Mr. Bingley was trying to encourage his friend to dance, pointing out how lovely the ladies of Meryton are, and encouraged Mr. Darcy to ask our Lizzy to dance."

Elizabeth's shoulders were shaking. Charlotte spared her a concerned glance before looking back at her mother. "And?"

"He said... he said... oh I cannot say it, Charlotte, it was quite dreadful!" Lady Lucas fanned herself.

Elizabeth gained control over herself and spoke, lowering her voice in an attempt to mimic Mr. Darcy's haughty tones. "He said I was *tolerable, I suppose, but not handsome enough to tempt me.*" Her voice broke on the last words and she began to laugh again, covering her mouth with her gloved hand.

Charlotte gaped for a moment before recollecting herself. "He... well, my goodness." Angry on Elizabeth's behalf, she looked across at the gentleman, only to find him watching them. "Well, perhaps he is determined to think himself above the company. Still." She took a deep breath. "Do not let Mr. Darcy's ill-mannered remarks wound you, Lizzy. First impressions are often misleading. There may be more to him than his proud exterior would suggest."

Elizabeth shook her head. "I very much doubt that, Stepmother. The man is insufferable." She seemed amused rather than hurt, which was a balm to Charlotte's mind.

Charlotte patted Elizabeth's hand. "Just promise me you will not judge too hastily. Keep an open mind, and observe his character further before deciding. *He* may have judged *us* quickly, but let us not be so hasty."

Elizabeth sighed. "Very well, for you I will try. But I confess, it will be difficult."

The young lady had heard him. There could be no other explanation for her laughter and the looks she was giving him, as she conversed with the two other ladies. Darcy felt an absolute fool, especially as he hadn't meant a word of it. The younger Bennet girl was quite beautiful, not perhaps so striking as her older sister, but the way her eyes sparkled as she genteelly concealed her laughter behind her gloved hand was really quite enchanting. He could hardly look away, and was already castigating himself for a fool. All he'd wanted was Bingley to stop badgering him to dance, but he was rethinking his stance on that now, staring at the beautiful young woman who clearly thought him a rude buffoon.

Just then, Caroline Bingley sidled up to Mr. Darcy. "Well! I had thought you were being overly pessimistic about this assembly, Mr. Darcy, but after an hour here I am quite in agreement. What a ghastly, provincial affair." She sneered as she looked about her, her gaze alighting on Elizabeth Bennet. "And these Bennet girls who are acclaimed as the beauties of the county! The eldest is pretty enough, I suppose, with that golden hair, but Eliza Bennet? Nothing out of the ordinary. And her manners are decidedly countrified."

Caroline cast her eye critically over Elizabeth's simple gown. "And her dress! She clearly has no taste or fashion." Fingering the gold-encrusted jewels at her throat, Caroline shook her head in a pitying gesture, though Darcy was quite sure she felt no such emotion. "Is that cross around her neck *silver*? On a *ribbon*? What a cheap little bauble, though I daresay she has no better."

Darcy made no reply. He was beginning to feel quite thoroughly ashamed of himself, and was debating asking Bingley to introduce him to Miss Elizabeth Bennet after all. At that moment, however, the music ceased and the supper bell rang, and Caroline Bingley latched onto his arm.

"Come, Mr. Darcy, let us go see what victuals are deemed adequate to serve at an assembly such as this." The scorn in her voice made him flinch.

"I have no doubt we will be able to find something to our liking," he murmured.

"Oh, you are too generous, Mr. Darcy! I am merely glad that I thought to instruct the servants to have tea and cake ready for us on our return to Netherfield!"

"Well, Jane seems to have made quite the impression on Mr. Bingley," Mr. Bennet said slyly to Charlotte, as he handed her up into the carriage for their return to Longbourn.

Charlotte smiled. "So it would appear. But let us not jump to conclusions just yet. There is still much to learn of Mr. Bingley's situation and character before determining if he would make Jane a suitable husband."

Mr. Bennet chuckled. "Quite right, my dear. We mustn't get ahead of ourselves." He climbed up and seated himself beside Charlotte.

Elizabeth lingered behind, gazing up at the starry night sky. It had been an evening full of new acquaintances and conflicting first impressions. Yet she had a hopeful feeling that good things lay ahead for them all. Linking arms with Jane, she joined her family in the carriage, her weariness overtaken by pleasant thoughts of the new friendships blossoming in their little village.

Chapter Three

THE SUN WAS LOW in the sky, casting long shadows upon the cobblestone streets of Meryton as the militia arrived with grand fanfare. Elizabeth stood by the window in Mrs. Phillips' apartment, observing the bustling scene, her thoughts a mixture of curiosity and wariness. The red-coated officers rode on horseback, accompanied by the steady drumbeat of marching soldiers. Excited chatter filled the air, with the townspeople gathering to welcome the newcomers.

"My father is holding a party for the officers tomorrow night," Charlotte said, joining Elizabeth at the window. "We must attend, of course, to welcome them to Meryton."

"Indeed," Elizabeth replied, watching as Sir William Lucas waved his hat enthusiastically. "It seems our quiet village has transformed into quite the spectacle."

"Surely you must be excited, Lizzy?" Maria Lucas exclaimed, her eyes wide with excitement. "Such handsome young men in uniform!"

Elizabeth raised an eyebrow at the younger girl, wondering if she would maintain the same ardour when confronted with the reality of young men seeking entertainment rather than commitment. She turned her gaze back to the crowd below, feeling an inexplicable unease settle within her.

"Let us bear in mind that their presence here is primarily for our safety, not our amusement," Charlotte reminded her sister, attempting to dampen Maria's enthusiasm.

"Indeed," murmured Elizabeth, grateful for her stepmother's level-headedness.

Lucas Lodge was a lively scene of music, laughter, and dancing. The officers seemed to revel in the attention they received from the townsfolk, their boisterous energy filling the room. Their bright red uniforms added a touch of vibrancy to the scene, but their presence did little to impress the three Bennet ladies.

"Though their company is lively," remarked Charlotte, "it is prudent for us to remember that it is highly unlikely a militia officer would have the necessary income to support a wife. We must be cautious not to let our hearts be swayed by mere appearances."

"Indeed, Stepmother," Jane replied with a gentle smile. "We must always be mindful of the true measure of a person, beyond mere surface charm."

Elizabeth nodded her agreement, her gaze drifting across the room to where Mr. Darcy stood aloof, watching the revelry. *His* appearance certainly belied his character, she thought with a little smile. A handsome face hiding a petty spirit!

As the music began, Mr. Bingley approached Jane, a radiant grin upon his face. "Miss Bennet," he said, extending his hand, "might I have the honour of this dance?"

"Of course, Mr. Bingley," Jane responded, accepting his hand with a delicate blush rising to her cheeks. As they proceeded to join the other couples, Elizabeth could not help but observe the way Mr. Bingley's gaze lingered on Jane, his enchantment with her evident in every glance and touch. It was clear that he was more enamoured of her than ever.

"Look at them, Lizzy," whispered Charlotte, leaning closer to her stepdaughter. "Mr. Bingley does seem completely taken with Jane."

Elizabeth smiled, her heart swelling with happiness for her sister. "Jane deserves all the love and joy that Mr. Bingley can offer."

"Indeed," agreed Charlotte, "but we must not forget your own prospects either, my dear. As we have discussed, the militia officers may not be suitable, but there are other gentlemen present who could make worthy matches." She glanced meaningfully towards Mr. Darcy, who stood on the opposite side of the room, his gaze fixed on Elizabeth. "He has not taken his eyes off you since arriving, I believe."

"Oh, Stepmother, no." Elizabeth let out a small laugh. "I am not handsome enough to tempt him, remember?"

"Do you not recall that conversation we had about first impressions, and how one should not rely on them, or be too quick to judge? Unless I miss my guess, Mr. Darcy has rethought his first impression of you." Charlotte nudged her lightly and laughed. "Do not be too hasty, my dear. Ten thousand a year and a grand estate in Derbyshire deserve the benefit of your consideration, at least."

"I am more inclined to measure a man by his character than the size of his fortune," Elizabeth said, striving to match Charlotte's light tone.

"And I should never tell you not to, but only caution you to take the time to make it out properly. Something you shall never do if you do not get to know him."

Too late, Elizabeth observed Sir William Lucas approaching, Mr. Darcy at his side. Charlotte was welcoming their approach with a smile and a nod.

"Dear Elizabeth," Sir William boomed jovially. "I cannot help but notice that you have not danced with our dear Mr. Darcy yet. He has expressed a desire to dance, and I thought to present you as a most suitable partner. What do you say?"

Elizabeth smiled, even while her mind worked frantically, trying to think of a way she could gracefully decline. "Why, Sir

William, I say that I am not accustomed to being asked to dance by proxy," she said lightly.

Sir William boomed a laugh, Charlotte sighed, and Mr. Darcy's already stiff posture seemed to grow even more rigid.

"Miss Elizabeth, may I have the pleasure of this dance?" Darcy clipped out.

Left with no escape, Elizabeth curtsied. "Thank you," she murmured distantly, only hoping that the dance should be a short one. Or even that Mr. Darcy might prove to be an interesting conversationalist, but it was not to be; he barely spoke until she provoked him, and then seemed more interested in provoking her in return than anything else.

When the apparently interminable dance finally ended, she curtsied to him and quickly retreated to Charlotte's side, feeling flustered and off-balance.

"Stepmother," she whispered urgently, her heart still racing from the encounter, "I cannot believe I was obliged to dance with Mr. Darcy."

"Indeed, Lizzy," Charlotte replied, her voice laced with amusement. "But do not let a bad beginning prejudice you against an extremely wealthy and influential man. Be pragmatic."

"Perhaps," Elizabeth admitted, her lips pursing in thought. "But I cannot help but feel that your pragmatism clouds your judgement when it comes to matters of the heart."

"Pragmatism has made me a very happy woman, Lizzy," Charlotte remarked gently, and Elizabeth was forced to concede the point.

Elizabeth was ten when her mother passed trying to bring a son into the world, and she well remembered Fanny Bennet's histrionic temper and silly ways. Charlotte's calmness and sensible manner had been like a breath of fresh air to Longbourn, and it had not taken long for Elizabeth to realise that Charlotte made her father far happier than ever his first wife had, even though his first marriage had ostensibly been for love and his second for practicality.

Perhaps Jane, at least, might have both, Elizabeth thought as she watched her sister dance with Mr. Bingley, Jane's angelic face aglow with happiness as she smiled at her partner. *But for both of us to fall in love with wealthy men seems so far-fetched! I shall have to settle for being an aunt to all of Jane's children, and teach them to play the piano very ill.*

Elizabeth laughed to herself at the thought, unaware of how her merriment enhanced her beauty and the sparkle in her dark eyes.

Mr. Darcy noticed.

And Charlotte noticed him noticing, and turned away, a smug smile on her lips she would not let Elizabeth see, lest her stepdaughter wanted to know what she found so entertaining.

A few days later, Elizabeth found herself seated in the parlour, her needlework lying forgotten in her lap as she listened to her father read aloud a letter he had just received. Mr. Bennet looked up at his wife and daughters with an expression that was a curious mixture of amusement and exasperation.

"Ah, my dear Mr. Bennet," he began, adopting the pompous tone of their cousin, Mr. Collins. "I write to inform you of my intention to visit Longbourn in the coming weeks. My esteemed patroness, Lady Catherine de Bourgh, has impressed upon me the necessity of a respectable clergyman to have a helpmeet in life. It is my fervent hope that I shall be able to make the acquaintance of your estimable daughters, and perhaps even find among them a suitable wife."

"Mr. Collins?" Elizabeth asked, her eyebrows raised in surprise. "Why ever would he wish to marry one of us?"

"Lady Catherine has told him to," Mr. Bennet replied dryly. "She seems to think Mr. Collins should make amends for the circumstances of the entail by marrying one of you."

"How ridiculous," declared Elizabeth, her eyes flashing with annoyance. "And to declare his intention to come among us and select one of us... as though choosing between different hats in a shop!"

"Indeed, Lizzy," agreed Charlotte, who had been listening quietly from her place near the window. "I believe I know how best to proceed. Mr. Bennet, it would be most prudent for you to fetch Mary from the Gardiners' residence in London. She is, I believe, the most suitable match for our cousin."

"Mary?" Elizabeth repeated incredulously, glancing over at Charlotte. "But she is hardly acquainted with him – more so than Jane and I, I admit, but she had little to say about him after they met."

"True," Charlotte conceded, her voice calm and pragmatic as ever. "However, as a clergyman, a lady of learning and piety would be the most suitable wife for Mr. Collins - qualities which Mary possesses in abundance. Moreover, she has been in London long enough to have acquired a certain polish and refinement that may serve to recommend her to our cousin."

"Very well," Mr. Bennet acquiesced, laying the letter aside and rising from his seat. "I shall make arrangements to travel to London and bring Mary back with me. Heaven knows what sort of wife she will make for that pompous fool, if she should choose to accept him, but at least we shall have done our best to accommodate his wishes."

"Indeed," Elizabeth murmured, her thoughts troubled as she contemplated the prospect of her sister being married to a man such as Mr. Collins. It seemed a cruel twist of fate that the very qualities which had always marked Mary as something of an oddity in their family should now be the means by which she might secure a husband - albeit one whose character left much to be desired.

"Take heart, Lizzy," Charlotte advised, noticing her stepdaughter's disquiet. "This may yet prove to be a fortuitous arrangement for all concerned. Mary has remarked more than once that she might like to be the wife of a clergyman. With one all but offering himself up on a platter, we would be foolish to refuse him before even giving them the opportunity to see if they should suit."

"True," Elizabeth conceded, though she could not shake the nagging sense of unease that had settled upon her. "We must simply trust that Mary will find a way to manage him - or, failing that, at least ensure that he does not make too great a nuisance of himself."

"Indeed," Charlotte agreed, her eyes twinkling with suppressed humour. "And who knows? Perhaps this union will serve to remind us all that there is more to life than wealth and influence. After all, even the most obsequious suitor cannot hope to compensate for a lack of genuine affection. Your father and I will not press Mary to accept him if she does not wish it, that I promise you."

Mr. Bennet nodded in firm agreement with his wife, and with those promises, Elizabeth had to be content.

Mr. Bennet's carriage had only just rattled out of sight, on his way to London to collect Mary, when a messenger arrived from Netherfield.

"Miss Bingley invites me to dinner," Jane murmured, reading over the message before passing it to Charlotte.

"Oh, the gentlemen are to dine with the officers. What a pity." Charlotte smiled slightly. "I see they did not include you in the invitation, Lizzy."

"Not that I should want to go," Elizabeth remarked dryly. "Miss Bingley and I have made poor impressions on each other thus far, I think. No, evidently they want to get to know Jane better, since their brother is obviously quite in love with her."

Jane blushed, and Elizabeth and Charlotte both laughed gently at her.

"Should you like to go, Jane?" Charlotte asked. "With your father having taken the carriage, and not back until tomorrow evening, you have a perfectly good excuse if you would like to decline."

"No, it is too kind of Miss Bingley to invite me to decline for such a reason! I should like to go," Jane said stoutly. "I shall ride Nellie."

"Very well, dear. But if the weather does turn – those clouds look suspiciously grey – I have no doubt the Bingleys will offer to send you back in their carriage," Charlotte said firmly. "It may feel like an imposition, but you must accept, for to insist upon staying the night would be a great deal more so."

"Oh, indeed!" Jane cried. "Thank you, Stepmother. I shall make you proud, I promise."

"You never do anything else, dearest Jane," Charlotte said, kissing her cheek. "I'll tell John to have Nellie saddled for you."

The sun shone weakly through the clouds, casting a pale, watery light upon the damp earth as Elizabeth Bennet gazed pensively out of the window. A restless urgency filled her chest, making it difficult to concentrate on anything but the news that had just arrived at Longbourn: Jane, caught in the rain during her ride to Netherfield the previous day, had fallen ill and was now confined to her bed at Mr. Bingley's estate.

"Dearest Lizzy," her hand trembled as she read aloud, "please do not be alarmed, but I find myself quite unwell this morning. I fear the damp air has taken its toll on me, and it is deemed best by both Miss Bingley and Mrs. Hurst that I remain here until I recover."

"Jane should never have gone!" Elizabeth exclaimed, crumpling the note in her fist. "How could we allow her to venture forth in such weather? And with the carriage away, no less!"

"Indeed," Charlotte agreed, her brow furrowed in concern. "It was a most unfortunate circumstance that the rain began much earlier than we expected; poor Jane must have been caught in it on her ride. However, we must make haste and see to her well-being."

"Quite right," Elizabeth said, determination lighting her eyes. "I shall walk to Netherfield at once and attend to my sister."

"Allow me to accompany you part of the way," Charlotte offered. "I must call in at Lucas Lodge to see my mother today."

"Thank you, Stepmother," Elizabeth replied gratefully. "Your company will be most welcome."

As they set out on their journey, the lingering moisture from the previous day's rain clung to the grass beneath their feet, leaving a trail of damp footprints in their wake. Elizabeth's heart pounded with worry for her sister, each step bringing her closer to Netherfield and the unknown state of Jane's health.

"Stepmother," she said, her voice tight with concern, "what if Jane's condition is worse than we feared? What if this illness should cause some lasting harm?"

"Take heart, Lizzy," Charlotte reassured her. "Jane is strong and will recover soon enough. In the meantime, it is our duty to care for her and ensure that she wants for nothing. Send to Longbourn if there is anything you need, and I will see it sent over at once, I will be home in an hour or two."

"Indeed," Elizabeth murmured, though her mind remained clouded with unease as she left Charlotte behind and strode onwards.

The imposing façade of Netherfield loomed before Elizabeth as she approached, her heart beating faster with a mixture of trepidation and urgency. Servants bustled about the grounds, attending to their numerous tasks, and the house seemed to hum with activity. With a deep breath, she ascended the broad steps and rapped on the massive door.

"Miss Bennet," said the butler, his voice coolly formal as he admitted her, "Miss Bingley is receiving this morning."

"Thank you," Elizabeth replied, her eyes darting around the opulent entrance hall as she followed him to the drawing room. The splendour of Netherfield did little to ease her anxiety; if anything, it served only to amplify her sense of unease.

"Ah, Miss Eliza," drawled Miss Bingley upon her arrival, her tone dripping with disdain, "how very... devoted you are, to walk all this way to tend to your sister."

"Indeed, Miss Bingley, I am here to ascertain Jane's well-being for myself," retorted Elizabeth, struggling to maintain her composure in the face of such blatant indifference. "I hope she is resting comfortably, at the very least."

"Of course," Miss Bingley replied dismissively, waving a hand as though the matter were of no real consequence. "She is abed, and the physician has been sent for. Do make yourself at home, Miss Eliza, although I must say, your attire is rather damp."

At Miss Bingley's pointed observation, Elizabeth glanced down at her sodden dress, acutely aware of the muddy hem and damp tendrils of hair clinging to her brow. She flushed with embarrassment, suddenly conscious of her dishevelled appearance.

"Your concern for your sister is commendable, Miss Bennet," came Mr. Darcy's deep voice, startling her. His dark eyes met hers, and she detected a glimmer of something akin to admiration in their depths.

"Thank you, Mr. Darcy," Elizabeth replied hesitantly, her pulse quickening at his unexpected praise. "I would do anything for Jane."

"Indeed," he said, his gaze never leaving her face. "If there is any assistance I might offer, please do not hesitate to ask."

"Your kindness is most unexpected, sir," Elizabeth stammered, taken aback by his offer. "I shall keep it in mind."

"Very well," he nodded, before taking his leave with a quiet determination that left her feeling both bewildered and strangely reassured.

As Elizabeth hastened to her sister's side, she could not help but puzzle over Mr. Darcy's sudden change in demeanour, nor could she shake the feeling that she had just glimpsed a hidden facet of his character that few were ever privy to. Her heart swelled with gratitude, even as her thoughts remained clouded by concern for her dear Jane.

The mellow morning light streamed through the windows, casting a warm glow upon the room where Elizabeth sat by Jane's bedside. Her fingers deftly smoothed the damp cloth across her sister's forehead, her heart swelling with affection and concern as she watched the rise and fall of Jane's chest.

"Excuse me, miss," a maid said from the doorway. "Mrs. Bennet and Miss Mary are here."

"Stepmother!" Elizabeth exclaimed, rising from her seat as Charlotte entered the room with Mary in tow. "Mary, you have returned! How glad I am to see you both."

"Elizabeth, we were most anxious to learn how Jane fares," Charlotte said, her brow furrowing with worry as she took in Jane's flushed features.

"Not well at all, I fear. The doctor has been, but he says she is a good deal too ill to be moved. She was quite feverish in the night." Elizabeth herself had slept little, sitting by Jane's bedside, trying to comfort her sister as she tossed restlessly, or coax a few sips of soothing tea between Jane's cracked lips.

"Poor Jane." Charlotte touched Jane's hot brow, shaking her head. "Well, I daresay I shall have to go and speak to Miss Bingley and see if she is willing to extend Netherfield's hospitality to Jane a while longer. And you, Lizzy? I know you well enough to be sure you will not leave Jane until she is better."

"Indeed I will not."

"Would you like me to stay with you?" Charlotte offered.

Elizabeth hesitated, glancing at Mary, who had spoken scarcely a word since greeting her. Mary looked well, dressed in a more flattering gown than her usual dull brown attire, with her hair prettily arranged. "No. You should be at Longbourn, preparing for our guest." Preparing Mary for her potential suitor, she meant, and Charlotte nodded, understanding the unspoken message.

"You are very capable to take care of Jane, dearest, but if you need me, send at once."

"I will," Elizabeth promised, knowing Charlotte would come, in the middle of the night if need be. "Jane is resting quietly for the moment; come, let us go downstairs and inform Miss Bingley that we must impose on her a while longer. And introduce Mary to everyone, of course."

"Oh, I... I could stay here with Jane," Mary offered quickly, clearly not delighted with the idea of meeting a group of strangers, but Charlotte shook her head to deny the request.

"Time you met our neighbours, Mary," Charlotte said quietly, and though Mary sighed, she also bowed her head in resignation.

"You look very well, Mary," Elizabeth said, linking her arm through Mary's as they made their way downstairs. "How did you find our uncle and aunt Gardiner?"

"They are so kind." A smile broke across Mary's face. "And our dear little cousins! Anna was forever begging me for another music lesson."

"How familiar that sounds," a deep voice said as they reached the bottom of the stairs, and both girls started to see Mr. Darcy emerging from a passageway. He made them a polite bow. "I do beg your pardon, I did not mean to startle you. It was only that what you said sounded so familiar... for the last few years, I have been constantly hearing my sister Georgiana beg me for more music lessons!"

Elizabeth gave him a pert smile. "And you have indulged her, Mr. Darcy? Certainly, according to Miss Bingley's accounts of Miss Darcy's accomplishments, you must have."

He bowed in response, eyes flicking to Mary, and Elizabeth felt her cheeks flush. "Mr. Darcy, please allow me to present my sister Mary, who is lately returned from visiting some relatives in London. Mary, this is Mr. Darcy of Pemberley, in Derbyshire."

"And how is your other sister, Miss Bennet?" Mr. Darcy inquired once the formalities were observed. Genuine concern etched his features.

"We are just about to speak to Miss Bingley about Jane, sir," Charlotte said. "Perhaps you would care to come into the drawing room with us and hear what Lizzy has to say about Jane's condition?"

"I would be honoured, Mrs. Bennet." Mr. Darcy made her a little bow, and indeed followed them into the drawing room. A little puzzled, Elizabeth watched him from the corner of her eye as Charlotte greeted the gathered Bingleys and Hursts and presented Mary to them.

"Another Bennet!" Caroline Bingley let out a false little trill of laughter. "Gracious. However many are there of you?"

"I have two more daughters, Miss Bingley, but they are too young to be Out in society and are presently away at school in Oxford," Charlotte replied equably.

"Well." Caroline seemed to be trying to think of something to critique in that statement. She settled for a little toss of her head instead. "And how does the eldest of your multitude of daughters do?" From the tone of her voice it was evident she did not care in the slightest how Jane was, and Elizabeth gritted her teeth.

"Jane is not well at all, I am afraid," Elizabeth said. "Doctor Jones has said that she is too ill to be moved at present."

"Miss Elizabeth," Bingley interjected, stepping forward from his position near the door. "Please do not trouble yourself on that account. I insist that your sister remains here at Netherfield until she has fully recovered. You have my word that she shall receive the utmost care and attention."

"Thank you, Mr. Bingley," Charlotte said, her tone and expression genteel and grateful, while Elizabeth nodded in earnest agreement. "Your kindness is much appreciated."

With their concerns momentarily assuaged, Charlotte and Mary took their leave. Turning back from the front door after seeing them off, Elizabeth's keen ears caught the sound of raised voices coming from the drawing-room.

"Goodness," Caroline Bingley's voice dripped with disdain, "I must confess that I find it rather tiresome to have our home turned into an infirmary."

"It will be an infirmary for as long as Miss Bennet needs it!" Mr. Bingley's voice was emphatic.

"Mr. Darcy, surely you must agree that there is nothing worse than undesired houseguests," Caroline said plaintively, obviously seeking an ally. "Especially ones with relations in *trade*."

"Miss Bingley," Mr. Darcy responded, his voice firm, yet calm. "I believe that the bond between sisters is something to be admired – the devotion and concern that Miss Elizabeth shows for her sister is a testament to the strength of their relationship, as is the fondness of Mrs. Bennet and Miss Mary. I only wish my own sister was blessed with such loving sisters." He paused a moment before adding, "And if I had objections to those with relatives engaged in trade, I would never have befriended your brother."

Caroline's retort died upon her lips, unable to withstand the weight of Mr. Darcy's words. Elizabeth, who had been listening in silent astonishment, felt a mixture of gratitude and confusion wash over her. Mr. Darcy's praise of herself and her family, and his setdown of Miss Bingley, was wholly unexpected, and yet it warmed her heart, even as she struggled to understand his motives.

Elizabeth stood by the window in Netherfield's library, her thoughts lingering on Mr. Darcy's praise of her family as she watched Mr. Darcy and Mr. Bingley riding their horses away from the house. It was a notion she could scarcely comprehend – that he, who had once looked upon them with disdain, should now speak highly of their bonds, even as Caroline Bingley sought to denigrate them.

"Miss Eliza," a voice called from behind her, and she turned to find Caroline Bingley entering the room. The woman's mouth was pursed in disapproval, an expression she seemed to wear whenever she looked at Elizabeth. "I must say, I am surprised you would abandon your sister's side for even a moment. Surely, you cannot think it proper to leave her unattended?"

Elizabeth smiled serenely, her composure unwavering. "Your concern is touching, Miss Bingley, but I assure you, Jane is presently resting, and I have been advised to take a brief respite, lest I become ill myself. We would not wish to trespass upon your generous hospitality any longer than need be."

Caroline Bingley's eyes narrowed. "Indeed," she said after a moment of fraught silence, but even she would not be so rude as to tell Elizabeth to her face that moment could not come too soon. Instead, she turned on her heel and swished out of the room, leaving Elizabeth alone to browse the meagre selection of books Netherfield's library had to offer.

Chapter Four

A FEW DAYS LATER, with Jane fully recovered, Mr. Bingley reluctantly conceded that they had best go home, and placed his carriage at their disposal, bidding farewell to Jane with his heart in his eyes. Elizabeth forebore to tease her sister, however. Jane's wistful longing was all too evident as she gazed back at Netherfield until the carriage took them beyond its view.

Upon their arrival home at Longbourn, the warmth of the hearth and the welcome of their family enveloped them. Charlotte received them with open arms and an affectionate smile, while Mr. Bennet peered over his spectacles with a playful quirk of his lips.

"It is a relief to see you returned in better health, Jane," Charlotte said, her concern evident in her eyes as she regarded her eldest stepdaughter.

"Yes, indeed," Mr. Bennet added, closing the book in his hands with a soft thud. "Our home has been rather too quiet without the pair of you."

The sisters settled happily into the parlour, sharing tales of their stay at Netherfield. Elizabeth could sense Charlotte's sharp eyes on her whenever she spoke of Mr. Darcy, and she had to admit that her first impressions of him might indeed have been wrong; he had been solicitous of Jane's comfort, attentive to Elizabeth herself, and even defended their family against Miss Bingley's sharp barbs.

As the dinner hour approached, the rattle of wheels could be heard outside, and Elizabeth looked at Charlotte.

"Today is the expected day of Mr. Collins' arrival," Charlotte answered the unspoken question with a quick glance at Mary, who began to smooth her skirt with an unexpected care for her appearance.

Elizabeth's interest, momentarily diverted from the account of the recent sojourn at Netherfield, now sharpened with curiosity at the prospect of meeting their cousin.

Mr. Bennet rose, gesturing to his daughters with a mix of resignation and mild amusement. "Let us greet our guest then," he said. "No doubt he is eager to make the acquaintance of his cousins."

Jane, Elizabeth, and Mary lined up beside their father as the door opened to admit Mr. Collins. Their graceful curtsies were met with his overly deep bow, which he executed with a flourish that bordered on the theatrical.

"Mr. Collins," Mr. Bennet greeted his cousin with a weary formality.

"What a pleasure it is to be welcomed to Longbourn once more, sir," Mr. Collins gushed, wringing his hands together.

Elizabeth took in her cousin with amused distaste; a tall, heavy-set young man in clergyman's black, he somehow appeared equally arrogant and obsequious, looking up at Longbourn's façade with a possessive air while simultaneously almost grovelling to her father. *Exactly the fool he appeared from his letters, I see.*

"Mr. Collins, welcome again to Longbourn," Charlotte greeted him with calm grace. "You remember our dear Mary, I trust. And these are our eldest daughters who were away from home on your last visit, Jane and Elizabeth."

"Ah, indeed, Mrs. Bennet," Mr. Collins replied, his eyes swiftly appraising the new faces before him. A gleam of appreciation flickered in his gaze as he beheld Jane's golden beauty and Elizabeth's lively eyes. Mary, who received but a cursory glance, shuffled her feet slightly, feeling the sting of being overlooked despite her efforts to put on a pretty gown and curl her hair.

"Such pleasure it brings me to meet the daughters of the house," Mr. Collins said, his voice taking on a tone of heightened interest. "I have heard much about the beauty and accomplishments of Miss Jane and Miss Elizabeth Bennet. I must confess that my curiosity has been most eager to verify these claims for myself. The accounts of your charms, it seems, were most understated!"

"Then we are equally curious, sir," Elizabeth replied with a playful smile, "to discover if your own reputation for wit and eloquence holds true as well."

"Ah, Miss Elizabeth," Mr. Collins chuckled, seemingly pleased by her remark, "I see that you possess not only beauty but also a keen and lively mind."

As the conversation unfolded, Elizabeth observed Mr. Collins with a mixture of amusement and bemusement, noting his overblown compliments and pondering what his visit might portend for the future of Longbourn and its inhabitants.

The parlour at Longbourn shimmered with the soft glow of candlelight, casting a warm and inviting atmosphere upon the assembled group. Mr. Collins, still basking in the admiration he believed he had inspired in his fair cousins, could hardly contain his delight.

"Ah, Mr. Collins," said Charlotte, gently drawing him aside after dinner as she sensed that Mr. Collins' attention was becoming too fixed on Jane, "I must inform you that our dear Miss Bennet has attracted the notice of a most eligible bachelor. Mr. Charles Bingley, a gentleman of considerable fortune, has shown great interest in her."

"Indeed!" exclaimed Mr. Collins, his eyebrows lifting in surprise. "Why, this is most gratifying news, Mrs. Bennet! Nothing could give me greater pleasure than to see my lovely cousins suitably matched."

"Mr. Bingley's attentions have been most assiduous," continued Charlotte, her voice tinged with just the right note of pride. "And I am sure you will agree that a gentleman of his standing would be an excellent match for our Jane."

"Undoubtedly," agreed Mr. Collins, his gaze shifting from Jane to Elizabeth, who was just then laughing at something her father was reading from his book. "And what of Miss Elizabeth? Does she too have a suitor?"

"Elizabeth has many admirers, as you may well imagine," said Charlotte, seizing the opportunity to redirect Mr. Collins' focus. "But, in knowing that part of your purpose of this visit is to consider one of Longbourn's daughters as a possible helpmeet for yourself, I would be remiss if I did not use my superior knowledge of my daughters to assist in your selection. Mary has just returned from a stay with her aunt and uncle in London, where she has been refining her accomplishments. I believe you will find her an engaging conversationalist, particularly on matters of moral improvement."

"Ah, Miss Mary," Mr. Collins said, turning his attention to the youngest of the three sisters present. His mouth turned down at the corners as he considered her, sitting in a shadow as she happened to be at that moment. Her thin, pointed face, mud-brown hair and glasses did not make her appear to advantage beside Jane's ethereal golden beauty and Elizabeth's vibrant dark looks.

"Mary has indeed previously espoused happiness at the thought of being a clergyman's wife," Charlotte said confidingly.

"Hm." Mr. Collins looked more thoughtful at that remark. "Miss Mary," he said, moving away from Charlotte. "Is that *Fordyce's Sermons* I spy on the table beside you?"

"It is, sir!" Mary started, catching the book up in her hand eagerly.

Mr. Collins smiled and took the seat beside Mary.

As the conversation between Mr. Collins and Mary unfolded, Elizabeth observed Charlotte's subtle machinations with a mixture of admiration and concern. She knew that her clever stepmother had only the best intentions for them all, but she could not help but wonder if Mr. Collins' attentions would prove a blessing or a burden for Mary.

"Stepmother," she whispered softly to her stepmother as they stood together at the edge of the room, "I cannot help but feel some apprehension about the direction of this evening's events. Mary is still only eighteen... perhaps too young to be married. Too young to know her own mind. You are serving her up to Mr. Collins on a platter!"

"Dearest Lizzy," replied Charlotte, "do not let your fears cloud your judgment. Your father and I will not press Mary into anything in haste."

"I know," Elizabeth accepted, her thoughts still troubled. "But I fear we may be meddling in affairs beyond our control."

"Trust in my judgment, dear one," said Charlotte, placing a comforting hand on Elizabeth's arm. "All shall be well, provided we proceed with care and discretion. Your father and I want what is best for all of you."

Elizabeth believed Charlotte meant what she said. However, she was also keenly aware that despite being married to her father for a decade, Charlotte had also failed to provide him with the son and heir needed to ensure the Bennets would remain at Longbourn after Mr. Bennet's demise. The entail meant that with no son, Mr. Collins would inherit Longbourn, and Charlotte and any remaining unmarried Bennet daughters would be entirely at Mr. Collins' mercy. If one of the sisters married Mr. Collins, however, Charlotte could be sure that their affection would see her always secure in her home.

Self-interest must be playing a part in Charlotte's decision making, Elizabeth considered as she watched Mary take a seat at the pianoforte. Elizabeth winced internally, hoping Mary did not intend to sing; while Mary's playing was adequate, her voice was thin and reedy, and she had difficulty holding to a tune.

Fortunately, Mary selected some music without a vocal accompaniment, and made a good showing of herself. Elizabeth could not help but notice, however, that Mr. Collins' attention did not fix on Mary for long during her performance; their cousin's gaze rested most often on Elizabeth, making her feel quite uncomfortable. Whether or not Mary wished to marry Mr. Collins, Elizabeth already knew that she herself quite definitively could never be happy as the wife of such a man.

Beneath the soft glow of candlelight, Jane Bennet stood quietly by the window, her gaze fixed on the tableau unfolding before her. Mr. Collins' earnest attempts to engage with Elizabeth and Mary were met by a mixture of subtle amusement from Elizabeth and poorly-concealed eagerness from Mary. Elizabeth's glance of appeal prompted Jane to intervene, and she moved across to request her sister's assistance on a trifling matter with her handiwork, leaving Mary as the exclusive focus of Mr. Collins' attention.

"Dear Lizzy," Jane said softly as she and Elizabeth retreated to the far side of the room, "I cannot help but be grateful that Mr. Collins seems to have chosen not to bestow his attentions upon me. I think I would find it rather disconcerting to be the object of such... persistent admiration."

"Indeed, dear sister," Elizabeth replied, her eyes sparkling with mirth, "you must count yourself fortunate to be spared such an experience. Mary is quite welcome to it."

As the sisters exchanged knowing glances, Charlotte approached them, her countenance calm and purposeful. She took Jane's hand and gave it a reassuring squeeze.

"See," she whispered, "though Mr. Collins at first showed little interest in Mary, he is certainly responding to her interest in him."

This was undeniable, and both Jane and Elizabeth nodded, watching Mr. Collins leaning in closer to Mary with interest as Mary talked, animation upon her subject brightening her eyes.

"None of us are unaware of Mr. Bingley's notice of you, Jane. It would be wise, I believe, to reciprocate his interest openly. A man of such fine character and fortune is not to be trifled with, after all," Charlotte said quietly. "I have planned a small dinner party, to celebrate your cousin's arrival to the neighbourhood, and of course the Netherfield party are invited. Welcoming Mr. Bingley into our home is an ideal opportunity to show him how you feel."

Jane's cheeks flushed with a delicate pink, and her heart fluttered in response to Charlotte's words. Though she had certainly noticed Mr. Bingley's growing affection, her innate reserve held her back from embracing the prospect of a courtship too eagerly.

"Thank you for your counsel, Stepmother," Jane murmured. "I shall endeavour to bear your advice in mind."

"Remember, my dear," Charlotte added gently, releasing Jane's hand, "that it is of the utmost importance to give a gentleman reason to believe his affections are not in vain. It is a delicate balance to manage while maintaining every appearance of propriety, but one that must be attempted for the sake of securing a suitable match."

As Charlotte withdrew with a nod and a smile, Jane's thoughts raced with conflicting emotions. On one hand, she was flattered by Mr. Bingley's attentions and found his company delightful; on the other, she hesitated to outstep the bounds of propriety and risk appearing forward.

"Let your heart guide you, dear sister," Elizabeth encouraged her, sensing her inner turmoil. "And remember, it is only natural to feel some degree of uncertainty when faced with matters of love and courtship. Trust yourself, and all will be well."

Taking a deep breath, Jane resolved to heed the words of both her stepmother and sister. She would walk the line between reserve and openness, allowing her true feelings for Mr. Bingley to shine through while retaining the modesty that defined her character. Despite her shyness at the thought of allowing Mr. Bingley to see her heart in such a way, her spirits rose at the thought of discovering the depth of their mutual affection.

The sun dipped below the horizon, casting a warm golden glow across Longbourn as final preparations were made for the intimate gathering Charlotte had planned for the evening. The fragrance of fresh flowers filled the air, and the sound of laughter mingled with strains of music drifting from within. Elizabeth stood in the parlour, surveying the scene and marvelling at Charlotte's ability to create such an elegant atmosphere. As the guests began to arrive, she noticed Jane standing off to the side, her gaze distant and thoughtful.

"Jane," Elizabeth said softly, approaching her sister, "I can see that you are still troubled by our conversation with Stepmama. Remember, it is only natural to have doubts and fears when faced with matters of the heart."

Jane smiled weakly, her eyes filled with gratitude for her sister's understanding. "Thank you, Lizzy. I shall try my best to trust my instincts and follow my heart, as you advised."

"Good," Elizabeth replied, her eyes twinkling. "Now, let us enjoy the evening and the company of those we hold dear."

As the evening progressed, the intimate gathering proved to be just what everyone needed. The few senior officers Charlotte had invited regaled the company with tales of their military prowess, while the Lucases engaged in lively discussions about the latest news from London. The Netherfield party shared stories of their travels and experiences, eliciting laughter and delight from the assembled guests.

Charlotte, ever attentive to the needs of her guests, kept a watchful eye on Jane throughout the evening. She noted with pleasure that Jane appeared to become more at ease as she conversed with Mr. Bingley, his genuine affection for her evident in every word and gesture.

"Jane seems to be faring well tonight, do you not think?" Charlotte remarked to Elizabeth, who nodded in agreement.

"Indeed," Elizabeth replied. "Your advice to her has not gone unheeded, and I believe she is beginning to trust herself more in matters of the heart."

"Let us hope that she and Mr. Bingley find their way to each other, for they are well-suited indeed," Charlotte said with a warm smile.

The candles flickered softly, casting a warm glow over the elegant assembly at Longbourn. Charlotte had outdone herself with the arrangements, and even Caroline Bingley, ever eager to find fault, could find little to complain about as the guests rose from the dinner table.

"Your home is quite delightful, Mrs. Bennet," she offered, attempting to sound gracious. "You have made it most... comfortable."

"Thank you, Miss Bingley," Charlotte replied, her eyes sparkling with satisfaction. "We are pleased to welcome you all here this evening."

As Mary sat down at the pianoforte and the music began, Mr. Darcy approached Elizabeth with a mixture of determination and trepidation. "Miss Bennet," he said, bowing slightly, "might I request the honour of this dance?"

Elizabeth hesitated for a moment, recalling their previous encounter on the dance floor, but she found herself willing to give him another chance. "Very well, Mr. Darcy," she replied, accepting his proffered hand. "I shall be happy to oblige."

As they moved gracefully through the steps of the dance, Elizabeth was surprised to find herself enjoying the experience far more than she had anticipated. The stiffness and formality that had characterized their earlier interactions seemed to have given way to a newfound ease and understanding.

A burst of laughter rang through the room as Jane, her cheeks flushed with pleasure, twirled around the floor in Mr. Bingley's arms. The warmth in his eyes was unmistakable, and for once, Jane allowed herself to bask in it unreservedly. She glanced over at Elizabeth, who was apparently laughing at something Mr. Darcy had just said to her, and the weight of uncertainty that had hitherto clouded Jane's thoughts began to dissipate.

"Your sister has a most charming laugh, Miss Bennet," Mr. Bingley observed, his own laughter mingling with hers. "One can scarcely help but be drawn to it."

"Indeed, her laughter is contagious," Jane agreed, emboldened by the genuine affection she saw reflected in Mr. Bingley's eyes. "I have always found such joy in her company, especially during trying times."

"Then we are alike in that respect," he replied warmly, pressing her hand ever so slightly. "For I, too, find your presence most enjoyable."

The sincerity in his words stirred something deep within Jane's chest, and she hesitated for a moment before responding. "Might I confess something, Mr. Bingley?" she asked, her voice soft and tentative.

"Please do," he encouraged, his eyes never leaving hers.

"Your companionship has become very dear to me," she admitted, quaking a little with trepidation at her own daring. "I find myself looking forward to our meetings with great anticipation."

"Miss Bennet," Mr. Bingley breathed, the corners of his mouth curling into a tender smile, "I must tell you that your confession fills me with joy, for my sentiments towards you echo your own."

"Truly, Mr. Bingley?" Jane's eyes widened with surprise and delight.

"Indeed," he assured her, his expression earnest. "I have found my thoughts occupied with you more often than not, and I cannot imagine a greater happiness than to secure your affections."

"Then, sir," Jane replied, her voice trembling with emotion as her hesitations melted away, "you have succeeded in that endeavour, for I am certain in my regard for you."

As they continued to dance, their conversation flowing effortlessly between them, Jane felt the last remnants of her uncertainty vanish like mist before the sun. In Mr. Bingley's arms, she had found a partner who valued her kindness and gentle nature as much as her beauty. And with the support of Elizabeth and Charlotte, she had learned to trust her own instincts and open her heart to love.

Chapter Five

THE AUTUMN SUN CAST warm, dappled light on the quaint streets of Meryton as Elizabeth Bennet walked with her sisters Jane and Mary, accompanied by their cousin Mr. Collins. The air was crisp, the leaves crunching beneath their feet as they strolled, the conversation between the sisters flowing with ease while Mr. Collins spoke at length about the many virtues of his esteemed patroness, Lady Catherine de Bourgh.

"Ah, my dear nieces," Mrs. Phillips exclaimed, suddenly appearing before them with a mischievous glint in her eyes. She took Elizabeth's arm with an excited grip. "I must acquaint you with a most charming young gentleman newly arrived in town."

"Indeed, aunt?" Elizabeth replied, raising an eyebrow and exchanging a quick glance with Jane. They had grown accustomed to their aunt's penchant for introducing them to any vaguely eligible bachelor who crossed her path.

"Indeed! Allow me to present Lieutenant Wickham," Mrs. Phillips continued, beckoning the newcomer forward.

As Wickham approached, Elizabeth noted his handsome countenance and the confidence with which he carried himself. He bowed gracefully to the sisters, his dark eyes twinkling with warmth.

"Miss Bennet, Miss Elizabeth, Miss Mary, I have heard much of your family and am pleased to finally meet you," he said in a smooth, melodic voice.

"Thank you, sir," Jane replied, a blush gracing her cheeks, while Mary offered a shy smile.

Mr. Collins, momentarily silenced by the arrival of such an imposing and personable gentleman, cleared his throat and extended his hand. "And I am Mr. Collins, their cousin and humble servant."

"Ah, Mr. Collins," Wickham replied, shaking his hand firmly. "It is a pleasure to meet you as well."

As they continued their walk through the streets, Elizabeth observed Wickham's easy manners and lively conversation. What little she knew of militia officers did not give her much hope for any deeper connection, but she could not deny the pleasure of his company, or that he had a truly handsome face and noble bearing.

"Come now, Miss Elizabeth," Wickham said, teasingly, as they discussed a recent novel. "Surely you cannot be so merciless in your judgement of the heroine's folly?"

"Perhaps I am too harsh," she conceded with a laugh, "but only because I recognise some of her faults in myself."

"Ah, but self-awareness is the first step towards improvement," he replied, a sparkle in his eyes. "And I must say, it is a rare quality among the fairer sex."

"Indeed, sir," Elizabeth retorted playfully, "and might I add that it is an even rarer quality among gentlemen?"

Wickham laughed heartily, clearly enjoying their spirited exchange. "Your sister Jane, she is truly a vision," Wickham remarked, casting a glance towards Jane who was engaged in conversation with Collins. "I must confess, I have seldom seen such beauty."

"Indeed," Elizabeth agreed. "Jane's beauty is matched only by her kindness and grace."

"Ah, but it is not only Miss Bennet who possesses such qualities," Wickham said, turning his gaze back to Elizabeth.

She felt a slight blush rise to her cheeks, unaccustomed as she was to such direct compliments. Though she appreciated his praise, she could not help but feel a pang of regret at the knowledge that a militia officer's income would likely prove insufficient to support the life of a gentleman's wife. She knew she ought not to entertain thoughts of matrimony with a man she had only just met, but there was something about Wickham's presence that made it difficult to quell such notions entirely.

"Thank you, sir," she replied, attempting to keep her tone light and unaffected. "It is fortunate, then, that my sisters and I are blessed with different strengths, for it would be most tiresome if we were all alike."

"Indeed," Wickham agreed, chuckling softly. "Variety is the very spice of life, as they say. And yet, I cannot help but think that your family has been blessed with an abundance of beauty and talent."

"Your flattery is most kind, Lieutenant Wickham," Elizabeth replied, a teasing smile playing at the corners of her lips. "But I must warn you, excessive praise will not endear you to my father; he values humility above all else in his daughters."

"Then rest assured, Miss Elizabeth, that my admiration is sincere, and not intended to pander to any vanity," Wickham said earnestly, his gaze locked on hers. "I believe it is important to acknowledge and appreciate the virtues of others, particularly when they are so clearly evident."

As they continued their walk, Elizabeth glanced up from her conversation with Lieutenant Wickham to find Mr. Darcy and Mr. Bingley approaching. Her pulse quickened at the sight of Darcy's tall figure, and she observed his expression change as he caught sight of Wickham. Mr. Darcy turned first pale, then red, and the shock and disquiet that flickered across his features were not lost on Elizabeth. Was Mr. Darcy somehow acquainted with Mr. Wickham, then? She speculated that perhaps they knew each other from some previous encounter – but what could have transpired between them to cause such a reaction in Mr. Darcy?

"Miss Bennet!" called Mr. Bingley, his cheerful countenance a welcome contrast to Darcy's brooding visage. "What a pleasant surprise to find you here. May I accompany you on your walk?" His tone conveyed an unmistakable sense of urgency as he glanced at Wickham, and Elizabeth suspected it was born of his desire to separate Jane from the handsome militia officer.

"Of course, Mr. Bingley," Jane replied, her cheeks suffused with a delicate blush as she accepted his proffered arm, her already happy smile widening further.

"Wickham," Darcy said stiffly, not even bothering to incline his head in greeting.

"Mr. Darcy. Fancy seeing you here." A smirk crossed Wickham's face, rendering him a good deal less handsome in Elizabeth's eyes.

Darcy's jaw clenched, but he didn't say another word. Just stared at Wickham until the other man's smirk faded and he dropped his gaze.

"If you'll excuse me, Miss Elizabeth." Wickham turned to her and offered his charming smile. "I must get to my duties. Until we meet again."

Elizabeth watched him go, pondering the enigma of his connection to Mr. Darcy.

"Miss Elizabeth," Darcy said softly, startling her from her reverie. He offered her his arm, his face betraying none of the conflicting emotions that raged within him. "Might I have the pleasure of accompanying you?" He nodded towards where Jane and Mr. Bingley were proceeding up the street, Mary and Mr. Collins following after them.

"Thank you, Mr. Darcy," Elizabeth replied hesitantly, placing her hand upon his arm. Her gaze lingered for a moment on the retreating form of Wickham before turning back to meet Darcy's eyes.

Inwardly, Darcy steeled himself against the barrage of questions he knew Elizabeth must be longing to ask.

"Your sister and Mr. Bingley appear to be enjoying their walk," Darcy remarked, hoping to divert her attention from the subject of Wickham. "And it seems Mr. Collins is quite taken with Miss Mary."

"Indeed," Elizabeth murmured, glancing ahead to where Jane and Bingley walked arm in arm, their conversation flowing easily. Behind them, Mary and Mr. Collins engaged in a more solemn discourse, the latter no doubt expounding at length upon some moral or religious topic.

"Mr. Darcy," Elizabeth began, her tone tentative, "I could not help but notice your reaction upon seeing Lieutenant Wickham. You appeared... troubled."

Darcy's jaw tightened. "I was merely surprised to see him in Meryton, Miss Bennet," he replied, his voice carefully controlled. "We have been acquainted since we were children; Mr. Wickham's father was a most excellent man, steward to my own late father. However, I had not expected our paths to cross here."

"Ah, I see," Elizabeth said thoughtfully, her eyes searching his face for any hint of the truth that lay behind his words. "I trust your surprise was not an unpleasant one, Mr. Darcy?"

"I confess I rarely find surprises to be pleasant, Miss Bennet," he replied, avoiding a direct answer. "But I have learned over the years that life has a way of confounding our expectations."

"Indeed, it does," she agreed.

Darcy half expected Elizabeth to question him further, but she did not speak, walking onward calmly with a peaceful expression on her lovely face. Darcy found himself struggling with an internal turmoil. While he desperately wished to rid Elizabeth and her sisters of Wickham's poisonous presence, he knew that divulging the full extent of the man's misdeeds could expose his beloved sister Georgiana to public disgrace.

"Miss Elizabeth," he began hesitantly, offering only a fraction of the truth in hopes that it would suffice. "I feel it is my duty to inform you that Mr. Wickham's character is not as it appears. Though I hesitate to speak ill of anyone, I fear for your family's wellbeing if I remain silent."

Elizabeth looked at him with an inquisitive expression, prompting Darcy to continue. "Wickham is the son of Pemberley's former steward, a most excellent man, greatly valued by my own esteemed father. George Wickham and I grew up together, but unfortunately, his nature proved... wild, as he matured."

"Wild, Mr. Darcy?" she asked, curiosity piqued. "In what manner do you mean?"

Darcy hesitated, weighing the potential harm of sharing more information against the need to protect those he cared for. "He grew careless with his friendships and associations, often disregarding the consequences of his actions. He has a penchant for creating discord and heartache in his wake, not to mention leaving significant debts whenever he departs a neighbourhood."

"Indeed?" Elizabeth raised a sceptical eyebrow, her keen mind already attempting to piece together the puzzle before her. "And why, pray tell, should this concern us? What bearing does Mr. Wickham's past have on our present acquaintance?"

"My father," Darcy began hesitantly, "held Wickham in high regard and, despite his wayward nature, sought to provide for him. He intended to leave him a living in the church—a respectable position that would have afforded him a comfortable life."

"Yet Mr. Wickham is not a clergyman?" Elizabeth inquired, her brow furrowed in confusion.

"Indeed not," Darcy confirmed, his voice tinged with regret. "Wickham declined the offer, demanding money instead after my father's passing. I obliged, since I knew his character was not fit to be a clergyman. I granted him a significant sum—enough to establish himself in any profession he chose, including purchasing a commission in the regulars."

Elizabeth's eyes widened at this revelation. "And yet," she mused aloud, "he has joined the militia rather than the regulars. Why would he do so if he had the means to secure a more advantageous position?"

"Miss Bennet, I fear that Wickham has already squandered the money," Darcy admitted, his countenance grave. "A militia position, though poorly paid in comparison to how he could be living, provides him with the opportunity to maintain appearances without revealing the extent of his financial ruin. I cannot fathom why a man with thousands of pounds to his name – the thousands I gave him – would take such a position; thus I can only conclude he no longer has the money. And knowing his bad habits, I can well believe it."

As they walked on, Elizabeth mulled over Darcy's words, struggling to reconcile the image of the charming officer with whom they had recently made acquaintance, and the irresponsible man described by the gentleman at her side. She stole a glance at Darcy, noting the concern etched upon his face, and could not help but feel a sense of gratitude for his revelations.

"Mr. Darcy, I am obliged to you for sharing this information with me," she said earnestly. "You have provided much to consider, and I assure you that your warning will not be disregarded."

"Thank you, Miss Bennet," Darcy replied, relief evident in his voice. As they continued their stroll through the picturesque streets of Meryton, he could only hope that his cautionary tale would be enough to protect Elizabeth and her family from the charming, yet dangerous, Mr. Wickham.

Wickham stood at a distance, keenly observing the unfolding scene as Elizabeth and Darcy walked arm in arm along the bustling streets of Meryton. He could not make out their words, but the intensity of their conversation was unmistakable. Wickham felt a pang of unease, imagining that the truth of his past might be revealed to the object of his newfound interest.

"Curse you, Darcy," he muttered under his breath, his gaze locked on the pair. "Why are you here, of all places?"

As Elizabeth and Darcy continued to converse, Wickham's thoughts raced. He knew he had to act quickly, lest his carefully crafted façade crumble before he had the chance to ingratiate himself with the people of Meryton. Watching Elizabeth's retreating form as she walked away with Darcy, Elizabeth looked radiant, her smile lighting her face. Wickham was not blind to her beauty, but more importantly, he noticed how Darcy's gaze lingered upon her, his usually stern expression softening ever so slightly.

"Mr. Denny," Wickham murmured to his fellow officer, nodding discreetly in the direction of the receding couple. "Do you not think that Mr. Darcy appears quite taken with Miss Elizabeth Bennet?"

"Ah, yes," Denny sighed. "Every officer in the militia has tried his luck with the Bennet girls, but they are too genteel to do more than accept a single dance every now and then. A shame, for they are exceptionally beautiful. Mr. Darcy is lucky enough to be rich enough to be of interest to them!"

"Indeed," Wickham concurred, his thoughts racing with newfound determination. While he could not deny the allure of the Bennet sisters, it was the opportunity to antagonize Darcy that truly quickened his pulse. Wickham considered and discarded several different strategies, his thoughts filled with schemes to thwart Darcy's interest in Elizabeth. Perhaps he'd begin that very evening, for her silly aunt had invited him to supper, and promised her nieces would be present.

It was easy enough to sidle up alongside Elizabeth Bennet in her aunt's parlour that evening, though he had to glare away a couple of other officers hopeful of catching a few moments with the beauty.

"Miss Elizabeth," Wickham began, his voice smooth and charming, "I find myself compelled to speak with you on a matter most pressing."

Elizabeth raised an eyebrow at him. "Indeed? What matter could be so pressing that it requires my immediate attention?"

"Forgive me for my forwardness, but I believe it is my duty to warn you about someone whose intentions may not be as honourable as they appear," Wickham replied, lowering his voice conspiratorially.

"Ah," Elizabeth said, her lips curling into a knowing smile. "You speak of Mr. Darcy, do you not?"

Wickham hesitated, surprised by her perceptiveness. "Yes, Miss Elizabeth. It seems you are already aware of the gentleman's... reputation."

"Your concern is duly noted, Lieutenant," she replied, her tone laced with scepticism. "However, I am not inclined to judge a person solely based on hearsay. I prefer to form my own opinions."

"Of course, Miss Elizabeth, and rightly so," Wickham said, attempting to hide his frustration behind a congenial smile. "But please, allow me to share some insight from our shared history. Perhaps then, you will understand the depth of my concern."

"Very well," Elizabeth relented, folding her arms across her chest. "Proceed."

As Wickham regaled her with tales of Darcy's alleged misdeeds and slights against him, Elizabeth listened intently, her expression remaining inscrutable. Occasionally, she would interject with a question or observation, making it abundantly clear that she was not one to be easily swayed by embellished stories.

"Thank you for sharing your experiences with me, Lieutenant Wickham," she said once he had finished his account. "I must say, your story is quite extraordinary. However, I maintain that I shall reserve judgment until I have had the opportunity to know Mr. Darcy better."

"Your caution is admirable, Miss Elizabeth," Wickham replied, his smile strained as he realized his efforts had not borne the desired fruit. What had Darcy already said about him? "I trust that you will keep our conversation in confidence."

"Of course," she assured him. "Now, if you will excuse me, I must return to my sisters."

As Elizabeth retreated from the conversation, Wickham watched her walk away, his thoughts racing with frustration and determination. If his words could not sway her, then perhaps his actions would prove more convincing. He resolved to redouble his efforts to thwart Darcy's potential courtship of Elizabeth Bennet, no matter the cost. After all, in matters of love and war, all was fair. Looking about the room, he considered his next target. The silly aunt was a possible point of leverage, but he thought he spied a better target, having heard Mr. Collins mention his patroness, Lady Catherine de Bourgh.

Lady Catherine would be very displeased indeed to hear that her nephew had eyes for anyone who was not her daughter.

Wickham observed Mr. Collins from a discreet distance, noting the clergyman's obsequious manner and his tendency to fawn over those whom he considered his social superiors. The man was weak and silly, and Wickham hoped he might be easily manipulated to serve Wickham's own ends.

"Mr. Collins," Wickham called out, approaching the man with a congenial smile. "I trust you are enjoying this charming evening?"

"Ah, Lieutenant Wickham!" Mr. Collins exclaimed, bowing deeply. "Indeed, I am. As a clergyman, of course, it does not do to partake in too much frivolity, but a pleasant occasion such as this, in the home of a family member, I feel may be safely enjoyed."

"Most certainly," Wickham replied, his eyes glinting with calculation. "In fact, I have been meaning to speak with you on a matter of some importance. It concerns our mutual acquaintance, Mr. Darcy."

"Mr. Darcy?" Mr. Collins echoed, his interest piqued. "Pray, do tell."

Wickham hesitated for a moment, feigning reluctance to share his concerns. "It is a delicate matter, sir, and I fear that sharing it may cause undue distress. However, as a man of the cloth and one who holds Lady Catherine de Bourgh's esteem, I believe you are the most fitting person to hear my concerns."

"Your confidence in me is most gratifying, Lieutenant," Mr. Collins said, swelling with pride at the thought of being entrusted with critical information. "Please, do continue."

"Very well," Wickham began, lowering his voice as if to impart a terrible secret. "I have reason to believe that Mr. Darcy may be in danger of falling prey to an... adventuress."

"An adventuress?" Mr. Collins gasped, scandalized by the notion. "Surely you do not mean to imply that a lady of ill-repute has designs on Mr. Darcy's affections?"

"Indeed, I am afraid so," Wickham confirmed solemnly. "I have observed their interactions and cannot help but feel a sense of foreboding for my former friend. It is my belief that this woman seeks to ensnare him into an unsuitable match, one that would be most detrimental to his reputation and standing."

"Good heavens!" Mr. Collins exclaimed, his face pale with shock. "This is indeed a grave matter. But what can be done to prevent such a calamity?"

"Perhaps, as a man under Lady Catherine's patronage, you could write to her and inform her of the situation," Wickham suggested, feigning reluctance. "She may be able to intervene and protect Mr. Darcy from making a disastrous error in judgment."

"Of course!" Mr. Collins cried, his eyes lighting up at the notion of being the instrument of Lady Catherine's will. "But you must tell me, so that I may advise her ladyship... who is this adventuress?"

Wickham hesitated. "Perhaps adventuress is too harsh a word," he said cautiously. "But the lady in question is decidedly inferior in her station to Mr. Darcy... who is of course, promised to his cousin, Miss Anne de Bourgh. It is quite understandable that many young ladies should set their caps for a gentleman such as Mr. Darcy, wealthy and influential as he is."

"Of course, of course," Mr. Collins agreed, leaning in closer as Wickham spoke in a confiding tone. "But this one... you believe Mr. Darcy returns her admiration?"

"I fear so." Wickham pasted on a regretful expression. "And I understand your loyalties may be torn, Mr. Collins, for Miss Elizabeth Bennet is your own cousin, but surely you see it is imperative that she cannot be allowed to distract Mr. Darcy from his duty."

"Miss Elizabeth!" Mr. Collins gaped, before turning to look across the room, at where Elizabeth was speaking with Colonel Forster and her uncle Mr. Phillips. "She is very beautiful," he said consideringly.

"She is," Wickham agreed, "but Miss Anne de Bourgh is promised to Mr. Darcy. Only imagine Lady Catherine's displeasure if your cousin were to come between them, Mr. Collins!"

Mr. Collins paled slightly, obviously only too well able to imagine Lady Catherine's fury. "Indeed, that cannot be allowed to happen," the clergyman said hastily. He frowned, apparently deep in thought, before turning to Wickham and nodding. "I thank you for the information, Lieutenant. I know how to act."

"With a letter to Lady Catherine?" Wickham pressed.

"We shall see," Collins replied. "I have plans of my own which may mean Lady Catherine's intervention is not required. Indeed, I should prefer not to bring down her wrath upon my cousins unless it becomes necessary. Let me see what I can do, first."

Annoyed, Wickham watched Collins move away, heading towards Elizabeth. Was the man going to write to Lady Catherine, or not? Wickham could not imagine what Collins thought he could do, that would thwart Darcy's interest in Elizabeth. "Stupid fool," Wickham muttered. Well, he would just have to focus on his first target, the silly aunt. Befriending her would at least ensure he had regular access to Elizabeth, so Wickham pasted his smile back on and crossed the room to coax Mrs. Phillips into giving him a dance.

Chapter Six

THE GRAND DRAWING ROOM at Netherfield bore the unmistakable signs of preparations for a ball: garlands of flowers adorned the walls, while gleaming candlesticks and silverware lined the mantelpiece. Mr. Darcy stood by the window, looking out at the autumnal landscape that stretched before him. He was lost in thought, considering his increasing attachment to Elizabeth Bennet, when the sound of an argument between his friend Mr. Charles Bingley and the latter's sister, Caroline, reached his ears.

"Charles, I implore you to reconsider," Caroline was saying, her voice sharp with disapproval. "The Bennets are hardly a suitable connection for a man of your standing."

"Caroline, I will not be swayed by your opinions on this matter," Bingley replied firmly, his easygoing nature momentarily replaced by uncharacteristic determination. "I am deeply in love with Jane Bennet, and I shall ask her to be my wife."

Darcy turned his gaze back into the room, watching as Bingley stood his ground against his sister's opposition. His heart warmed at the sight of his friend's devotion to the gentle Jane Bennet, for he knew it to be earnest and true.

"Besides," Bingley continued, "the Bennet family, though not wealthy, is reputable; their family have been at Longbourn for over a century, and they are very well-regarded in the neighbourhood. I cannot see why we should not marry, despite Jane's small dowry; I have no need of more money."

Caroline's eyes darted towards Darcy, seeking support. "Mr. Darcy," Caroline appealed to him, her voice tight with restrained frustration. "I hope you will agree with me that my brother's intended match with Miss Bennet is most unsuitable. Surely you cannot support such an alliance?"

Darcy found himself in an uncomfortable position. While he could not deny his own initial reservations about the suitability of the match, he had seen firsthand the sincerity of the affection between Bingley and Jane. It was true that the Bennet family was not as wealthy as some, but they were reputable, and Jane was a gentleman's daughter.

"Miss Bingley," Darcy began slowly, choosing his words with care. "While I understand your concerns, I must confess that I can see no reason why your brother should not marry Miss Bennet. Her family may not be wealthy, but they are reputable, and she is a gentleman's daughter. Furthermore, there is very clearly mutual affection between the couple."

Caroline stared at Darcy in disbelief, her mouth agape. She had expected him to share her disdain for the Bennets and their lack of fortune, not support the match. Her cheeks flushed with indignation, and she struggled to find words to express her outrage.

"Surely you jest, Mr. Darcy!" she exclaimed, her voice rising in pitch. "You, of all people, must see the imprudence of such a pairing! I had thought you would share my concern for my brother's happiness and future."

"Miss Bingley, your brother's happiness is of great importance to me," Darcy replied firmly. "But I do not believe that happiness is solely dependent on wealth or social standing. Mr. Bingley himself has stated that he loves Miss Bennet, and I have observed their mutual affection. Why should you or I ask them to deny their affection, to undoubtedly be miserable without each other, without good cause?"

Caroline's eyes flashed with anger, but she could find no argument against Darcy's words. She was forced to accept his support of the match, however reluctantly, and retreated from the drawing room without another word.

"Ah, Darcy!" Bingley said, turning to face his friend with a beaming countenance. "I cannot express how glad I am to have your approval in my choice of Miss Bennet. Your opinion holds great weight in my esteem."

"Indeed, Bingley," replied Darcy, clasping his friend's shoulder affectionately. "I am truly delighted that you have found such happiness with a lady who is so eminently well-suited to you. Your good taste is unquestionable, and it seems fortune has smiled upon you."

As they engaged in conversation, Darcy could not help but reflect on the irony of the situation. Despite his own reservations about the social divide between their families, he had chosen to support Bingley's desires above Caroline's objections. The truth was, he could no longer deny the genuine love that existed between Jane Bennet and his dearest friend. Moreover, as he himself had begun to entertain thoughts of a union with a certain spirited sister of Jane's, he could hardly stand in opposition to Bingley's wishes.

"Miss Bennet is indeed a most amiable and accomplished young lady," Bingley continued, his voice filled with warmth and admiration. "And I believe her family, though perhaps not as elevated in society as some might wish, will come to hold a special place in my heart as well."

Darcy nodded in agreement, his mind wandering to the impertinent yet captivating Elizabeth Bennet. As much as he tried to suppress these feelings, she had somehow managed to capture his heart, and he could no longer ignore this fact. He knew that supporting Bingley's match might lead him to question his own prejudices and perhaps even consider a future with Elizabeth.

"Your happiness is of the utmost importance, Bingley," said Darcy earnestly. "And I am certain that you will find it with Miss Bennet and her family."

"Thank you, my friend," Bingley replied, his eyes shining with gratitude. "I cannot wait for the day when Jane becomes my wife, and we can begin our life together."

As they stood by the window, both men lost in their thoughts of love and the future, Darcy could not help but wonder whether he too would one day know the same joy as his friend. He hoped that, perhaps, if he allowed himself to embrace the changes in his heart, such happiness might also be within his grasp. With this thought filling his mind, Darcy vowed to seize any opportunities that may arise in the pursuit of his own felicity.

Days later, the long-awaited Netherfield ball had finally arrived. The grand hall buzzed with animated conversation and laughter as couples gracefully paraded around the polished dance floor. However, amidst the gaiety of the evening, Caroline Bingley's sullen expression stood out like a dark cloud threatening to eclipse the sun.

"Mr. Darcy," Elizabeth greeted him as he approached her, her eyes sparkling with mirth and excitement. "I trust you are enjoying the ball?"

"Indeed, I am, Miss Elizabeth," he replied, a small smile gracing his lips as he took in her radiant beauty. Her dress, though not as ostentatious as those worn by other ladies, displayed both elegance and taste, accentuating the natural loveliness that had so captured his attention. Tiny pearls and crystals threaded into her dark hair shimmered in the light of the candles, and she seemed almost to glow as he gazed at her. "And may I say, you look particularly enchanting this evening."

"Thank you," she said, a hint of a blush dusting her cheeks. "How charming Netherfield looks tonight!"

As they spoke, Darcy could not help but steal glances at Caroline, whose narrowed eyes were fixed upon them with thinly veiled resentment. He knew that his attentions towards Elizabeth would only serve to fuel Caroline's ire, yet he could not bring himself to feign indifference to this lovely, intriguing young lady.

"Miss Elizabeth," he began hesitantly, feeling an unfamiliar nervousness take hold. "Might I request the honour of the next dance?" His voice was low, almost a whisper, as if he feared that the mere utterance of his desire would shatter the fragile hope that had taken root within his breast.

"Mr. Darcy, I would be delighted," Elizabeth replied, her eyes shining with genuine warmth and pleasure. The simple words, spoken without any hint of artifice or pretence, sent a thrill through Darcy.

As they joined hands and stepped onto the dance floor, Darcy could not help but notice the sullen expression on Caroline's face grow even more severe. Her jealousy was palpable, yet he found himself unable to summon any sympathy for her plight. Although he knew that propriety and societal expectations demanded a certain level of civility towards Miss Bingley, he would not feign affection where none existed. Caroline had not made it a secret that she had hopes of being the next mistress of Pemberley, but Darcy had never given her cause to think he might entertain such an idea.

The world seemed to fall away as Darcy danced with Elizabeth, leaving only the two of them in a realm of their own creation. In between the elegant turns and sweeping steps, Elizabeth glanced up at him, her eyes bright, and began to speak, raising a topic Darcy would much rather not address.

"Mr. Darcy, I must ask your opinion on a matter," she began. "I recently had the opportunity to converse with Mr. Wickham. He made certain claims about your character, which I admit left me somewhat perplexed."

Darcy's brow furrowed momentarily, his mind whirring with the potential implications of Wickham's deceitful tongue. He took a steadying breath before responding, his voice tinged with restrained emotion.

"Miss Elizabeth," Darcy began, trying to maintain equilibrium despite the anger which flooded through him at even the mention of Mr. Wickham's name, "I must confess that Mr. Wickham possesses a certain charm which has long beguiled those around him. He is skilled at making friends with great ease, much to the sorrow of those friends when they inevitably find themselves betrayed by his true nature."

Elizabeth raised an eyebrow archly. "Indeed, sir? It seems then that his charm serves as both a gift and a curse."

"Quite so," Darcy replied, his gaze briefly darkening with recollections of Wickham's past indiscretions. "In truth, I would not wish anyone to be unfortunate enough to cross paths with Mr. Wickham, for it is only a matter of time before they discover the extent of his duplicity."

"A tragic outcome indeed," Elizabeth said sombrely. She leaned a little closer then, an absolutely bewitching smile touching her lips. "Do you think I should intervene?" She nodded towards the side of the ballroom.

Darcy glanced across to see Bingley leading Jane Bennet out onto the darkened terrace, both of them obviously attempting to remain unobserved.

"Absolutely not," Darcy said firmly. "I have reason to believe Bingley has a particular question he wishes to put to your sister, and certainly I do not think an audience would be required."

Had he thought Elizabeth's smile bewitching before? In that moment, Darcy wished for nothing more than to see that smile before him every day, for the rest of his life.

The entire ballroom seemed to hold its breath as Mr. Bingley and Jane stood in the centre, their hands clasped and eyes filled with the tender glow of love. A murmur of anticipation rippled through the throng of guests as Mr. Bingley raised his voice, addressing the assembly.

"Dear friends," he began, his expression somehow both overwhelmed with joy and incredulous at his own good fortune, "it is with great happiness that I announce my engagement to the lovely Miss Jane Bennet."

A symphony of congratulatory exclamations burst forth as the news was met with delight, and the couple found themselves besieged by well-wishers eager to offer their felicitations.

Caroline Bingley's carefully composed smile hid a tempest of vexation and disappointment as she watched the scene unfold. She had schemed and plotted, hoping to dissuade her brother from this match, only for her efforts to come to naught. Now, she was forced to face the reality that she would be forever connected to the family she deemed so inferior.

"Dearest Jane," Caroline uttered through clenched teeth, approaching with a practiced air of grace and warmth, "allow me to offer you my most heartfelt congratulations on your engagement."

"Thank you, Miss Bingley," Jane replied, her gentle countenance radiating sincere gratitude, seemingly oblivious to the insincerity that lurked beneath Caroline's words.

As Caroline retreated from the happy couple, her thoughts were consumed with bitterness and envy. In her mind's eye, she envisioned herself as the bride-to-be, standing beside Mr. Darcy with the admiration of all those in attendance. This was the future she had desired, the future she believed she deserved, yet it seemed to slip further from her grasp with each passing moment.

"Miss Bingley," said Mr. Darcy, appearing at her side, "you have been most gracious in offering your felicitations to your brother and Miss Bennet."

"Thank you, Mr. Darcy," Caroline replied, her voice strained as she struggled to maintain her façade of composure. "It is only fitting that I extend my best wishes to them, for they are to be joined in holy matrimony, after all. Jane will be my sister."

"Indeed," agreed Mr. Darcy, his keen gaze betraying an understanding of the turmoil that roiled within Caroline's heart. "May their union be a testament to the power of love and the importance of finding one's equal in both mind and heart."

Caroline could barely contain her ire at these words, for they served as a reminder that Mr. Darcy, the object of her affections, had deemed the match between her brother and Jane Bennet as suitable and worthy of praise. As the celebrations continued around her, Caroline found herself adrift in a sea of discontent, unable to shake the sense that the future she had envisioned was slipping through her fingers like grains of sand. Those horrible Bennets! Here came Mrs. Bennet now, that plain creature, coming up to congratulate her stepdaughter. Scheming, dreadful woman!

"Mr. Bingley, my dearest Jane," Charlotte said, "may I offer my most sincere congratulations on your engagement. Your love for one another is evident to all who know you, and Mr. Bennet and I are delighted at the prospect of your union."

"Thank you, Stepmama," replied Jane, her cheeks flushed with happiness. "Your kind words mean a great deal to us both."

"Indeed," agreed Bingley, his face the picture of contentment. "We are most fortunate to have found each other."

"Fortune, perhaps, played a part," Charlotte said thoughtfully, "but it is your own good hearts that have brought you together.

Now, if I may be so bold as to make a suggestion?" She paused, a twinkle in her eye, before continuing, "It would be most fitting, I believe, for your wedding to take place before Christmas. The season lends itself to joy and celebration, and such an occasion would only serve to enhance the festivities."

Bingley's eyes brightened at the thought, and he turned to Jane, seeking her approval. "What do you think, my love? A Christmas wedding would indeed be a magical event."

Jane's smile grew even wider, and she nodded enthusiastically. "Oh, Charles, I can think of no better time to begin our life together. A Christmas wedding would be perfect."

"Then it is settled!" declared Bingley, the excitement evident in his voice. "We shall be married before Christmas."

Caroline wondered if she was going to be ill. Turning away from the sickening sight before her, her gaze fell on a face almost as discontented as her own; that silly clergyman cousin of the Bennets. Wondering what displeased him about the match, she moved a little closer, thinking perhaps to at least find an ally to listen to her displeased sentiments. Mr. Collins was just approaching Elizabeth Bennet at that moment, however, soliciting her hand for the dance. Caroline watched with amusement. Seeing Elizabeth get her toes stepped on would be some small consolation for the miseries of the evening.

"I thank you, Mr. Collins, but I find myself quite done in," Elizabeth said quickly. "The excitement of the evening, you know. Have you made your congratulations yet to Mr. Bingley and Jane?"

"An impressive match indeed for your sister," Mr. Collins said, "but I confess I have my reservations as to its suitability. Surely you must agree that the disparity between Jane's modest background and Mr. Bingley's generous fortune is a cause for concern?"

Caroline smiled as she listened. An unexpected ally indeed! But Mr. Collins was no match in wit for Elizabeth Bennet, and the minx very nearly laughed in his face.

"Mr. Collins," replied Elizabeth, with that disgusting arch smirk on her face, "I would like to remind you that Mr. Bingley is a gentleman, and Jane is the daughter of a gentleman. Their match is perfectly appropriate, and any concerns about their union are unfounded."

Mr. Collins humphed and folded his arms.

"Indeed," Elizabeth added, "what matters most is that they are well-suited in temperament and love each other dearly. Surely even a man of your esteemed position can appreciate the importance of such qualities in a marriage?"

The expression on Mr. Collins' face shifted from indignation to discomfort as he stammered out a response, clearly taken aback by Elizabeth's reasoning. He sought refuge in the crowd, leaving behind an air of satisfaction among the gathered family... and a furious Caroline Bingley, vowing to find a way to disrupt her brother's plans if it was the last thing she did.

Chapter Seven

THE MORNING AFTER THE Netherfield ball, Charlotte and Jane were quickly absorbed in planning for the wedding. Mr. Bennet, in the face of far more talk about lace than he ever wished to hear, retreated to his study posthaste, and Mary elected to practice on the pianoforte. With inclement weather preventing Elizabeth from taking her customary walk, she made her way to the parlour and was sitting alone with a book when Mr. Collins came upon her. He had been waiting for this moment with bated breath, anticipating the opportunity to secure his future. Elizabeth Bennet, he thought, would make him an excellent wife. Her wit would entertain Lady Catherine de Bourgh, and her alluring form would be a pleasure to Mr. Collins himself.

"My dear Miss Elizabeth," he began, approaching her with a mixture of trepidation and self-assurance, "you can hardly doubt the purport of my discourse, however your natural delicacy may lead you to dissemble; my attentions have been too marked to be mistaken. Almost as soon as I entered the house, I singled you out as the companion of my future life. But before I am run away with by my feelings on this subject, perhaps it would be advisable for me to state my reasons for marrying—and, moreover, for coming into Hertfordshire with the design of selecting a wife, as I certainly did."

He began a speech about the merits of his suit and the advantages of proximity to Lady Catherine de Bourgh which his wife would enjoy, not noticing the expression on Elizabeth's face, which slid slowly towards horror as he continued.

"And now nothing remains for me but to assure you in the most animated language of the violence of my affection," he concluded happily, "and suggest that perhaps, as a matter of economy, we might share in the wedding celebrations of Miss Bennet and Mr. Bingley."

Elizabeth paused a moment, and he smiled smugly, sure that she was overcome with the honour of receiving his attentions.

At last, however, Elizabeth spoke. "You are too hasty, sir! You forget that I have made no answer. Let me do it without further loss of time. Accept my thanks for the compliment you are paying me. I am very sensible of the honour of your proposals, but it is impossible for me to do otherwise than to decline them."

This was entirely impossible. He smiled. "I do understand that it is usual with young ladies to reject the addresses of the man whom they secretly mean to accept, when he first applies for their favour; and that sometimes the refusal is repeated a second, or even a third time. I am therefore by no means discouraged by what you have just said, and shall hope to lead you to the altar ere long."

"Upon my word, sir, your hope is a rather extraordinary one after my declaration. I do assure you that I am not one of those young ladies who are so daring as to risk their happiness on the chance of being asked a second time. I am perfectly serious in my refusal. You could not make *me* happy, and I am convinced that I am the last woman in the world who could make you so."

She looked composed, calm, and not in the slightest bit as though she might change her mind. Or even as though she was flattered by his attentions! For a brief moment, Mr. Collins' carefully constructed façade crumbled, revealing a flash of hurt and indignation. How could she refuse him so readily, he wondered, when he had been so certain of her acquiescence?

"Miss Elizabeth," he pressed, struggling to maintain his composure, "I understand that my proposal may come as a surprise, but I assure you that my intentions are sincere. I am prepared to offer you all the comforts and security that a gentleman of my position can provide."

"Your generosity is commendable, Mr. Collins," Elizabeth replied, her voice unwavering. "However, I must be true to my own feelings, and they do not align with the future you propose. Please forgive me for any distress my decision may cause, but I cannot accept your offer."

Mr. Collins' face flushed with embarrassment and frustration, his earlier confidence ebbing away like sand through an hourglass. His thoughts raced, grappling with the implications of Elizabeth's refusal. Had he misjudged her character? Was there some insurmountable obstacle he had failed to perceive? Or was it simply that she did not find him desirable enough to consider as a husband?

As Mr. Collins turned away, his heart heavy with disappointment, he could not help but feel that he had suffered a grievous injustice. He had offered Elizabeth Bennet everything a woman could desire – a comfortable home, a respectable income, and the esteem of his noble patroness, Lady Catherine de Bourgh – and yet, she had spurned him without hesitation.

"Perhaps," he mused bitterly, "I was mistaken in my choice of a wife. But I shall not allow this setback to deter me from my ultimate goal." He would speak with Mr. and Mrs. Bennet; they had both been encouraging of his motives to seek a wife from among their daughters! Surely, they would make Elizabeth see reason.

In the quiet solitude of Mr. Bennet's library, Mr. Collins found both his cousin and Mrs. Bennet, apparently discussing the budget for Miss Bennet's wedding clothes. Mr. Collins had no compunctions about interrupting such a trivial conversation with his concerns.

"Mr. Bennet, Mrs. Bennet," he began after a deep, aggrieved breath, "I am at a loss. Miss Elizabeth has refused me despite the many advantages I laid before her. I cannot fathom her reasons."

The Bennets shared a glance of apparent confusion.

"I am sorry, Mr. Collins," Mr. Bennet said, "did you just say that you proposed to *Elizabeth*?"

"Indeed, sir! Almost as soon as I entered this house, I singled her out as the companion of my future life." Aggrieved, Mr. Collins slumped into a chair and glared at his cousin. "But she has, incomprehensibly, refused me! You have raised a very silly daughter, cousin, who does not understand the very great advantages which would..."

"Mr. Collins," Charlotte interrupted him, her voice even, "Elizabeth has the right to decline your proposal if she does not feel it would lead to her happiness."

"Mrs. Bennet," Mr. Collins said, exasperated, "surely you can understand my confusion. I have a very fine living to offer, as well as the patronage of Lady Catherine de Bourgh!"

Mr. Bennet covered his mouth and looked away. Embarrassed, perhaps, at his daughter's foolishness, Mr. Collins thought, and leaving the conversation therefore to his wife.

"Of course, Mr. Collins," Charlotte assured him with a gentle smile. "But I did mention upon your arrival that I believed Mary to be more suited to you. I hoped you might consider her as a potential partner."

"Mary is a sensible girl," Mr. Bennet added, steepling his fingers. "She shares your passion for order and propriety. Perhaps a courtship with her would be more successful."

But Mary isn't nearly as pretty as Elizabeth, Mr. Collins thought rebelliously.

"You will not intercede with Miss Elizabeth?" he asked, desperately hoping they would change their minds.

"I shall speak to her, of course," Mr. Bennet said, after a glance at his wife. "But no, Mr. Collins, we will not bring pressure to bear on her to change her decision. Lizzy knows her own mind, and if she has determined against you, certainly we will honour her choice. I urge you to reconsider yours."

He could listen to no more of this. Angry at being thwarted, Mr. Collins jumped to his feet and left the library without taking his leave of his cousins, seriously displeased. Stamping up the stairs to his room, he stood for a moment staring out of the window before whirling to his writing-desk.

He knew how to act, now. Mr. Wickham had been quite right. His pen scratched against the paper as he laboriously composed a letter to Lady Catherine de Bourgh. In it, he detailed the unfortunate turn of events that had led to Elizabeth Bennet's refusal of his hand in marriage.

Surely, your ladyship will concur with my reasoning, he wrote, *that Miss Elizabeth's hopes of marrying a man of great consequence like Mr. Darcy have blinded her to the honourable and advantageous match I offered her.*

With a flourish of his pen, Mr. Collins signed his name and set the letter aside to dry. He pondered the advice given to him by Charlotte and Mr. Bennet about the suitability of Mary as a potential spouse. Though his pride smarted from Elizabeth's rejection, he knew it would be wise to consider their counsel.

"Mary is a diligent and prudent young woman," he mused aloud, his voice barely audible above the crackling fire. "She shares my values and understands the importance of fulfilling one's duties in life. Perhaps she is better suited to the role of Mrs. Collins than her sister."

Resolved in his decision, Mr. Collins sought out Mary Bennet, finding her practicing on the pianoforte. The sombre tones of her music filled the air, and he hesitated for a moment before interrupting her performance.

"Miss Mary," he began, clearing his throat nervously. "Might I have a word with you in private?"

"Of course, Mr. Collins," Mary replied, her brow furrowing with curiosity as she closed the piano lid. They retired to a quiet corner of the room, away from the prying ears of others.

"Miss Mary, I must confess that I have spent much time reflecting on the qualities of a suitable wife," Mr. Collins began, his voice quavering with emotion. "After much deliberation, and in light of recent events, it has become clear to me that you possess the necessary virtues and disposition that would make us a most compatible match."

He paused, taking a deep breath before continuing. "Therefore, I am honoured to offer you my hand in marriage, Miss Mary, if you will accept it."

Mary stared at him in a mixture of surprise and uncertainty. "Mr. Collins," she said hesitantly, "I am flattered by your proposal and grateful for your kind words. However, I must request some time to consider your offer and weigh it against my own desires and aspirations."

"Of course, Miss Mary," Mr. Collins replied, trying to mask his disappointment that she had not eagerly accepted him. "I understand that this is a matter of great importance, and I shall eagerly await your response."

As they parted ways, Mr. Collins could not help but feel a twinge of uncertainty gnawing at his heart. Would he ever find a Bennet daughter willing to accept his hand? Or would he be doomed to face further rejection and disappointment?

A delicate sunbeam pierced through the lace curtains of Darcy House in London, casting a warm glow upon Georgiana Darcy's slender fingers as they traced the elegant script of her brother's letter. The news within its pages was both exciting and disconcerting – an upcoming wedding at Netherfield, and Fitzwilliam's decision to remain in Hertfordshire with the Bingleys until just before Christmas.

"Miss Darcy," Mrs. Annesley, her companion, observed with a gentle smile, "you appear quite lost in thought. Is there news of great import in your brother's letter?"

"Indeed, there is, Mrs. Annesley," Georgiana replied. "Fitzwilliam writes of a wedding soon to take place at Netherfield, and he has chosen to stay with the Bingleys for some weeks longer. He will not join us here until Christmas Eve."

"Ah, that is most delightful news, Miss Darcy. Your brother must be quite taken by the society in Hertfordshire."

"Perhaps," Georgiana murmured, her heart fluttering with a mixture of worry and curiosity. Would her beloved brother find happiness in these new friendships? And what of herself? Without his steady guidance, she felt adrift amidst the swirling currents of London society.

"Is something troubling you, my dear?" Mrs. Annesley inquired, her brow furrowed with concern.

Georgiana hesitated, then sighed. "I cannot help but feel... left behind, Mrs. Annesley. Fitzwilliam's letter is filled with warmth and excitement, while I remain here in London, confined by propriety and circumstance."

"Ah, I understand your feelings, Miss Darcy," Mrs. Annesley said sympathetically. "But remember that your brother's first duty is to ensure your safety and well-being. He would not leave you without good reason."

"Of course, you are right," Georgiana conceded, a wistful smile gracing her lips. "I must trust in Fitzwilliam's judgment and cherish our reunion at Christmas."

"Indeed, my dear," Mrs. Annesley agreed, patting Georgiana's hand comfortingly. "With patience and fortitude, the days will pass swiftly, and soon you shall be reunited with your brother amid the joys of the festive season."

Yet as Georgiana gazed out upon the bustling streets of London, she couldn't shake the feeling that something was amiss – a quiet, nagging whisper that hinted at secrets yet untold. And though she endeavoured to banish such thoughts from her mind, they lingered like shadows, their presence an unwelcome reminder of the distance between herself and her dearest Fitzwilliam.

The following morning found Georgiana pacing the length of the drawing room, her fingertips brushing against the delicate petals of an arrangement of hothouse flowers as she passed. Her thoughts were consumed by the contents of Fitzwilliam's letter and the troubling notion that she had been intentionally excluded from the celebrations at Netherfield.

"Mrs. Annesley," Georgiana began hesitantly, pausing in her restless movements to face her companion. "Do you not think it is strange that I was not invited to accompany Fitzwilliam to Hertfordshire? Surely, he must have forgotten to include me."

"Miss Darcy," Mrs. Annesley replied with a gentle smile, "I am certain your brother would never intentionally leave you out. Perhaps there are practical reasons for his decision that we are not aware of."

"Even so," Georgiana countered, her cheeks flushed with determination, "I cannot bear the thought of missing such an important event in his life. I must go to Netherfield immediately."

"Are you quite sure, my dear?" Mrs. Annesley asked, concern flickering in her gaze. "It is a long journey, and we may arrive unannounced and unwelcome."

"Indeed, I am certain," Georgiana declared, her chin lifted in quiet resolve. And though she felt a tremor of doubt pass through her, she silenced her misgivings with the conviction that her presence at the wedding was of the utmost importance – not only for her own happiness but for the bond between herself and her beloved brother.

"Very well," Mrs. Annesley conceded with a sigh, sensing that Georgiana's resolve would not be swayed. "I shall arrange for our departure in the morning."

"Thank you, Mrs. Annesley," Georgiana said, gratitude shining in her eyes. "I do hope Fitzwilliam will understand my actions and forgive any inconvenience I may cause."

"Your brother loves you dearly, Miss Darcy," Mrs. Annesley assured her. "I have no doubt that he will be pleased to see you, even if our arrival is unexpected."

The carriage rattled and shook with every jolt of the uneven road, but Georgiana remained steadfast in her determination, despite the mounting concern for Mrs. Annesley's health. Even though it was only a day's journey in the well-sprung coach, the older lady had grown more and more feverish as the journey progressed, and Georgiana could not help but feel responsible for her companion's illness.

"Mrs. Annesley," Georgiana ventured softly, reaching out to touch her hand. "I am truly sorry that you have fallen ill on my account."

"Think nothing of it, Miss Darcy," Mrs. Annesley replied weakly, offering a wan smile. "I was not feeling quite the thing yesterday, but I am sure this present malady is merely the consequence of our hasty departure."

"Nevertheless," Georgiana insisted, her eyes filling with remorse. "Had I been less stubborn, we might have avoided this situation altogether. I pray that Fitzwilliam will not be too harsh when he learns of our arrival."

"Your brother loves you dearly, my dear," Mrs. Annesley reassured her. "He will understand your desire to be present at such an important occasion."

Arriving at Netherfield, the sight of the grand estate filled Georgiana with both excitement and trepidation. When the carriage finally came to a halt, she hesitated a moment before stepping down, her heart racing at the thought of facing her brother's reaction to their unexpected presence.

"Georgiana!" Mr. Darcy exclaimed, his voice tight with surprise and alarm as they were announced into the drawing-room. "What brings you to Netherfield?"

"Forgive me, Fitzwilliam," Georgiana said, her gaze lowered in deference to her brother's evident displeasure. "I was eager to attend Mr. Bingley's wedding and feared that my invitation had been overlooked."

"Georgiana, you should not have come without warning," Darcy scolded, concern etched upon his features as his eyes fell upon Mrs. Annesley's pallid countenance. "Mrs. Annesley, you are unwell!"

"Indeed," the older woman admitted, her voice barely a whisper. "I fear the journey has taken its toll on me."

"Then there is no other option," Darcy declared with an authoritative air. "You must remain at Netherfield until Mrs. Annesley is well enough to travel. However, Georgiana, I must insist that you confine yourself to the grounds of the estate during your stay."

"Dearest Fitzwilliam," she began, hesitating before continuing in a voice barely audible even to herself, "I understand your concern for my safety, but surely there must be some way for me to make friends without exposing myself to danger."

"Georgiana," Darcy replied, "I wish only the best for you, but we must be cautious. You are young, and there are those who would take advantage of your innocence." His expression was ungiving, and Georgiana realised he would not bend from his decision.

"Am I to remain caged like a bird at Netherfield, then?" she asked, her heart heavy with disappointment.

"Only until Mrs. Annesley has recovered," Darcy reassured her. "I promise that once she is well, you will have the freedom to explore and make friends as you please. For now, however, it is vital that we prioritize her health and your safety."

"Very well," Georgiana murmured meekly. She longed to trust her brother's judgement, but in the depths of her heart, she could not help but question whether the price of protection was too steep.

They removed upstairs, where the housekeeper at once set a very comfortable suite of rooms at their disposal, and two competent maids briskly hurried to make Mrs. Annesley comfortable, assuring Georgiana that they would see to her every need.

Georgiana found herself alone in her room, standing at the window. Footsteps behind her made her turn, forcing a smile to her lips as she saw her hostess entering the room. Caroline Bingley had always been polite to her – almost fawning, in fact – but Georgiana could not bring herself to warm to the older lady, perhaps because Caroline's pursuit of Fitzwilliam was so obvious. Georgiana suspected Caroline was only nice to her because Caroline thought it might increase Darcy's good opinion.

"Miss Darcy," ventured Caroline Bingley, with a practiced air of congeniality, "might I offer you some solace in your confinement to Netherfield's grounds? Perhaps we could take tea together and discuss the latest fashions or share our thoughts on recent novels?"

"Thank you for your kind offer, Miss Bingley," Georgiana replied politely. "However, I am rather weary from our journey and would prefer to rest."

"Of course," Caroline conceded, hiding disappointment beneath a polite smile. "But should you change your mind, do not hesitate to call upon me. I am certain we could become fast friends."

As she watched Caroline leave the room, Georgiana could not deny the pang of loneliness that gnawed at her heart. Yet, despite her craving for companionship, she found herself unable to overlook the air of condescension that clung to Miss Bingley like a second skin. Even at her young age, Georgiana recognized the unmistakable scent of a social climber, and she was reluctant to align herself with such a person.

"I only hope my brother sees her for who she really is, too," Georgiana murmured, turning back to the window to gaze wistfully out at the view once more. "Caroline Bingley as my sister is too awful a prospect to contemplate!"

Chapter Eight

Elizabeth watched her sister Mary, brow furrowed in thought, as Mary accompanied their cousin to the door of Longbourn and the chaise waiting outside to take him back to Kent.

"Mr. Collins," Mary said with a polite nod, "I trust you will have a safe journey back to Hunsford. I shall give your proposal due consideration and write to you soon with my decision."

"Thank you, Miss Mary," replied Mr. Collins, his obsequious grin firmly in place. "I eagerly await your response and hope for a favourable outcome."

As the door closed behind him, Elizabeth could not help but feel a sense of relief at his departure. She glanced at Mary, whose contemplative demeanour indicated that the prospect of her decision weighed heavily upon her. Elizabeth could only hope that her sister would make the choice that would best suit her own happiness.

"Mary," she ventured cautiously, "are you quite well?"

Mary looked up, meeting Elizabeth's concerned gaze. "Yes, Lizzy, I am well. I merely find myself... pondering the future."

"Whatever you decide, dear sister," Elizabeth reassured her, "know that you have my full support."

"Thank you, Lizzy," Mary replied softly.

Elizabeth had made no attempt to conceal the fact that Mr. Collins had proposed to her and been rejected, telling Mary and Jane about it as soon as they saw Mr. Collins leave the house, saying he had a letter to post in Meryton. On hearing that Mr. Collins had proposed to Elizabeth, Mary had grown quite grave, before admitting she too had received a proposal.

Elizabeth had wished at once that she had said nothing, but Mary shook her head, saying she was glad she knew.

"I do not think I like being his second choice," Mary murmured quietly. "I am pleased that I hesitated and asked for time to make my decision." She evinced a small smile. "I am not sure I could be brave enough to reject him to his face like you, Lizzy. If I do decide against him, it will be much easier to let him know by a letter."

Seeing Mary now, not even bothering to watch as the chaise rattled away, Elizabeth suspected Mary had already made her choice, but avoided sharing her decision as she wanted to avoid any confrontation before Mr. Collins departed. As Mary had said, a rejection by letter would be far less painful, though possibly not for Mr. Collins, twice rejected by Bennet sisters.

Mr. Bennet departed shortly after Mr. Collins, headed once again for Oxford. He and Charlotte had decided to bring Kitty and Lydia home from school, to spend time with Jane before she married. Late that afternoon, the carriage returned, its occupants alighting with a flurry of excited chatter and rustling skirts. The door flew open and Kitty and Lydia burst into the house, their faces flushed with excitement and anticipation.

"Jane!" cried Lydia, flinging herself into her eldest sister's arms. "Oh, how we have longed to see you! What wonderful news, that you have found a rich man to marry!"

"How good it is to see you, my dear," Jane replied with a radiant smile, enfolding her younger sister in a tender embrace but tactfully ignoring Lydia's unladylike observation.

"Such thrilling news!" exclaimed Kitty, clasping her hands together in delight. "We shall have such wonderful celebrations, and just imagine all the handsome gentlemen who will be in attendance!"

"Kitty, do try to contain your enthusiasm," Elizabeth chided gently, though she could not quite suppress a smile at her sisters' unrestrained gaiety.

"Very well, Lizzy," Kitty sighed dramatically, but her eyes danced with mischief. "But surely, we cannot be blamed for our excitement. After all, it is not every day that one's sister becomes engaged to such an eligible gentleman!"

"Indeed not," Elizabeth agreed, her gaze shifting to Jane, whose cheeks now glowed with a becoming blush. "But let us remember that it is the affection and understanding between two hearts that truly matters, rather than the trappings of wealth and rank."

"Of course, Lizzy," Lydia conceded, rolling her eyes playfully. "But just think of the balls, the gowns and the carriages she will have! Not to mention the dashing gentlemen who will no doubt flock to our sister's side when Mr. Bingley takes her to London for the Season!"

"Lydia!" Jane admonished with a laugh, shaking her head at her sister's incorrigible good spirits.

"Very well, dear sister," Lydia relented, grinning impishly. "In any case, we are all thrilled for you and eager to play our part in your happiness. Especially since Papa has agreed we are all to have new gowns for your wedding!"

"Thank you, my dears," Jane replied, her eyes shining with unshed tears as she regarded her sisters fondly. "Your love and support mean more to me than words can express."

"And when are we to meet your betrothed?" Lydia demanded, eyes sparkling with excitement.

"Tomorrow." Jane smiled patiently as Kitty and Lydia squealed and clapped. "We shall go over for a morning call, and you shall meet Mr. Bingley, and his sisters."

The following morning, the Bennet carriage once again rolled up Netherfield's grand carriageway, carrying the Bennet ladies, all bar one – Mary had elected to stay at home, saying that she wanted to write a letter.

Elizabeth, arm-in-arm with Jane and Charlotte, led Kitty and Lydia up the steps to the grand entrance, her heart filled with a mix of anticipation and concern. She knew that introducing her younger sisters to Mr. Bingley's circle would be an important step in their social development, but she could not help but worry about their propensity for mischief and frivolity. School did not seem to have improved either of them particularly; Lydia was still fearless and feckless, though at least had learned to moderate the volume of her voice slightly, possibly because she had learned her noisiness was likely to get her caught out more often. Kitty was still too easily led and did not seem to think through the consequences of her actions.

"Remember, my dear sisters," Elizabeth cautioned as they neared the door, "we are here to make a favourable impression upon our new acquaintances. Please conduct yourselves with decorum and restraint."

"Of course, Lizzy," Kitty replied, rolling her eyes with mock exasperation, while Lydia merely smirked and nodded with a teasing glint in her eye.

As they were ushered into the drawing-room, they found the Bingleys already assembled, along with a young lady Elizabeth did not recognise. The girl, no more than sixteen, stood beside

Mr. Darcy, her hands clasped tightly in front of her and her eyes shyly downcast.

"Ah, Miss Bennet, Miss Elizabeth, and Mrs. Bennet!" Mr. Bingley greeted them warmly, coming over to make his bows. "How wonderful to see you again! And these must be your other sisters. I am delighted to make their acquaintance."

Lydia and Kitty were introduced, and then Bingley turned to gesture the young lady with Mr. Darcy to step forward. "And please, allow me to present a new arrival of our own... Miss Darcy."

"Miss Darcy," Elizabeth said graciously. "It is a pleasure to make your acquaintance at last. Your brother has said so many good things about you."

"Th-thank you, Miss Elizabeth," Georgiana stammered, her cheeks flushing as she curtsied nervously.

As they all took their seats, Elizabeth could not help but observe the contrast between her lively, boisterous sisters and the quiet, demure figure of Georgiana. She hoped that the meeting would serve to broaden their horizons and offer them a glimpse of a different kind of refinement and grace.

"Georgiana plays the pianoforte quite beautifully," Mr. Darcy remarked, as if reading her thoughts. "Perhaps, once we have finished our tea, she might be persuaded to favour us with a performance?"

"Indeed," Elizabeth agreed, smiling warmly at the young girl, who blushed and nodded in response. "I am certain that we would all be most delighted to hear her play."

Georgiana's heart fluttered as she took in the animated faces of Kitty and Lydia, their eyes wide with wonder as they surveyed her attire. It was a mixture of admiration and envy that Georgiana could not help but notice, even though she wished to shrink away from their attention.

"La! Such a lovely silk gown!" Lydia exclaimed, reaching out to touch the fabric before stopping herself just in time. "I dare say you must have the most exquisite taste, Miss Darcy!"

"Indeed," Kitty chimed in, her gaze lingering on the delicate lace adorning Georgiana's sleeves. "And your hair is arranged so elegantly. I do wish we had a maid as skilled as yours."

"Thank you both for your kind words," Georgiana replied softly, feeling slightly abashed by their effusive compliments. She cast a glance towards Elizabeth, who appeared to be watching the exchange with a mixture of amusement and concern.

"Miss Darcy," Lydia said, leaning in conspiratorially, "do you ever wear such fashionable dresses when you attend balls? I imagine you must be quite the belle of the season!"

"Lydia!" Elizabeth scolded gently, though there was a hint of laughter in her voice. "Surely you can find more appropriate topics of conversation."

"Apologies, sister. But truly, Miss Darcy, you must tell us what it is like to attend a ball at Pemberley," Lydia persisted, undeterred by her elder sister's rebuke.

"Um, well..." Georgiana hesitated, unsure how to respond to the other girl's eagerness. "I... I am not yet out, I'm afraid. I have never attended a ball, and I don't believe there has been one held at Pemberley since before I was born."

"Lydia, perhaps Miss Darcy would rather discuss something else," Elizabeth interjected kindly, sensing Georgiana's discomfort. "I am certain she has many other interests besides fashion and dancing."

"Of course," Lydia agreed, though her curiosity remained unabated. "Like music, for instance! That piece you played on the pianoforte was absolutely beautiful, Miss Darcy."

"Thank you," Georgiana murmured, feeling a mixture of pride and embarrassment at their praise. It was true that she loved music passionately, but she had always been shy about performing in front of others.

"Miss Darcy," Kitty ventured hesitantly, "do you think... Would it be possible for you to show us some of your favourite pieces sometime? We have both been studying the pianoforte at school, but even our music mistress is not half so skilled as you."

"Indeed," Lydia added eagerly, "we would be ever so grateful for any advice or instruction you could offer!"

Georgiana hesitated for a moment, considering the sincerity in their expressions. Despite their forwardness, she could not deny that their enthusiasm was genuine. And perhaps, she thought, this might be an opportunity to forge a connection with these lively young ladies who were so unlike herself.

"Very well," she agreed softly, her decision made. "I would be honoured to share my love of music with you both, should we have an opportunity."

"Girls," Charlotte said then, "It is a dry, pleasant day. Why don't you take a walk in the grounds?"

Georgiana suspected that Mrs. Bennet just wanted to get the noisy younger girls out of the drawing room so the older people could have a more civilized conversation, but getting out of the house – and away from Caroline Bingley's fawning, false friendship – sounded like a lovely idea, even if it was only for a walk in the grounds. She glanced appealingly at her brother.

Darcy did not hesitate before nodding amiably, saying to her quietly; "You should take advantage of this opportunity to become better acquainted with your new friends. I trust Miss Catherine and Miss Lydia to be sensible companions for you."

"Thank you, Fitzwilliam," Georgiana replied, touched by her brother's unexpected support. She could sense that he felt guilty for having been harsh with her on her arrival, and his encouragement seemed to stem from a desire to make amends. She knew he approved of the older Bennet ladies, and obviously felt that their younger sisters would be suitable friends for her. Georgiana felt her spirits lifting as she put on her bonnet and pelisse in the hallway before stepping outside into the crisp, chill air.

"Come, Miss Darcy!" Lydia exclaimed, her enthusiasm barely contained. "We shall take you on a delightful walk to Meryton.

It is the most charming village, and we are quite anxious to meet all the militia officers who have taken up residence there!"

Kitty nodded vigorously in agreement, her curls bouncing with each movement. "Yes! Our friend Maria Lucas has written to us, telling us about them. They are such fine, handsome men, and we simply cannot wait to meet them!"

Georgiana hesitated, recalling her brother's admonition to remain on the estate. Yet she found herself unwilling to disappoint her new friends, whose eagerness was infectious. Her heart raced with a mixture of excitement and trepidation as she considered the prospect of venturing beyond the safe confines of Netherfield.

"Very well," she acquiesced, her voice quiet but determined. "I shall accompany you to Meryton."

As they set out on their journey, Georgiana's mind was a whirlwind of conflicting emotions. She was thrilled by the prospect of meeting new people and experiencing the world beyond her sheltered existence, but also deeply aware of the potential consequences should her brother discover her disobedience. The weight of his expectations weighed heavily upon her, and she could not help but wonder if her newfound freedom might come at too great a cost.

"Miss Darcy, you are unusually quiet," Lydia observed, breaking through Georgiana's reverie. "Are you not excited to meet all the dashing young officers?"

"I am," Georgiana replied hesitantly, unwilling to voice her concerns. "I merely hope that my brother will not be displeased with our excursion."

"Your brother need never know," Kitty chimed in, her eyes sparkling with mischief. "What he does not know cannot hurt him, after all."

"Indeed," Lydia agreed, grinning conspiratorially. "We shall be back before he even realises we have gone, and no harm will have been done."

As they continued their walk, Georgiana could not help but marvel at the exuberance and vivacity of the two younger Bennet sisters. They chattered incessantly about their activities in Oxford, the local gossip and the various families in the neighbourhood, their voices lilting with laughter as they shared amusing anecdotes. Though she felt somewhat overwhelmed by their energy, Georgiana also found herself envying their ease and confidence.

"Miss Darcy," Kitty began hesitantly, "I hope you do not think us too forward or impertinent, but we truly wish to become friends with you."

"Indeed," Lydia added earnestly, "we are most eager to know you better and to learn from your excellent example."

Georgiana bit her lip, touched by their sincerity yet unsure how to respond. She had spent much of her life sheltered from the world, and the idea of forming close friendships was both intriguing and daunting.

"Thank you," she managed finally, her voice barely audible above the rustling leaves. "I would be honoured to count you both as my friends. And to that end, you must both call me Georgiana, please."

"Excellent!" Lydia cried, clapping her hands together in delight. "We shall have no end of fun together, Georgiana, I promise you that!"

The bustling streets of Meryton greeted the three young ladies with a cacophony of sights, sounds, and scents. Shopkeepers called out their wares, children darted about underfoot, and the intoxicating aroma of fresh bread wafted from a nearby bakery. Kitty and Lydia's eyes sparkled with delight as they eagerly scanned the crowd for familiar faces, while Georgiana hesitated, feeling a sudden wave of trepidation.

"Lydia! Kitty!" A cheerful voice rang out above the din, and Maria Lucas hurried towards them, her cheeks flushed from exertion. "You are home!"

"Maria!" Lydia exclaimed, embracing her friend with enthusiasm. "You must meet Miss Darcy, Mr. Darcy's sister. She has joined us for our little excursion."

"Miss Darcy, it is an honour," Maria said, curtsying politely before turning to Lydia with a conspiratorial grin. "Now, come and let me introduce you to all the officers, they're all just dying to meet you!"

"Come along, then," Lydia replied, grabbing Maria's arm and pulling her into the throng. "Let us waste no time!"

Georgiana hesitated on the edge of the lively throng of officers and young ladies. The laughter and flirtatious chatter filled the air, creating an atmosphere that was at once exhilarating and overwhelming for the gentle, timid girl.

"Georgiana," Lydia called out, beckoning her forward with an impish grin. "Do come and meet Captain Carter! He has been regaling us with tales of his most recent exploits!"

Kitty nodded enthusiastically, adding, "Oh, yes! You simply must hear about the time he escaped from a band of French spies by swimming across a river in the dead of night!"

Though Georgiana longed to share in their excitement, she could not help but feel a pang of unease at the thought of engaging in such frivolous pursuits. Her brother's stern disapproval seemed to hang in the air like a dark cloud, casting a shadow over even the simplest of pleasures.

"Please excuse me, Lydia," she said softly, attempting to extricate herself from the situation while still maintaining a semblance of politeness. "I fear I am not good company today."

Lydia waved away her concerns, replying with a laugh, "Nonsense! A little merriment is just what you need to banish those sombre thoughts. Come along now, there is no use in being shy!"

Despite her reservations, Georgiana found herself unable to resist the forceful pull of Lydia and Kitty's enthusiasm. With a reluctant sigh, she allowed them to lead her further into the crowd, her heart pounding with a mixture of anxiety and anticipation.

"Captain Carter," Lydia announced, presenting Georgiana with a flourish, "May I present Miss Georgiana Darcy, sister to Mr. Darcy of Pemberley?"

The captain bowed gallantly, taking Georgiana's hand and pressing a chaste kiss to her knuckles. "Enchanted, Miss Darcy."

"Thank you, Captain," she murmured, her cheeks flushing at his bold gesture.

As the conversation continued around her, with Lydia and Kitty vying for the attention of the various officers present, Georgiana found herself growing increasingly uncomfortable. Their boisterous laughter and suggestive remarks grated on her sensitive nature, causing her to shrink further into herself with each passing moment.

"Miss Darcy," Captain Carter said, observing her distress, "Are you feeling quite well?"

"Thank you, Captain, but I believe it is time for me to return to Netherfield," she replied, forcing a polite smile onto her face. "My brother will be expecting me."

"Of course," he said, understanding in his eyes. "Shall I escort you back?"

"No, thank you," she insisted, relief washing over her at the prospect of escape, but also horror at what her brother would say if she arrived back at Netherfield escorted by a militia officer. "I shall manage just fine on my own."

Kitty and Lydia did not even seem to notice as she slipped quietly away.

Upon her return to Netherfield, Georgiana found the drawing-room occupied by a small party: the Hursts played a game of whist with Mrs. and Miss Bennet, and Elizabeth Bennet, seated serenely near the window, was absorbed in a book. A soft smile touched her lips as she turned each page with unhurried elegance.

"Miss Darcy," Elizabeth greeted, looking up from her reading with a warm smile. "I hope your walk was enjoyable?"

"Indeed it was, Miss Elizabeth, thank you," Georgiana replied, hesitating at the threshold of the room, uncertain of her next move.

"Please, do join me," Elizabeth offered, motioning towards an empty seat beside her. Though still somewhat shy, Georgiana could not refuse such a kind invitation and gratefully accepted the indicated chair.

"Thank you, Miss Elizabeth," she said quietly, settling herself into her seat.

"My sisters do not accompany you?" Elizabeth asked, glancing towards the door.

"They decided to walk a little while longer," Georgiana prevaricated, not wanting to get Kitty and Lydia into trouble. "I felt tired, so I came inside."

With a calmly accepting nod, Elizabeth returned her attention to the pages before her, allowing Georgiana a moment's respite to gather her thoughts.

As she sat there, Georgiana observed that Elizabeth possessed a certain grace which had been absent from her interactions with Kitty and Lydia. Her voice, though soft, carried evident strength of character. It was a quality Georgiana admired and longed to emulate, yet feared she lacked entirely.

"Miss Elizabeth," Georgiana ventured hesitantly, "Might I ask what it is you are reading?"

Elizabeth looked up from her book once more, her eyes shining with enthusiasm. "It is a collection of poetry by Lord Byron. I find his work quite enchanting."

"Indeed?" Georgiana said, her interest piqued. "My brother has often spoken of his admiration for Lord Byron's verse, but I have not yet had the pleasure of reading any myself."

"Would you like me to read aloud some passages?" Elizabeth suggested, her voice laced with genuine warmth.

"Very much so," Georgiana responded, a tentative smile forming on her lips.

And so they passed the remainder of the afternoon together, Elizabeth's voice weaving a tapestry of words that resonated deep within Georgiana's soul. The shy young girl began to feel a sense of ease in Elizabeth's presence, as though she had finally found someone who could understand her innermost thoughts and dreams.

Chapter Nine

Georgiana Darcy stood at the window of Netherfield's drawing room, her breath ghosting on the glass as she watched the tall figures of her brother, Mr. Darcy, and his friend, Mr. Bingley, striding across the crisp lawn. A thin layer of frost crunched beneath their boots, and their breaths misted in the chilly air, a testament to the cold yet dry weather that had taken hold. Gamekeepers followed behind with guns and dogs, for the two gentlemen planned to take advantage of the dry weather and spend the morning shooting.

Despite the chilly air outside, Georgiana felt a twinge of envy at their freedom, the ease with which the men took to the outdoors, leaving the confines of the house behind. She, on the other hand, was bound to the drawing room and the company of Miss Caroline Bingley, whose presence seemed to fill the space with a frost of its own.

The sound of a carriage approaching drew Georgiana's gaze, and she watched as the Bennet family's arrival prompted the men to pause and offer polite greetings. From her secluded spot behind the window, she noted the subtle shift in her brother's posture, the softening around his eyes and the subtle curve of his lips as he spoke to Elizabeth Bennet. She had never seen such an expression on her brother's face before, and it made her wonder.

Caroline Bingley, who had been hovering nearby with thinly veiled interest, let out a soft huff of annoyance. "It seems we can never be free of those blasted Bennets, even in this frosty weather," she remarked with icy disdain, before letting out a sneeze.

The comment, meant only for Georgiana's ears, resonated with a bitterness that left the younger woman feeling even more isolated. Georgiana turned away from the window, her gaze falling on the embroidery in her hands, but her thoughts remained outside – with the cold, the freedom, and the warmth of her brother's uncharacteristic smile. She did not design to acknowledge Caroline Bingley's catty remark, and with a sigh, Miss Bingley walked away, constrained by her duties as hostess to greet her guests.

Left alone once more, Georgiana sank into a nearby chair, her heart heavy with anxiety and uncertainty. She had wanted only to be here with her brother, but now that she was, could not seem to find happiness.

"Miss Darcy?" Elizabeth Bennet's gentle voice pulled Georgiana from her reverie. "I know your brother has left us for the day, but I do hope you will find some enjoyment in our company."

"Thank you, Miss Elizabeth," murmured Georgiana, grateful for Elizabeth's kindness and warmth. "I shall endeavour to do so."

"Excellent!" Elizabeth beamed, her eyes sparkling with sincerity. "Now, let us find some amusement to occupy our time."

As the morning wore on, Georgiana found herself drawn to Elizabeth's lively conversation and quick wit. She marvelled at the ease with which the other lady navigated the complex social dynamics of their small gathering. It was honestly a delight to witness the way Elizabeth parried every barb of Caroline Bingley's with total aplomb.

"Miss Darcy," Lydia exclaimed suddenly, "it is such a lovely day outside, do you not think we should venture outdoors for a walk?"

"Indeed," chimed in Kitty, her eyes sparkling with anticipation, "it would be a terrible waste to spend such a beautiful day cooped up indoors."

Georgiana's heart tightened with reluctance at their proposal, remembering the previous day's unfortunate encounter. Yet she could not deny that the prospect of fresh air was tempting, especially after spending so much time in the confines of Netherfield.

"Perhaps it is a good idea," Elizabeth offered gently, sensing Georgiana's hesitation, "a brisk walk might do you some good. I only wish I might accompany you."

Georgiana wanted to beg Elizabeth to do just that, but Caroline Bingley was being particularly petty and mean towards Jane, and Georgiana could see Elizabeth was fully occupied in shielding her sister. Removing Lydia and Kitty – potential fuel for Caroline's spite – from the situation would be doing Elizabeth a favour.

"Very well," Georgiana acquiesced, attempting to muster a smile, "I shall accompany you."

"Capital!" cried Lydia, clapping her hands together with glee, while Kitty nodded her agreement enthusiastically.

Sure enough, as soon as they were out of view of the house's windows, Lydia and Kitty turned towards Meryton, deaf to Georgiana's quietly voiced suggestion that perhaps they need not go there today. With them securely clasping her arms and chattering nineteen to the dozen, Georgiana had perforce little choice but to go with them.

In the quaint village of Meryton, the lively chatter of the market square surrounded them as they strolled amidst the bustling stalls. Lydia and Kitty seemed barely able to contain their excitement as they spotted a group of officers nearby, resplendent in their red uniforms. As if drawn by an invisible force, they gravitated towards the soldiers, giggling behind gloved hands and casting flirtatious glances their way.

"Lydia, do be mindful of your manners," Georgiana chided softly, her brow furrowing with concern. She could not help but feel a sense of unease at the thought of encountering more strangers.

"Lighten up, Georgiana!" Lydia cried, her eyes shining with mischief. "We are simply having a bit of fun. Besides, you never know when you might meet someone who will sweep you off your feet."

"Or lead you astray," Georgiana muttered beneath her breath, though she doubted her words would be heeded.

"Lydia! Kitty!" Maria Lucas called out as she caught sight of them, waving them over excitedly. "I have someone I would like you to meet."

Curiosity piqued, the sisters exchanged bemused glances before making their way to Maria's side. As they neared, Georgiana's heart skipped a beat; standing beside Maria was none other than Mr. George Wickham, his roguish grin as charming as ever, dressed now in the red coat of an officer of the militia.

"Mr. Wickham," Maria began, her voice infused with warmth, "may I present Miss Lydia Bennet and Miss Catherine Bennet? They did not have the pleasure of meeting you yesterday. And our new friend, Miss Darcy."

"Delighted, I am sure," Wickham declared, bowing low before the wide-eyed girls. "And may I say that Meryton has certainly been blessed with an abundance of beauty."

"Thank you, sir," Lydia simpered, a blush stealing across her cheeks, while Kitty merely giggled in response.

Georgiana watched the scene unfold with a mixture of horror and disbelief. How could Wickham be here, in Meryton, so brazenly engaging with her acquaintances? She felt the blood drain from her face, leaving her feeling light-headed and disoriented. The truth became painfully clear: this was why her brother had been so cautious in his instructions. He had known all along that Wickham would be in the village, waiting like a serpent in the grass to strike at the heart of their family once more.

Wickham, ever the consummate performer, wasted no time in regaling Kitty and Lydia with stories of his exploits as a militia officer, his anecdotes peppered with just enough wit and daring to keep them on the edge of their seats. As he spoke, he made a point of including Georgiana in his gaze, as though to remind her of the connection they once shared.

"Indeed," Wickham continued, his voice lilting as he described a particularly harrowing skirmish, "it was only through the grace of Providence, and the courage of my fellow officers, that we emerged victorious from that dreadful encounter."

"La!" cried Kitty, her eyes alight with excitement. "What an adventure! I do so wish that I could have been there to witness it!"

"Would that you could," replied Wickham, his smile somehow both rakish and tender. "I am certain that your presence would have inspired us to even greater feats of valour."

Georgiana, still reeling from the shock of Wickham's unexpected appearance, struggled to maintain her composure. Her mind raced with questions, chief among them the matter of how she ought to proceed. Should she confront him, demand an explanation for his sudden return? Or should she remain silent, trusting her brother to deal with the situation when he returned from his shooting?

As these thoughts swirled within her head, Georgiana's attention was drawn back to the conversation at hand. Wickham had turned his charm on Lydia now, drawing her into a lively debate about the merits of various military tactics. It was all too much; Georgiana could feel her resolve crumbling beneath the weight of his magnetism. She knew that she must distance herself from Wickham, lest she be drawn back into his web of deceit.

"Excuse me," she murmured, her voice barely audible above the laughter and chatter of her companions. "I believe I require some air."

"Of course, dear Georgiana," said Lydia, her eyes still shining with excitement. "We shall not be long; surely a few more moments in Mr. Wickham's delightful company will do us no harm."

As Georgiana stepped away from the group, her heart pounding in her chest, she could not help but wonder at the cruel twist of fate that had brought Wickham back into her life. It was as though the very universe conspired against her peace of mind, determined to remind her of the folly she had so narrowly escaped. Retreating around a corner, she stood with her back to the wall of a shop, hand pressed to her throat, valiantly attempting to catch her breath.

"Miss Darcy," Wickham's voice was smooth, like honeyed silk, as he approached her with a warm smile. "Might I have a word with you? In private?"

Georgiana hesitated, her eyes darting over to where Kitty and Lydia were engaged in animated conversation with several other militia officers. She could not help but feel a shiver of apprehension at the thought of being alone with Wickham, even for a moment. Yet, she could not refuse him without drawing unwanted attention, and so, she nodded her assent.

"Of course, Mr. Wickham."

"Splendid," he replied, gesturing towards a secluded bench beneath a towering elm tree. "Shall we?"

As they walked, Georgiana found herself unable to shake the feeling of unease that had settled over her like a heavy shroud. She glanced back at Kitty and Lydia, who seemed entirely oblivious to her plight, their laughter ringing through the air as Wickham's friends entertained them with tales of their exploits.

"Miss Darcy," Wickham began, his voice low and intimate as they reached the bench. "I must tell you how very much I have missed your company these past months."

"Indeed?" Georgiana murmured, feigning disinterest as she stared down at her gloved hands, which were clasped tightly in her lap.

"Indeed," he confirmed, leaning closer so that his words tickled her ear. "And I cannot help but wonder if perhaps you have missed me, as well."

"Mr. Wickham," Georgiana said carefully, her heart hammering in her chest. "I do not think it appropriate for us to discuss such matters."

"Ah, but we are not merely acquaintances, Miss Darcy," he countered, his eyes glittering with hidden intent. "We share a history, and I believe that entitles me to be frank with you."

"Very well," she replied, steeling herself against the onslaught of emotions his words were sure to provoke. "What is it that you wish to say?"

"Simply this," he whispered, reaching out to take her hand in his. "I love you, Georgiana Darcy. And I cannot bear to spend another day apart from you. Elope with me, and together we shall find the happiness we both so desperately crave."

For a moment, Georgiana was stunned into silence, her mind reeling at the audacity of his proposal. She knew that she should reject him outright, that to consider his words for even an instant was tantamount to betrayal. Yet, there was something within her that could not help but yearn for the love and affection he seemed to offer so freely.

"Mr. Wickham," she began, her voice trembling with emotion. "I... I do not know what to say."

Wickham's eyes blazed with intensity, holding Georgiana captive in their magnetic grip. "You must understand, my dear," he implored earnestly, "that your brother has always harboured an irrational hatred for me. Your dear father, the late Mr. Darcy, was fond of me, and I dare say his son's jealousy knew no bounds."

Georgiana's thoughts raced, her heart torn between what she knew of her brother and the seductive words that now poured forth from Wickham's lips. She desperately sought a way to reconcile these conflicting narratives, but found herself unable to dismiss his claims out of hand.

"Is that truly the reason for my brother's dislike of you?" she asked hesitantly, her mind still grappling with the implications of this revelation.

"Indeed it is," he replied fervently. "And it is that same jealousy which has driven him to keep us apart all these years. But we need not be pawns in his petty game any longer, Georgiana. You have the power to choose your own path, and I stand before you as living proof that love can conquer all."

The sweetness of his words left Georgiana's head swimming, and for a wild, reckless moment, she considered giving in to the temptation he offered. However, the practical concerns that had been ingrained in her by years of strict upbringing could not be entirely silenced.

"Mr. Wickham," she ventured cautiously, "even if I were inclined to accept your proposal, how could you possibly leave your post with the militia to elope with me? Surely such an action would bring disgrace upon us both."

"Ah," he stammered, obviously taken aback by her question, "well, I... you see, there is a certain... arrangement that can be made with my commanding officer, one that would allow for a temporary absence from my duties..."

Before he could finish this rather unconvincing explanation, a carriage came to an abrupt halt beside them, and the door swung open with a sharp, imperious snap. To Georgiana's dismay, Lady Catherine de Bourgh emerged from the interior, her stern features set in an expression of utter disapproval.

"Miss Darcy!" she exclaimed, fixing her piercing gaze upon the young girl. "What on earth do you think you are doing, consorting with a soldier in the middle of the street? Have you no thought for your reputation, or for the honour of your family?"

Georgiana, too flustered to form a coherent response, merely stared at her feet, her cheeks burning with shame. She knew that Lady Catherine was right; even if her intentions had been entirely innocent, the mere appearance of impropriety could have disastrous consequences for her social standing.

Lady Catherine's withering glare then turned towards Wickham, who seemed to shrink before her formidable presence. "As for you, sir," she said icily, "I suggest you remember your place and keep your distance from young ladies of quality."

"Ma'am," Wickham began, attempting to sound contrite even as his eyes flashed with indignation, but Lady Catherine raised a hand to silence him.

"Enough!" she snapped. "Georgiana, get into the carriage this instant. We shall have a serious discussion about your conduct when we arrive at Netherfield."

The world seemed to tilt beneath Georgiana's feet as she stumbled towards the carriage, her mind a whirlwind of shock and confusion. She felt Lady Catherine's eyes boring into her, her aunt's admonishments echoing in her ears like the tolling of an ominous bell. As she reached the door of the carriage, she hesitated for a brief moment, casting a final glance towards Wickham. He stood where she had left him, his handsome features twisted into a mask of frustration, but whether it was directed at her or at Lady Catherine, she could not tell.

"Georgiana," Lady Catherine said sharply, reminding Georgiana of her command. With a quiet sigh, Georgiana obediently stepped inside the carriage, the door closing behind her with a sense of finality that made her heart sink. The interior was dim and suffocating, a stark contrast to the bright sunshine that had greeted her earlier in Meryton. It felt as if she were being swallowed by a great, dark beast, one whose maw would forever silence the whispers of love and adventure that Wickham's words had ignited within her.

As the carriage lurched into motion, Georgiana sank back against the plush cushions beside her cousin Anne, feeling as though she were being torn apart from within. A part of her wanted nothing more than to fling open the door and run back to Wickham, to surrender herself to the wild, reckless passion he had promised her. Another part, however, recoiled at the very thought, horrified by the potential consequences of such a choice.

"Did I do wrong?" she wondered silently. "Could there have been truth in his words, or was it all a cruel deception?"

Her thoughts raced as she tried to reconcile the conflicting emotions churning within her. How could someone who professed such love be so willing to jeopardize her reputation and the honour of her family? And yet, was it not possible that Wickham had been sincere in his intentions - that he truly believed their love could conquer all obstacles, even those placed before them by Darcy's unjust enmity?

"Georgiana," Lady Catherine's voice broke through her tumultuous thoughts like a dousing of cold water. "You must understand that your conduct today was most unbecoming of a young lady of your station. I trust you will take this as a lesson in the importance of propriety and decorum."

Georgiana nodded meekly, though inwardly she seethed at the injustice of the situation. She knew she had acted naively, perhaps even recklessly, but she also felt a fierce protective instinct towards the tender feelings that had blossomed within her heart. To have them dismissed so cavalierly by Lady Catherine left her feeling both angry and ashamed.

"Your brother would be most disappointed in you, Georgiana," Lady Catherine continued, her tone softening somewhat. "I am certain, however, that with time and guidance, you will learn to navigate the treacherous waters of society without further scandal."

"Thank you, Aunt Catherine," Georgiana murmured, her voice barely above a whisper. She stared out of the window, lost in thought. Her future seemed as uncertain as the landscape that blurred past her, but one thing remained clear: her path forward lay not with Wickham, but within the constraints of duty and propriety.

And yet, as the carriage rumbled on towards Netherfield, she could not help but wonder if there might still be room for love and passion in her life - or if such dreams were destined to remain forever out of reach.

Chapter Ten

Georgiana Darcy sat on the plush seat of her aunt's carriage beside her cousin Anne, her hands folded neatly in her lap, watching the scenery pass by through the window. Georgiana couldn't help but feel a sense of unease as the carriage rolled inexorably on towards Netherfield. *Fitzwilliam will be furious with me*, was all she could think, panic welling that her brother was about to find out she had defied his edict to remain on Netherfield's grounds.

"Georgiana," Anne de Bourgh whispered, leaning towards Georgiana, her dark eyes filled with curiosity. "Pray tell me, who was that handsome officer I observed you speaking with? He seemed quite taken with your company."

Georgiana's cheeks coloured at the mention of Mr. Wickham. Her heart raced as she recalled his charming smile and the way his eyes sparkled when he spoke. She hesitated before replying, finding it difficult to speak of him without betraying her own tangled emotions. "He is... an acquaintance of my brother's," she finally said, keeping her voice steady.

Anne leaned in closer. "Indeed? How fascinating. He appeared to be quite attentive to you. I must admit, I am rather envious of the attention."

Georgiana glanced at her cousin, noting the flush of excitement on her pale cheeks. She knew Anne rarely experienced such thrills in her sheltered existence under Lady Catherine's strict supervision. It saddened her to think of the limited world Anne inhabited, but she could not bring herself to encourage any interest in Mr. Wickham. Instead, she offered a gentle smile and turned her gaze back to the passing scenery, hoping the conversation would shift to a different topic.

As the carriage continued to roll on, the weight of their silence hung heavy in the air. Georgiana's thoughts turned inward, pondering the complex web of relationships and deceptions that seemed to surround her. She wondered how much more there was to learn about Mr. Wickham and, indeed, about her own heart.

"Here we are at last," Lady Catherine announced with an air of grandiosity as they arrived at Netherfield. "I shall demand to speak with my nephew immediately."

The carriage came to a halt, and a footman opened the door to assist the ladies in their descent. Lady Catherine swept out of the carriage with all the pomp and circumstance befitting her rank, her gaze sweeping over the grounds of Netherfield as though appraising them for potential faults. Anne followed her mother with more grace than might have been expected, given her often fragile health.

Georgiana struggled to suppress her unease as she followed after her aunt and cousin. There was something ominous about the way her aunt had insisted upon speaking with Mr. Darcy as soon as they had arrived at Netherfield. Georgiana did not dare ask why Lady Catherine had come – certainly it could have nothing to do with Georgiana herself, despite her guilty conscience. Georgiana had not even been in Hertfordshire long enough for Lady Catherine to have become aware of her presence. No, her aunt was here because of Fitzwilliam.

"Georgiana, dear," Lady Catherine said, turning to her niece with a stern gaze. "I trust you understand the gravity of the situation we find ourselves in?"

"Yes, Aunt," Georgiana replied softly, her eyes downcast. She knew better than to question Lady Catherine, but she couldn't help wondering what exactly was going on. Was it something to do with Mr. Wickham? No, surely not; her aunt had not even seemed to recognise him.

"Good," Lady Catherine said curtly, turning away from her niece. "Your brother must be made aware of the danger that lurks in Meryton. It is my duty as his aunt – and yours as his sister – to ensure that he does not fall prey to the machinations of unscrupulous individuals."

Georgiana contemplated her aunt's words, her confusion deepening with each passing moment. How little she understood of the world beyond Pemberley; how much more there was to learn about loyalty, betrayal, and the tangled webs people wove in pursuit of their desires.

It fell to Caroline Bingley to play the hostess to Lady Catherine de Bourgh.

"Welcome to Netherfield, Lady Catherine," Caroline began with a forced smile. "We are honoured by your presence. I am Miss Caroline Bingley, and..."

"Your pleasantries are appreciated, Miss Bingley, but I have not come for idle chatter," Lady Catherine replied, brushing past Caroline and striding over to the hearth to seat herself in the best armchair. "Where is my nephew?"

"Mr. Darcy is out this morning with my brother," Caroline answered, struggling to maintain her composure. "He is expected to return shortly."

"Very well," Lady Catherine said, her eyes narrowing. "I shall wait, but not idly. There is a matter of great import that must be addressed, and I would be remiss in my duties as his aunt were I to let it pass unremarked. It seems there is a scheming woman seeking to entrap my nephew, and I am most relieved that Mr. Collins saw fit to warn me of this peril."

A sudden silence fell upon the drawing room, as if the very air had been sucked out by Lady Catherine's arrival. From her vantage point near the window, Elizabeth could not help but observe the exchange between Caroline and the formidable matron with both amusement and trepidation.

"Lady Catherine, I assure you that my intentions towards Mr. Darcy have always been of the most honourable nature," Caroline stammered, her voice trembling and her face white.

"*Your* intentions?" Lady Catherine echoed, raising a single eyebrow in a manner that sent an involuntary shudder down Elizabeth's spine. "You speak as if you presume to know what is best for my nephew. Pray, enlighten me as to how you deign to possess such insight."

Caroline opened her mouth to respond, but before she could utter a single syllable, her face contorted with a sudden grimace. A moment later, she sneezed violently into her handkerchief, the force of her action propelling her forward and causing her to unwittingly stumble into Lady Catherine herself.

Lady Catherine shrieked in horror at the unexpected contact, recoiling. The entire room seemed to hold its breath, waiting for the impending explosion of indignation.

"Miss Bingley!" she bellowed, her cheeks flushed with rage. "Have you no sense of propriety? First, you dare to insinuate yourself into matters that do not concern you, and now you inflict your illness upon me! This is intolerable!"

Caroline, her face ashen with terror, could only stammer out a weak apology, her gaze fixed on the ground as if she hoped it might swallow her whole.

"Lady Catherine, I…" she began, but Lady Catherine silenced her with a single, imperious wave of her hand.

"Enough!" she snapped. "I have heard quite enough from you, Miss Bingley, and certainly I cannot risk exposing Anne to whatever illness you may be suffering! Georgiana, show us to another parlour. We shall wait there for Darcy's return!"

Elizabeth watched as the door slammed shut behind Lady Catherine, her heart pounding in her chest. She exchanged a glance with Jane, who looked as shaken as she felt. It was at this moment that Charlotte, ever the epitome of grace and tact, stepped forward and gently placed her hands on Elizabeth's and Jane's shoulders.

"Come, let us take our leave," Charlotte said in a hushed voice. "We shall collect Kitty and Lydia and return to Longbourn."

"Indeed," agreed Elizabeth, grateful for her stepmother's intervention. "I do not think we could bear another moment here."

As they made their way out of Netherfield and towards the waiting carriage, Jane spoke up.

"Stepmama," she began hesitantly, "what do you make of Lady Catherine's accusations? Do you believe there is any truth to them? Was Mr. Collins referring to Miss Bingley, do you think?"

"Jane," interjected Elizabeth, "now is not the time for such discussions. Let us focus on returning home."

"Very well," conceded Jane, shaking her head. "Poor Caroline, with such a house guest inflicted upon her!"

They deserve each other, Elizabeth thought a little uncharitably, but she did not voice the thought aloud.

"Now where are Kitty and Lydia?" Charlotte murmured, looking towards the gardens as though debating whether she should go and look for them.

"They must have walked towards Meryton," Elizabeth noted. "How else could Lady Catherine have picked Georgiana up, on her way to Netherfield? Let us drive that way and I am certain we will find them."

Indeed, they found Kitty and Lydia in Meryton itself, near the inn, speaking with their Aunt Phillips.

"Finally!" exclaimed Lydia, throwing her hands in the air as she spotted their carriage approaching. "What has taken you so long?"

"Lydia," chided Charlotte gently, "patience is a virtue."

Kitty simply scowled as she climbed into the carriage, followed by Lydia, who continued to grumble under her breath. The atmosphere inside the carriage was tense and uncomfortable, and Elizabeth found herself longing for the relative peace of Longbourn.

"Lydia, Kitty," Charlotte began as they set off once more, "I trust you behaved yourselves while we were occupied at Netherfield?"

"Of course we did!" retorted Lydia with a roll of her eyes, while Kitty gave a noncommittal shrug.

"Very well," replied Charlotte, though her expression betrayed her doubts. She turned her gaze to Elizabeth, who met it with a weary smile and a silent promise to discuss these matters further once they were safely home.

As the carriage rolled along, an uneasy silence hung heavy in the air, broken only by the occasional jolt of the wheels over a rutted patch of road.

"Really, it's too bad," Lydia burst out at last, her impatience finally getting the better of her. "We were having such a fine time with Mr. Wickham and his friends before Georgiana left, and then all he could talk about was her! As if she were some sort of angel!"

"Indeed," Kitty chimed in, her eyes narrowed resentfully. "I do not see why she should have left so abruptly. It was very ill-mannered of her."

Elizabeth exchanged a look with Charlotte, who merely raised an eyebrow in response. She turned her attention back to her younger sisters, struggling to keep her tone even as she asked, "And what, pray tell, did Mr. Wickham have to say about Miss Darcy?"

"Nothing particularly interesting," Lydia pouted. "He simply spoke of how he had known her since she was a child, and how they were once quite close. I do not see why that should matter now – we are far more entertaining company than some dull girl who barely speaks a word!"

"Lydia!" Elizabeth admonished, her voice sharp. "You must not speak so unkindly of Miss Darcy. She has done nothing to warrant such animosity."

"Perhaps not," Lydia grumbled, sinking back into sullen silence.

"I cannot like that the two of you took Miss Darcy into Meryton and were speaking with officers, unchaperoned," Charlotte said then, her tone cool. "This is not appropriate behaviour, and I expect better from you. Neither of you are yet out."

"We were with Maria Lucas," Lydia said defiantly, "and our Aunt Phillips. You cannot deny she is an adequate chaperone!"

"We will also have words about the manner in which you are speaking to me, Lydia." Charlotte's expression did not change. "I had thought that school was improving your manners and sense, but perhaps not."

Lydia turned red, but said nothing more. Elizabeth noted that Kitty, at least, looked a little ashamed of herself.

As the conversation lulled, Elizabeth's thoughts turned inward, her mind racing with the implications of her sisters' words. She recalled Mr. Wickham's tales of his own history with Mr. Darcy, of the injustices he claimed to have suffered. Yet, there was something more here, another layer she had not yet uncovered. She resolved to speak with Mr. Darcy when next they met, to seek answers from him directly. After all, if there was one thing Elizabeth had learned over the course of her tumultuous acquaintance with the gentleman, it was that things were rarely as simple as they appeared.

"Elizabeth," Charlotte murmured softly, drawing her from her reverie. "You seem deep in thought, my dear."

"Indeed, I am," Elizabeth replied with a wry smile. "There is much that remains unclear to me, and I fear it is only through further inquiry that the truth will be brought to light."

"Then let us hope that your inquiries prove fruitful," Charlotte said, her eyes warm with understanding. "And that your discoveries bring you peace."

"Thank you, dearest," Elizabeth whispered, her heart swelling with gratitude for Charlotte's unwavering support.

Retiring to the parlour once they arrived back at Longbourn, Jane, Elizabeth and Charlotte found Mary seated with a book. Mary set the book aside and smiled as she saw them enter.

"You are back earlier than I expected," Mary noted. "Did the visit not go well?"

"It certainly took an unexpected turn. You will not believe who arrived at Netherfield, Mary," Jane said, taking a seat as Charlotte rang for tea.

"Do enlighten me," Mary said, her expression curious.

"Lady Catherine de Bourgh," Elizabeth announced. "In response, it seems to a summons from Mr. Collins, warning that there is a lady here in Hertfordshire with designs upon Mr. Darcy, tempting him away from his engagement to Miss Anne de Bourgh! Who, I must assume, was that young lady who accompanied Lady Catherine," she noted, looking at Jane and Charlotte.

"I barely noticed her, to be honest," Jane admitted. "I was too busy quaking in fear of Lady Catherine."

"Oh, you have nothing to fear from her," Elizabeth said with a laugh. "You are not the one with designs on Mr. Darcy! I could almost feel sorry for Caroline Bingley."

"You think Mr. Collins was referring to Caroline Bingley?" Charlotte queried.

"Of course." Puzzled, Elizabeth turned to her stepmother. "Whom else could he have meant?"

"Hm," was all Charlotte said in response.

"But why?" Mary asked, her expression serious as she considered this news. "What could have possessed him to write such a letter?"

"Mr. Collins' motives are often unfathomable, but in this case, I believe it was his misguided sense of duty to Lady Catherine," Charlotte explained. "He felt it necessary to warn her of the situation."

"Regardless of his intentions, his actions display an extraordinary level of pettiness," Mary declared, her lips pressed into a thin line of disapproval. "I cannot condone such behaviour, nor can I align myself with it through marriage."

"Then you mean to reject his proposal?" Charlotte inquired gently.

"Indeed, I do," Mary replied firmly. "Though I am well aware of the benefits such a match would bring, I cannot bring myself to marry a man whose character I find so fundamentally lacking."

"Your determination is admirable, Mary," Charlotte said, placing a reassuring hand on her arm. "You deserve a partner who will treat both you and those around you with respect."

"Thank you, Stepmama," Mary replied with a small smile, one that made her look quite pretty, Elizabeth noted. "It is comforting to know that you understand my position, and support it."

"Always, my dear," Charlotte assured her.

"Mary, I am very glad you have decided not to accept him," Elizabeth said, reaching out to take Mary's hand and squeeze it with affection. "I think you would have been wasted, married to a man as silly and petty as Collins."

"Thank you, Lizzy," Mary responded, obviously touched by her sister's sentiment. "I feel similarly. I would rather not marry at all than settle for the first man who asks me when he is not the right choice."

"Such maturity is rare, and admirable," remarked Jane, smiling gently at her sister.

"Indeed," agreed Elizabeth. "We must all learn from Mary's example, and strive to make choices based on our own happiness, rather than the expectations of others."

Mary's steps were heavy as she ascended the stairs to her bedroom, seating herself at her small writing-desk. She took no pleasure in what she was about to do, but putting it off was an intolerable notion. She dipped her quill into the inkwell, exhaling deeply as she contemplated the weight of the words she was about to write. This letter would put an end to any possibility of marriage between herself and Mr. Collins, and although she felt confident in her decision, there was still a part of her that could not help but wonder what would become of her in the future.

Dear Mr. Collins, Mary began, her hand steady as she penned the opening lines, *I hope this letter finds you in good health and spirits. Your recent proposal has given me much cause for thought and reflection.*

"Mary, do you require any assistance with your letter?" Elizabeth asked, peeking in through the half-open door.

"Thank you, Lizzy, but I must do this on my own," Mary replied, offering her sister a weak smile.

"Very well, then," Elizabeth nodded, understanding the importance of Mary handling the matter herself. "If you need anything, just call for me."

"Thank you," Mary murmured, returning her focus to the task at hand.

She continued to write, her thoughts flowing onto the page: *Upon careful consideration, I must regretfully inform you that I cannot accept your offer of marriage. While I am grateful for your kind attention and regard, it is my belief that we are not suited for one another.*

Pausing for a moment, Mary considered how best to explain her decision without causing undue offense. It was important for her to be honest and forthright, yet she wished to remain respectful and considerate.

Since spending time in London with my aunt and uncle, I have come to understand more about myself and my desires for the future, Mary wrote, hoping that by sharing a piece of her personal journey, Mr. Collins might better comprehend her choice. *I have learned that I value my independence and the pursuit of knowledge above all else, and while marriage is undoubtedly an honourable institution, I cannot in good conscience enter into such a union unless I am certain it will contribute to my happiness and personal growth.*

Furthermore, she continued, her words growing bolder as she articulated her convictions, *I firmly believe that both parties in a marriage must be well-matched in temperament and values, lest their union become a source of strife and discontent. I fear that our differing outlooks on life would prevent us from achieving true harmony and understanding within a marriage.*

As Mary penned the closing lines of her letter, she felt a mixture of relief and trepidation. She knew that her refusal might displease Mr. Collins and perhaps even Lady Catherine de Bourgh; however, she also recognized that she owed it to herself and her future to make choices based on her own convictions rather than the expectations of others.

Please accept my sincerest apologies for any disappointment this decision may cause you. I wish you every happiness in your future endeavours, Mary concluded, her hand trembling slightly as she signed her name.

With a sigh, Mary folded the letter and carefully sealed it with wax. As she gazed upon the finished product, she could not help but feel a sense of pride in her newfound strength and resolve. In choosing her own path, she had taken the first step toward defining her own destiny – and that, she knew, was worth more than any marriage proposal could ever offer.

Chapter Eleven

It was late when Mr. Darcy and Mr. Bingley returned from their day out, having been invited to and accepted an invitation to take dinner at Lucas Lodge. The amiable companionship of the Lucases had been a welcome respite from the tensions within Netherfield, and the two gentlemen found themselves in high spirits.

As the door opened, Mrs. Hurst stood before them, her countenance etched with worry. Her usual detached air of haughty disdain seemed to have abandoned her entirely, replaced by a palpable sense of panic.

"Oh my dear brother, and Mr. Darcy!" she exclaimed breathlessly, approaching them with hurried steps. "Thank goodness you have returned! I must speak with you immediately."

"Louisa, whatever is the matter?" inquired Mr. Bingley, concern evident in his voice as he observed his sister's disordered appearance.

"Caroline..." she hesitated, wringing her hands anxiously, "she has taken ill after... Well, after your aunt arrived and confronted her, Mr. Darcy."

"My aunt?" Darcy stared at her, confused. "Which aunt?"

"Lady Catherine de Bourgh! She accused Caroline of... of..." Mrs. Hurst clearly did not want to say the words, but with Darcy and her brother both staring at her, she had to admit the truth. "Of setting her cap for you," she confessed, in a near-whisper.

"And Lady Catherine came here to confront her about it?" Darcy queried, struggling to contain his surprise. It was hardly news to him that Miss Bingley imagined herself as the future mistress of Pemberley, but he had never anticipated Lady Catherine's involving herself in the matter.

"Caroline appears to have contracted the same influenza that has kept Mrs. Annesley abed since her arrival," Mrs. Hurst added, her voice laden with worry. "I fear the distress from Lady Catherine's tirade has only exacerbated her condition."

"I shall send for the doctor immediately," Bingley said. "Where is Lady Catherine now?"

"When you and Mr. Darcy did not return for dinner, she demanded rooms for herself and her daughter. I ordered the housekeeper to prepare the best guest suites we had available for them." Mrs. Hurst took a deep breath and seemed to pull herself together.

"Wait, my cousin Anne is here as well?" Darcy asked, wondering what his aunt could possibly be about. "Forgive me, Bingley. I did not anticipate my aunt's intrusion upon your hospitality."

"Think nothing of it, Darcy," Bingley replied, ever the amiable host. "We shall manage as best we can, even if Caroline is not well. Indeed, I am sure my dear Jane will be eager to step into the breach and learn the ways of Netherfield; you will not have to manage alone, Louisa!"

Mrs. Hurst hardly looked delighted at the prospect, but said nothing, perhaps realising that if she declined Jane's help she would have to manage everything herself until her sister recovered, which would not suit her inclination to indolence at all well.

Despite Bingley's assurances, Darcy could not shake the sense of foreboding that settled over him as he retired for the night. He braced himself for the confrontation with his imperious aunt that he knew would inevitably come.

The following morning, as Darcy descended the staircase to join his companions for breakfast, Lady Catherine appeared suddenly at his side. Her countenance was stormy, her eyes flashing with indignation as she launched into her tirade without preamble.

"Darcy, I must speak with you," she declared, her voice a mixture of wrath and hauteur. "It has come to my attention that a certain woman of inferior status has been pursuing you!"

Darcy opened his mouth, but she did not give him even a moment to speak.

"Surely you must know that such a match is out of the question," Lady Catherine continued, her words a veritable torrent of disapproval. "You are duty-bound to make a more advantageous alliance, one befitting a man of your station."

"Indeed, madam," Darcy replied, struggling to maintain his composure in the face of her accusations. "I assure you I have no intention of marrying any woman who does not meet the standards required of me by both family and society."

"And what if you are trapped by a designing female such as this? One who has rejected a perfectly suitable proposal from Mr. Collins! I can only assume that she believes she will receive a better offer!" Lady Catherine gave him a meaningful look.

Darcy's brow furrowed in confusion. *Mr. Collins? Mr. Collins had proposed to Caroline Bingley?* "Aunt Catherine," he ventured cautiously, "are you referring to Miss Bingley? Has she truly received a proposal from Mr. Collins?"

Lady Catherine's eyes widened in disbelief, her countenance betraying her incredulity at his suggestion. "Miss *Bingley*?" she echoed, a sneer forming on her lips. "Heavens, no! She is even less suited to be your wife than the lady I speak of... at least that one is a gentleman's daughter."

"Madam, I am still at a loss as to whom you are referring!" Darcy exclaimed, running out of patience.

"Miss Elizabeth Bennet!" his aunt cried, infuriated.

"Miss Elizabeth?" Darcy repeated, his heart eluding his attempts to quell its sudden, inexplicable acceleration within his chest.

"Indeed," Lady Catherine confirmed, her voice laced with disdain. "It appears that she has spurned his suit, despite the fact that a match with such an upstanding clergyman would have secured the future of her entire family as well as herself."

Darcy struggled to conceal his astonishment, his mind whirring with the implications of this revelation. He had always known Elizabeth to be a young woman of exceptional wit and discernment, yet it seemed she had surpassed even his estimations in her refusal of Mr. Collins. Still, he could not allow his feelings to cloud his judgment or to betray him in front of his imperious aunt.

"Your concern for my welfare is most touching, Aunt," he replied evenly, striving to maintain a semblance of detachment. "However, I can assure you that there is no need for alarm. The situation is entirely under control."

"Under control, you say?" Lady Catherine scoffed, her eyes narrowing as she scrutinized Darcy. "I find it most alarming that a man of your consequence should be linked to a woman so clearly beneath you. I had expected better judgment on your part, nephew."

Darcy's jaw tightened, and he willed himself not to betray his true feelings. It would not do to give Lady Catherine any further ammunition.

"Your concern is noted, Aunt," he replied, forcing a polite smile. "Yet I must inform you that I have given no indication of any interest in Miss Elizabeth Bennet. I fear there has been some misunderstanding on Mr. Collins' part."

"Indeed," Lady Catherine huffed, clearly doubting his sincerity. "And yet, Mr. Collins appears quite convinced that you are enamoured with the young lady and that she is at any moment expecting your declaration, which is what has led her to refuse the most suitable proposal which Mr. Collins offered! Whatever could have given him such an impression?"

"Perhaps Mr. Collins is simply prone to flights of fancy," Darcy suggested, his voice dripping with false nonchalance. Inwardly, he cringed at how easily the falsehoods slipped from his lips. He *did* admire Elizabeth Bennet, far more than he should.

"Be that as it may," Lady Catherine said icily, "I intend to see this matter resolved forthwith. Pray tell me, where might one find this Elizabeth Bennet?"

Darcy hesitated, knowing full well that his aunt's interference would only serve to complicate matters further. Yet the truth was that he could not bear the thought of Lady Catherine confronting Elizabeth, and perhaps even damaging her reputation in the process.

Before Darcy could devise a plan to prevent Lady Catherine from confronting Elizabeth, Mrs. Hurst eagerly stepped forward and provided detailed directions to Longbourn. Her voice was tinged with malicious satisfaction, her eyes glinting at the prospect of scandal, especially one which might damage the Bennet family.

"Longbourn is but a short ride from here," she informed Lady Catherine, who listened attentively. "Merely follow the main road through Meryton, and you shall arrive there soon enough."

"Excellent," Lady Catherine said, nodding curtly. "You have been most helpful, Mrs. Hurst."

"Always at your service, my lady," Mrs. Hurst replied, inclining her head in a shallow courtesy.

As Lady Catherine turned to leave, Darcy felt a surge of desperation. He could not allow his aunt to descend upon Elizabeth like a vengeful storm, wreaking havoc on the young woman's life. With a resolution born out of his growing affection for Elizabeth, he made a hasty decision.

As soon as Lady Catherine's carriage began rolling away, Darcy wasted no time in summoning his horse and urging it into a swift gallop, hoping to reach Longbourn before his aunt arrived.

With each thundering stride, Darcy's thoughts raced, consumed by the need to protect Elizabeth from Lady Catherine's wrath. Though he knew it would be impossible to deter his aunt entirely, he hoped that his presence might somehow shield Elizabeth from the worst of the confrontation.

As Darcy neared Longbourn, he prayed that he would arrive in time to provide whatever support Elizabeth might need in the face of Lady Catherine's formidable presence. He could not, and would not, allow her reputation or happiness to be marred by the machinations of his overbearing aunt. His heart pounded with urgency as he dismounted his horse and rushed to the door, praying that he had arrived before Lady Catherine. Upon reaching the entrance, he hesitated for a moment, taking a deep breath to calm himself before lifting the knocker.

"Mr. Darcy!" Elizabeth exclaimed, her eyes widening with surprise as he was shown into the parlour, where she was sitting alone. "To what do we owe this unexpected visit?"

"Miss Elizabeth," Darcy began, struggling to catch his breath, "I have come to warn you of an impending visit from my aunt, Lady Catherine de Bourgh. She is under the impression that there is some... understanding between you and I, and has taken it upon herself to intervene."

Elizabeth raised an eyebrow, clearly bemused. "And pray tell, Mr. Darcy, what sort of understanding does your aunt believe exists between us?"

"An engagement, Miss Elizabeth," Darcy confessed, feeling his cheeks flush with embarrassment. "She believes that you have refused an offer of marriage from Mr. Collins due to some connection between us."

Elizabeth looked quite stunned, before beginning to laugh. "So that is what Charlotte meant," she murmured, almost to herself, before looking back at him. "Well, I must say, that is quite the imaginative tale. As much as I appreciate your warning, Mr. Darcy, I assure you that I am not intimidated by your aunt's impending visit."

"Elizabeth," Darcy implored, so concerned for her welfare he slipped and addressed her only by her first name, "please reconsider. My aunt can be quite... forceful, and I fear the repercussions should she confront you directly."

"Mr. Darcy," Elizabeth responded calmly, a mischievous smile playing at the corners of her lips, "if anything, your presence here is likely to give precisely the opposite impression to the one you intend. You must leave at once if you wish to avoid further fuelling your aunt's suspicions."

Darcy hesitated, torn between his desire to protect Elizabeth and his need to respect her wishes. In the end, it was her steady gaze and resolutely calm expression that convinced him to relent.

"Very well," he conceded, his voice heavy with reluctance. "I shall take my leave, but please know that I stand ready to support you should the need arise."

"Thank you, Mr. Darcy," Elizabeth replied softly, holding his gaze. "But rest assured, I am quite capable of handling Lady Catherine on my own."

As Darcy turned away from Longbourn, he could not help but be struck by the undeniable strength and courage that lay beneath Elizabeth's delicate exterior. It only served to deepen his admiration for her, even as he resigned himself to the reality that his presence might only complicate matters further.

Upon his return to Netherfield, Darcy's thoughts were consumed by Elizabeth and the potential confrontation with Lady Catherine. His admiration for her had only grown due to her unwavering resolve in the face of such an imposing figure as his aunt.

Entering the drawing room, Darcy found Bingley engaged in a game of cards with the Hursts. His friend looked up at his arrival and noted the troubled expression on Darcy's face.

"Is everything quite well, Darcy?" Bingley inquired, genuine concern in his voice. "You seem rather perturbed."

Darcy hesitated, unsure how much to reveal about the situation at Longbourn. He settled for a vague explanation, unwilling to betray Elizabeth's confidence.

"Merely a minor family matter," he replied, forcing a tight smile. "Nothing that need cause you any concern, Bingley."

"Very well," Bingley acquiesced, though he still eyed Darcy with concern. "If you are certain, my friend."

"Indeed, I am," Darcy assured him, though he could not completely shake the nagging worry that gnawed at him. As he joined his friends at the card table, his mind remained focused on Elizabeth, fervently hoping that she would emerge unscathed from her encounter with Lady Catherine.

As the afternoon wore on, Darcy found it increasingly difficult to concentrate on the game at hand, his thoughts constantly straying back to Longbourn and the spirited woman he was beginning to fear had captured his heart. He could only wait, and trust in her strength and courage to see her through the storm that awaited her.

Chapter Twelve

The air at Netherfield had taken on a distinctly frigid chill, despite the roaring fires blazing in every hearth. Mr. Darcy surveyed his aunt, Lady Catherine de Bourgh, as she paced the drawing room like a caged lioness, her sharp eyes darting about and her mouth set in a thin, furious line.

"I cannot believe the impertinence of that foolish, headstrong girl!" Lady Catherine exclaimed, her voice rising with each word. "To think that Elizabeth Bennet dared to defy me - *me*! The daughter of an earl! It is beyond the pale."

Darcy shifted uncomfortably in his seat. He longed to press his aunt for details of her confrontation with Miss Elizabeth, to learn what exactly had transpired between them, but he sensed now was not the opportune moment. Lady Catherine's temper was legendary and unpredictable. Better to let her vent her spleen first before venturing any inquiries.

"And now, to add insult to injury," Lady Catherine continued, her cheeks flushed an angry red, "I discover that everyone in this wretched place seems to think that upstart Miss Bingley has also set her cap for you, Darcy! The audacity! As if a man of your station and breeding would ever consider such an unsuitable match – your friendship with her brother is bad enough, but marriage! Their money came from *trade*!"

Darcy's jaw tightened at the slight to his friends. He was grateful that he and Lady Catherine were the only ones in the room at the present moment; he would not like Bingley to hear what Lady Catherine was saying.

"I have half a mind to whisk you back to Rosings this very instant, Darcy," Lady Catherine declared. "I'll not have you falling prey to the machinations of ambitious young ladies and their scheming families!" She whirled to face him, her eyes glinting with steely determination. "Yes, I believe that would be for the best. You must leave Hertfordshire at once."

Darcy shook his head, affecting a calm he did not feel. "Come now, Aunt Catherine," he said in a placating tone. "There's no need for such drastic measures. I assure you, I am in no danger from either Miss Elizabeth Bennet or Miss Bingley."

Lady Catherine studied him for a long moment, her shrewd gaze seeming to penetrate the very depths of his soul. At last, she gave a curt nod. "Very well, Darcy. I suppose I cannot exactly drag you away from here by the scruff of your neck. But mark my words - I will not stand idly by and watch you throw yourself away on some country nobody, *or* an upstart from a family of doubtful antecedents. The shades of Pemberley will not be thus polluted."

They sat in silence for a few moments, an uneasy truce reached, until Darcy ventured to speak again.

"Aunt Catherine," he began, his voice carefully measured, "I must speak with you about your conversation with Miss Elizabeth Bennet."

Lady Catherine's lips thinned into a tight line. "There is nothing to discuss, Darcy. The girl is entirely unsuitable for you, and I will not stand by and watch you throw away your future on a mere whim."

Darcy bristled at her words, his jaw clenching with barely suppressed anger. "Lady Catherine, I am not in any way involved with Miss Elizabeth Bennet, and I cannot conceive where Mr. Collins gained the notion that I am... or the audacity to seek to interfere in my personal life!"

That gave Lady Catherine a moment's pause. "Perhaps it was not Mr. Collins' place," she allowed, "but you must make allowances for his feelings of hurt after being so summarily rejected by a woman who should have been grateful for his attentions."

"Grateful!" Darcy scoffed. "Mr. Collins is a foolish, fawning man with not one tenth of Miss Elizabeth's wit. It would have been a most unequal match and frankly, I applaud her decision to reject him."

"You *do* admire her." Sensing weakness, Lady Catherine leaned forward, her eyes narrowing.

"I do," Darcy admitted it freely. "But I have not made any pursuit or led Miss Elizabeth on in any way. I have been considering, in truth, the possibility of choosing to align myself with a family such as the Bennets, rather than pursuing a match for connections and wealth. I am leaning towards following the genuine emotion Miss Elizabeth has inspired in me."

"Genuine?" Lady Catherine scoffed. "What can you possibly know of genuine feeling? You are a Darcy, and with that comes certain obligations and expectations. You cannot simply follow your heart without considering the consequences!"

"And what consequences might those be?" Darcy asked, his tone growing more heated. "To marry for love, to find a partner who challenges and inspires me? I fail to see how that could be anything but a blessing."

Lady Catherine shook her head, her expression a mixture of pity and exasperation. "You are blinded by infatuation, nephew. Miss Bennet may have a pretty face and a sharp tongue, but she is far beneath you in every way that matters. Her family, her connections, her fortune – all are woefully inadequate for a man of your station."

Darcy paced the room, his agitation growing with every step. "I care nothing for her fortune or her connections. It is her mind, her spirit, that I admire."

"You are a fool, Darcy," Lady Catherine said coldly. "A fool who is willing to throw away everything for the sake of a passing fancy. I will not stand by and watch you ruin yourself and your family name."

"Then do not watch," Darcy said quietly, his voice filled with a steely resolve. "I am my own man, Aunt, and I will make my own choices. They are absolutely none of your concern, and should you seek to interfere further, I will have no choice but to show you exactly who is senior in our family."

Lady Catherine's face turned red, and her jaw worked as though she was chewing, but she said nothing. Darcy eyed her with a touch of pity.

"It gives me no pleasure to remind you that your husband saw fit to leave everything to his daughter in trust and not name you as one of the trustees," Darcy said quietly. "My cousin Fitzwilliam and I have chosen to allow you as much leeway to run Rosings as we are able, only visiting occasionally to handle such legal matters as require our presence or one of our signatures. But do not mistake me; attempting to interfere in my choice of a wife is considerably beyond your purview and I will not tolerate it."

A tense silence hung in the room as the two strong personalities eyed each other, Lady Catherine obviously considering if she could push Darcy further. "It was your mother's fondest wish..." she began, but Darcy held up his hand to stop her.

"Anne and I will never be married," he said flatly. "On that, the two of us agreed years ago. It is an idea you have clung to far too long, and it is clearly your bruiting it about that led Mr. Collins to run to you with his invented tale in the first place. I will tolerate it no longer. I have offered, numerous times, to assist you to take Anne to London for a Season, where no doubt she would be fêted as the great heiress she is, and have her choice of husbands. That offer remains open. Despite your claims of Anne being too weak for it, I think the only thing wrong with Anne is that you have spent years telling her she is sickly. She is too over-protected, and it is high time she saw a little more of the world. If you will not see to it, I will take it up with Lord and Lady Matlock when next I write to them."

Lady Catherine humphed. "You never used to be so impertinent, Darcy," she said, a little petulantly. "That Bennet girl has been a bad influence, I fear!"

Darcy would have dearly loved to ask just what Elizabeth had said to Lady Catherine that was so impertinent, but was prevented from trying once again to get the information out of his aunt as Mr. Bingley entered the drawing room at that moment, his usual affable smile firmly in place, even though he must have been able to hear their raised voices in the hall.

Darcy introduced his aunt and Bingley, who had not previously met.

Bingley bowed very deeply, and said; "Lady Catherine, I do hope you will extend your stay with us at Netherfield. It would be our great pleasure to have you as our guest for as long as you wish."

Lady Catherine sniffed, her eyes narrowing as she appraised the young man before her. "I suppose I have no choice but to accept your offer, Mr. Bingley. Someone must be here to ensure that my nephew does not make a complete fool of himself over that impertinent girl. Or any other girl who imagines herself worthy of him." She flicked a sideways glance at Darcy.

Bingley's smile faltered slightly, but he maintained his composure. "I am quite sure, my lady, that Mr. Darcy is more than capable of managing his own affairs."

As Bingley continued to make polite conversation with Lady Catherine, Darcy found his thoughts drifting to Elizabeth. He longed to see her, to speak with her, to assure himself that she had not been too distressed by his aunt's visit. But he knew that he must bide his time, that he must allow the situation to calm before he could approach her again.

For now, he would have to content himself with the knowledge that Elizabeth had refused to be intimidated by Lady Catherine's threats and ultimatums.

Lady Catherine allowed herself to be just a little charmed by Mr. Bingley, who Darcy thought sourly was probably capable of charming the birds from the trees if he put his mind to it, and he soon persuaded her to join him in the dining parlour where a light nuncheon buffet had been set out. Mr. Hurst was already there, as was Georgiana, and Anne walked in a few moments later.

Anne greeted Darcy with a smile, and he bowed to her before introducing her to Hurst and Bingley.

Bingley bowed. "A pleasure to make your acquaintance, Miss de Bourgh."

Anne curtsied awkwardly. "The pleasure is mine, sir."

"I will leave you two to get acquainted," Darcy said. "If you'll excuse me..."

He moved to help himself to some food, half-listening as Anne attempted stilted small talk with Bingley. After a few banal pleasantries about the weather, he noticed Anne's tone shift.

"It must be so dull for you here in the country," she said, fluttering her eyelashes in what Darcy presumed was an attempt at flirtation.

"Oh, not at all," Bingley replied obliviously. "The shooting is excellent."

Anne tittered and laid a hand on Bingley's arm in a way that made Darcy cringe. Bingley gently extracted himself, looking bemused.

Just then, the sound of an approaching carriage saved Bingley from further awkwardness. "Ah, I believe that will be the Bennets now. I am eager to introduce my fiancée, Miss Jane Bennet, to your notice, Miss de Bourgh!"

Anne's face fell comically as Bingley hurried away. Darcy had to stifle a chuckle at her failed flirtation. *Some amusement after all,* he thought wryly.

"Why are the Bennets here?" Lady Catherine demanded, her tone outraged.

"Aunt Catherine," Darcy said warningly. "The eldest Miss Bennet is Mr. Bingley's fiancée. With Miss Bingley indisposed and the wedding date fast approaching, Miss Bennet's presence at

Netherfield daily is both expected and welcome. Generally she is accompanied by one or more of her sisters, and sometimes Mrs. Bennet too. Indeed, the younger Bennet girls have been very kind in befriending Georgiana; they are clever and lively, and I daresay Anne might like to get to know them too. Indeed, this is a good opportunity for Anne to encounter more people in social situations, is it not?" He gave Lady Catherine a pointed look. She pursed her lips, but finally gave a reluctant nod.

"Very well," she said, rather ungraciously. "Anne, you will befriend the younger Bennet daughters."

"Yes, Mama," Anne said, obviously startled, but Darcy could see excitement dawning on her face.

This would be good for Anne, he thought. She had too little opportunity to make friends her own age. Perhaps it was not so bad that Lady Catherine had come to Hertfordshire after all, if it led to Anne being able to live a little.

But his thoughts were soon interrupted by Georgiana, who approached him with a troubled expression on her face when he finished eating. "Brother," she whispered, drawing him aside, "I must speak with you privately."

Darcy followed his sister out of the room and into the library, where she took a deep breath and began to speak, her words coming out in a hasty rush. "Fitzwilliam, I must confess something to you. I... I walked into Meryton with Lydia and Kitty, and I saw Mr. Wickham there."

Darcy felt a surge of anger and fear at the mention of Wickham's name. "Did he speak to you?" he demanded, his voice low and urgent.

Georgiana looked away, not meeting his eyes. "I know he saw me, and I... I was afraid," she said.

Darcy wondered if she was prevaricating, but considering that she had just come to confide in him of her own free will, decided not to press her. Instead, he sighed and took his sister's hands in his own. "Georgiana, I am sorry that you had to face that alone. I should have been there to protect you."

Georgiana looked up at him with tearful eyes. "I am sorry, Fitzwilliam. I know I should not have gone into town without your permission. I promise I will not do so again."

Darcy nodded, his heart heavy with regret. He realised that he should have been more honest with Georgiana from the beginning, that he should have trusted her and told her about Wickham's presence in Meryton. But he had wanted to protect her, to shield her from the pain of the past. Instead, he had made her more vulnerable by concealing the truth.

Now, as he looked into his sister's eyes, he saw a new maturity there, a strength that he had not noticed before. Perhaps it was time for him to trust her, to treat her as the young woman she was becoming, rather than the fragile child he had always seen her as.

"Georgiana," he said softly, "I am proud of you. You have shown great courage in facing your fears, and I know that you will continue to grow in strength and wisdom. I am sorry that I did not trust you with the truth about Wickham, but I promise that from now on, I will be honest with you about everything."

Georgiana smiled through her tears and embraced her brother tightly. "Thank you, Fitzwilliam," she whispered. "I love you."

As they stepped back from their embrace, Georgiana's eyes shone with a newfound determination. "Brother," she began, her voice steady despite the slight quiver of her lip, "I understand now why you forbade me from leaving Netherfield. Seeing Mr. Wickham in Meryton brought back all the pain and shame of my foolish actions last summer. But I realize that I cannot hide from my past forever. I must learn to face it with courage and dignity, as you have taught me."

Darcy felt a surge of pride at his sister's words. She had grown so much in the past year, and he marvelled at the strength and resilience she now displayed. "Georgiana, I am sorry for not trusting you with the truth from the beginning. I thought I was protecting you, but I see now that you are capable of handling far more than I gave you credit for. It was wrong of me to keep you in the dark about Wickham's presence here."

Georgiana nodded, a small smile gracing her features. "I appreciate your apology, Fitzwilliam. I know that you only want what is best for me, but I am no longer a child. I want to be treated as an equal, as someone who can be trusted with the truth, no matter how painful it may be."

Darcy took his sister's hand in his, his eyes conveying the depth of his affection and respect for her. "You have my word, Georgiana. From this day forward, I will be honest with you about everything. No more secrets between us."

Georgiana's smile widened, and she squeezed her brother's hand in return. "Thank you, Fitzwilliam. That means more to me than you can know. And I promise, I will not leave Netherfield again without your permission. I understand the importance of propriety and the need to protect our family's reputation."

As they stood there, hand in hand, Darcy felt a weight lift from his shoulders. He had always carried the burden of protecting Georgiana, of shielding her from the harsh realities of the world. But now, he realized that she was stronger than he had ever imagined, and that together, they could face whatever challenges lay ahead.

A knock at the door interrupted their moment of sibling bonding. Bingley entered, his usually jovial expression tinged with a hint of nervousness. "Darcy, might I have a word with you?"

Darcy nodded, releasing Georgiana's hand and turning to face his friend. "Of course, Bingley. What is on your mind?"

Bingley fidgeted with his cravat, a sure sign that he was anxious about something. "Well, you see, I need to go to London for a few days to consult with my solicitor regarding the marriage settlements. I was hoping that you might accompany me, as I value your opinion and could use your support."

Darcy considered the request, weighing his desire to be there for his friend against his reluctance to leave Georgiana at Netherfield. He glanced at his sister, who gave him an encouraging smile, as if to say that she would be fine in his absence. "Of course, Bingley. I would be happy to accompany you to London. When do you plan to depart?"

Bingley's relief was palpable. "I was thinking we could leave tomorrow morning, if that suits you. I do not wish to be away from Jane for too long, but I know that this is an important matter that requires my attention."

Darcy nodded, his mind already turning to the practical matters of the trip. "Very well. I will make the necessary arrangements and inform my staff. We can take my carriage, as it will be faster and more comfortable than yours."

As Bingley left to attend to his own preparations, Darcy turned back to Georgiana. "Will you be well here while I am gone, Georgiana? I do not like the idea of leaving you alone with our aunt and Miss Bingley."

Georgiana lifted her chin, a determined glint in her eye. "I will be fine, Fitzwilliam. I am stronger than you think. And besides, I am by no means friendless. I will have Mrs. Annesley to keep me company. She is improving from her illness. I would like to spend more time sitting with her, keeping her company, and I have a desire to come to know the elder Bennet sisters better too."

Darcy smiled, pride swelling in his chest at his sister's newfound courage and resilience. Perhaps this trip to London would be good for both of them - a chance for Bingley to settle his affairs and for Darcy to gain some much-needed perspective on his own feelings for Elizabeth. With a final squeeze of Georgiana's hand, he set off to make the necessary arrangements, his heart lighter than it had been in weeks.

As Darcy made his way through the halls of Netherfield, his thoughts turned to the other benefits of this impromptu trip to London. With any luck, his absence would allow Lady Catherine's infamous temper to cool. Darcy hoped that a few days apart might help to soothe her ruffled feathers.

And then there was the matter of Miss Bingley. Darcy suppressed a sigh as he thought of the calculating gleam he had seen in her eyes of late. It was clear that she had set her sights on him as her future husband, despite his repeated attempts to discourage her attentions. Perhaps with Lady Catherine present to discourage her in the inimitable way only Lady Catherine could, Miss Bingley would finally realize the futility of her pursuit and turn her attentions elsewhere.

Lost in thought, Darcy nearly collided with a servant carrying a stack of linens. He apologized, his cheeks heating with embarrassment. It was not like him to be so distracted, but then again, nothing about his life had been normal since he had first laid eyes on Elizabeth Bennet.

As he entered his chambers to pack for the journey, Darcy's thoughts once again turned to Elizabeth. He wondered what she was doing at that very moment - perhaps taking a walk through the countryside, her cheeks flushed with the crisp wintry air. Or maybe she was curled up with a book, her clever mind absorbed in some new tale of adventure and romance.

Darcy shook his head, trying to banish such thoughts from his mind. It was time to put his feelings aside and focus on the matter at hand. Bingley needed his help, and Darcy would not let his friend down. And if, in the process, he managed to gain some clarity on his own heart's desire...well, that would be a most welcome development indeed.

Chapter Thirteen

ANNE STOOD AT THE window, gazing out at the carriage containing Mr. Darcy and Mr. Bingley as it rolled away from Netherfield. A slight frown creased her brow. With the gentlemen gone, the house felt hollow and vapid, devoid of any stimulating companionship. Resting her forehead against the cool windowpane, Anne sighed.

Suddenly, there came an urgent rap on the door and her maid bustled in, flushed with import. "Miss de Bourgh! Your lady mother has taken ill with the influenza - the same malady that afflicts Miss Bingley."

Anne's eyes widened in alarm. "Mother? Ill? But she is never ill!" And yet, a traitorous part of her felt a twinge of relief. With Lady Catherine confined to bed, Anne would be free, at least temporarily, from her mother's constant critique and commandments. Certainly, she would be banned from her mother's presence, for fear that Anne herself would catch the sickness.

But what would she do with this unexpected reprieve? Anne wrung her hands as she walked, at a loss. Her entire life had been structured around obeying her mother's whims and wishes. She had never before been presented with unfettered time.

Anne paced the drawing room, unsure how to occupy herself with Lady Catherine ill and the gentlemen away. She paused as the sound of an arriving carriage drew her to the window.

Four elegantly dressed young ladies stepped down. Anne recognised the tall, lovely blonde as Miss Bennet, Mr. Bingley's fiancée, which meant the others would be her younger sisters. Miss Bennet had come alone the previous day, but spoke much of her sisters, intriguing Anne.

Upon entering, Miss Bennet greeted Anne respectfully. "Miss de Bourgh, how lovely to see you again. Mrs. Hurst begged me to come to assist while dear Miss Bingley and your mother are unwell. Please, allow me to introduce my sisters Elizabeth, Kitty and Lydia."

Anne nodded shyly as Miss Bennet and Miss Elizabeth took charge, directing the servants and tending to Lady Catherine.

"Kitty, Lydia, I think Miss de Bourgh might enjoy your company," Elizabeth said briskly. "Please do your best to see to her amusement while Jane and I attend to matters here."

The girls curtsied and seized Anne's hands eagerly. "It's a delight to meet you!" exclaimed Lydia, as Elizabeth and Jane left the room. "We shall be the greatest of friends."

"Indeed," Kitty nodded sagely. "It must be ever so dull, cooped up here with Lady Catherine unwell and the gentlemen gone away. We thought you might enjoy some companionship."

Anne blinked at them, nonplussed by their eager overtures. She did not know these girls in the slightest. Why should they take any interest in her welfare? And yet...the prospect of diversion, of something novel after so many years of staid routine, sparked an unfamiliar sensation within her breast. Excitement.

A smile bloomed across Anne's wan face. "Thank you both, truly. Your kindness touches me." She gestured for them to resume their seats. "I confess, I am quite at a loss for how to occupy myself. What do you suggest?"

Lydia and Kitty exchanged a gleeful glance before Lydia leaned forward conspiratorially. "Well, Miss de Bourgh, Kitty and I have several friends among the militia officers currently stationed in Meryton. Perhaps you would like to accompany us on a few social calls?"

Anne felt a frisson of trepidation at the boldness of the idea. Call upon unknown gentlemen? Without a chaperone? Lady Catherine would be horrified by the impropriety.

And yet, in that moment, Anne decided she was tired of being timid, obedient Anne. This was her chance for a taste of independence, of living, before the yoke of her predestined future settled around her neck. Her chin lifted a notch.

"I would be delighted to join you," she said firmly. "When do we begin?"

"Oh, today, of course!" Lydia laughed, tossing her glossy curls exuberantly. "It is a fine dry day, and Meryton is not a mile from here; we shall be there in barely a quarter-hour!"

Anne did not think she had ever walked a mile in her life, but a quarter-hour was not a very long time, so she smiled gamely, not wanting Lydia and Kitty to think her feeble. "Then let us be off!"

The three young ladies set out arm-in-arm, giggling and chattering as they made their way into Meryton. The usually sedate town seemed to hum with energy, the streets thronged with dashing officers in scarlet coats. Anne felt a thrill of excitement at the prospect of meeting these handsome strangers.

Their first stop was the home of Mrs. Phillips, Lydia and Kitty's aunt. The lady was delighted to see them and immediately welcomed them into her parlour to take refreshments. No sooner had they sat down than several officers came in, having seen them arrive and eagerly followed them. As the group sipped tea and nibbled on cakes, the conversation flowed easily, punctuated by frequent laughter.

Anne marvelled at the easy camaraderie between the Bennet girls and the officers. They bantered and flirted with a freedom that she envied. For the first time, she wondered what it would be like to have such uncomplicated friendships, such light-hearted interactions with the opposite sex.

Lost in thought, she started when Lydia laid a hand on her arm. "Miss de Bourgh, allow me to introduce Mr. Wickham, one of the most charming gentlemen of our acquaintance."

Anne looked up to find herself face-to-face with a strikingly handsome officer, his eyes sparkling with intelligence and humour. He bowed deeply over her hand, his lips brushing her knuckles in a manner that sent a shiver down her spine.

"Miss de Bourgh, it is an honour to make your acquaintance," he murmured, his voice rich and smooth as honey. "I confess, I have been eager to meet the illustrious daughter of Lady Catherine de Bourgh."

Anne flushed with pleasure at his words, at the undisguised admiration in his gaze. "The honour is mine, Mr. Wickham. I must say, I am quite impressed by the gallantry and charm of the officers I have met today. You are a credit to your regiment."

He smiled, a slow, devastating smile that made her heart flutter in her chest. "You are too generous, Miss de Bourgh. I assure you, we pale in comparison to the loveliness and grace of the ladies present."

As he held her gaze, Anne felt a frisson of something unfamiliar, a warmth that suffused her cheeks and quickened her breath. She had never experienced such an instant connection with anyone, let alone a handsome stranger.

She barely noticed as Lydia and Kitty continued to chatter and flirt with the other officers, so entranced was she by Mr. Wickham's attentions. He drew her out skilfully, asking her opinion on books and music, listening intently to her responses. For the first time in her life, Anne felt truly seen, truly heard.

The hours slipped by in a haze of laughter and stimulating conversation. When at last they took their leave, Mr. Wickham bowed over her hand once more, his eyes holding hers. "Until we meet again, Miss de Bourgh. I shall count the hours."

Anne floated back to Netherfield on a cloud of happiness, her head spinning with the events of the day. The exhilaration of new friendships, the thrill of Mr. Wickham's regard...it was like something out of a dream.

And yet, in the back of her mind, a small voice whispered a warning. She had strayed so far out of her usual sphere, had behaved with an impropriety that would shock her mother. Was she prepared for the consequences of her actions?

But as she recalled the warmth of Mr. Wickham's smile, the flutter of her heart at his touch, Anne pushed those doubts aside. For the first time in her life, she was truly living. And she was determined to savour every moment of it.

For the rest of the day, even after returning to Netherfield, Anne found herself thinking of little else but Mr. Wickham. His charming words echoed in her mind, his handsome face appeared in her dreams. She longed to see him again, to bask once more in the glow of his attention.

An opportunity presented itself sooner than she had dared to hope. Kitty and Lydia, delighted by the success of their first outing, insisted on another visit to the officers the following morning. Anne, her heart leaping at the prospect, readily agreed.

As they walked along the main street of Meryton, Anne's eyes searched the crowd, seeking out one figure in particular. And there he was - Mr. Wickham, resplendent in his regimentals, his face lighting up as he caught sight of her.

"Miss de Bourgh," he greeted her warmly, bowing low over her hand. "What a pleasure to see you again so soon. I had feared I would have to wait an eternity for another glimpse of your lovely face."

Anne blushed at his bold words, a thrill running through her. "The pleasure is all mine, Mr. Wickham. I must confess, I have thought of little else but our last meeting."

His eyes sparkled with delight. "Then we are of one mind, for you have scarcely left my thoughts either. Come, let us walk together and talk. I am eager to hear more of your views on the world."

As he settled her hand on his arm, Mr. Wickham leaned in conspiratorially. "I must say, Miss de Bourgh, you are a revelation. So different from the other ladies of my acquaintance. There is a depth to you, a fire that burns beneath the surface. I find myself quite captivated."

Anne's heart raced at his words. No one had ever spoken to her like this before, had ever seen beyond her shy exterior to the passionate soul within. "You flatter me, Mr. Wickham. I am not used to such attentions."

"Then more fool the men of your acquaintance," he declared. "For they are blind not to see what a treasure you are. A woman of intellect, of spirit. A rare jewel indeed."

As he spoke, his hand rested over hers, sending a jolt of electricity through her even through the layers of their gloves. Anne knew she should pull away, should maintain a proper distance.

But she found herself leaning in, drawn to him like a moth to a flame.

Mr. Wickham smiled, a slow, seductive curve of his lips. "Tell me, Miss de Bourgh, have you ever longed for adventure? For something more than the staid confines of society?"

"I..." Anne hesitated, then plunged ahead, emboldened by his interest. "I have always dreamed of seeing the world. Of experiencing life beyond the narrow bounds of my existence. But I fear I shall never have the chance."

"Never say never," Mr. Wickham murmured. "For where there is a will, there is a way. And I believe, Miss de Bourgh, that you have the will to shape your own destiny. With the right companion by your side, of course."

His words hung in the air between them, heavy with promise and possibility. Anne's breath caught in her throat, her pulse pounding in her ears. She knew she was treading on dangerous ground, that she was straying far from the path of propriety.

But in that moment, lost in the depths of Mr. Wickham's eyes, Anne found she did not care. For the first time in her life, she felt truly alive. And she was determined to hold onto that feeling, no matter the cost.

The following day, the weather was too wet to walk to Meryton. Anne chafed at being trapped at Netherfield, even with the lively Kitty and Lydia to keep her company, until it occurred to her that she could order her mother's carriage made ready to take them into Meryton. Who would gainsay her, with the gentlemen absent and her mother confined to bed? Certainly not the gentle Miss Bennet, nor Mrs. Hurst, who seemed utterly incapable of managing anything without her sister's presence.

Lydia and Kitty both brightened considerably when Anne suggested ordering the carriage, exclaiming how clever she was and what a wonderful friend. Anne blossomed under their praise, and in a very short time the de Bourgh carriage was drawing up outside the Phillips' house.

As it was in the early afternoon rather than the morning when they usually called, Mrs. Phillips was busy belowstairs, but she was happy to receive them and settle them in her little parlour, and very shortly several officers arrived to keep them company. Mr. Wickham as usual came immediately to Anne's side.

Anne had been sharing tales of her sheltered life at Rosings, the quiet monotony broken only by her mother's infrequent but imperious demands, when Kitty and Lydia came up to her, their cheeks flushed with merriment.

"Oh, Anne, you simply must take a turn about the room!" Lydia exclaimed, her eyes sparkling with mischief. "Mr. Wickham, you are being quite dreadful, monopolising Miss de Bourgh this way. The other officers are most eager to make her acquaintance."

Kitty giggled, nodding enthusiastically. "Indeed, they have been asking after you all afternoon. You have quite captured their attention, Anne."

Mr. Wickham leaned in conspiratorially, his voice low and intimate. "It seems you have admirers, Miss de Bourgh. Shall we indulge them with your charming presence?"

Anne hesitated, torn between the thrill of the attention and the nagging sense that she was straying into uncharted territory. But the allure of the moment, the heady rush of being sought after and desired, was too powerful to resist.

"I suppose a short turn about the room would be agreeable," she said, a slight tremor in her voice betraying her nerves.

As Mr. Wickham offered his arm, Anne caught the approving glances of Kitty and Lydia, their eyes alight with vicarious excitement. They seemed to revel in her newfound daring, eager to see their friend embrace the delights of society.

"Remember, Anne," Lydia whispered as they passed, "fortune favours the bold. Do not be afraid to seize the moment."

With those words ringing in her ears, Anne allowed Mr. Wickham to lead her into the throng of officers, their scarlet coats a dizzying blur of colour. She could feel the weight of their gazes upon her, the murmur of their voices as they speculated about the young heiress in their midst.

But it was Mr. Wickham who commanded her attention, his presence a steady anchor in the swirling sea of sensations. He guided her through the crowd with practiced ease, his hand at the small of her back a gentle but insistent pressure.

As they walked, Anne found herself confiding in him further, sharing her hopes and dreams, her fears and insecurities. The words tumbled from her lips, unbidden, as if his very presence had unlocked a floodgate within her.

"I have always longed for a life beyond Rosings," she admitted, her voice barely above a whisper. "A life of my own choosing, where I might be free to follow my heart. But my duty is to my mother."

"Duty is a heavy burden to bear, Miss de Bourgh. One that can crush the very life from you, if you let it." His words sent a shiver down her spine, a thrill of both fear and excitement. Kitty regretfully called to Anne that it was time they departed, and they stepped apart, but the intimacy of the moment lingered between them.

"Meet with me tomorrow," Mr. Wickham whispered, his eyes dark with promise. "And let us speak further of freedom and the pursuit of happiness."

Anne could only nod, her heart pounding in her chest. As Mr. Wickham bowed and took his leave, she felt a rush of exhilaration, tinged with the bittersweet knowledge that she was venturing into dangerous territory.

But for the first time in her life, Anne felt truly alive, truly awake to the possibilities that lay before her. And as she made her way back to Netherfield once more, she knew that she would risk everything for the chance to seize them.

The following evening, a small soirée was being held at Lucas Lodge. Lady Catherine was still too ill to rise from her bed, as was Miss Bingley, but upon eager pleas, Mrs. Bennet agreed that Anne might accompany her stepdaughters to the event, as well as Georgiana. Georgiana immediately declined, however, claiming she was not feeling well enough to leave Netherfield, and though Elizabeth looked at her with concern, nobody thought anything of the shy Miss Darcy not particularly wishing to be exposed to a crowd of strangers.

Anne had barely settled herself beside Mrs. Bennet in the front parlour at Lucas Lodge when Kitty and Lydia descended upon her, their cheeks flushed and eyes bright with mischief.

"Come, Anne!" Lydia whispered, tugging at her arm and giggling. "The officers have opened a bottle of port, and invited us to have a taste!"

"Port?" Anne repeated, her eyes widening. "But surely that is not proper..."

"Oh, hang propriety!" Lydia squealed. "We are among friends here, are we not?"

Anne hesitated, glancing nervously at Mrs. Bennet, who was deep in conversation with Lady Lucas. The temptation to join in the revelry, to shed the constraints of her sheltered life, was overwhelming.

"Very well," she said at last, rising to her feet. "But only a small taste."

Lydia clapped her hands in delight, and the three young ladies made their way to the corner where the officers had gathered. Mr. Wickham was there, his eyes lighting up as he saw Anne approach.

"Miss de Bourgh," he greeted her, his voice low and intimate. "I am honoured that you would join us."

He pressed a glass into her hand, his fingers brushing against hers in a way that sent a shiver down her spine. Anne took a tentative sip, the rich, fruity flavour exploding on her tongue.

"It is delicious," she murmured, feeling a warm glow suffuse her cheeks.

Mr. Wickham smiled, his gaze never leaving her face. "A taste of freedom, is it not?"

Anne nodded, taking another sip of the fortified wine. She could feel her inhibitions melting away, her usual reserve giving way to a giddy sense of rebellion.

"Tell me, Miss de Bourgh," Mr. Wickham said, leaning in closer. "What would you do, if you could do anything in the world?"

Anne's mind raced with possibilities, with dreams she had never dared to voice aloud. "I would travel," she said at last, her voice barely above a whisper. "I would see the world beyond Rosings, beyond Kent."

"And so you shall," Mr. Wickham promised, his eyes glinting with something that might have been triumph. "If you are brave enough to reach for it."

Anne's heart raced at his words, at the promise of adventure and excitement that lay ahead. She knew that she was playing with fire, that the path she was contemplating could lead to ruin and disgrace.

But in that moment, with the alcohol singing in her veins and Mr. Wickham's gaze holding her captive, Anne could not bring herself to care. For the first time in her life, she felt truly alive, truly free. She knew that her feelings for Mr. Wickham were deepening, transforming from a mere infatuation into something far more profound and consuming.

"Mr. Wickham," she said softly, her voice trembling with emotion, "there is something else I must tell you, something that weighs heavily on my heart."

He looked at her intently, his eyes filled with concern and tenderness. "You can tell me anything, Miss de Bourgh. I am here for you, always."

Anne took a deep breath, steeling herself for the revelation she was about to make. "My inheritance, Mr. Wickham. It is not entirely my own, even though my father left Rosings and everything else he owned to me. Until I marry, it is under the control of my cousins, Mr. Darcy and Colonel Fitzwilliam."

She saw a flicker of surprise cross Mr. Wickham's face, quickly replaced by a look of understanding and sympathy. "I see," he said softly, taking her hand in his. "That must be a great burden for you, Miss de Bourgh, to feel that your future is not entirely your own."

Anne nodded, her eyes filling with tears. "It is, Mr. Wickham. I feel trapped, not only by my mother's expectations but by the very terms of my own inheritance. I long for freedom, for the ability to make my own choices and chart my own course in life."

"I understand, Miss de Bourgh. Truly, I do. But you must not lose hope. There is always a way to find happiness, to break free from the chains that bind us."

Anne looked up at him, her heart swelling with love and gratitude. In that moment, she knew that she would follow Mr. Wickham anywhere, that she would do anything to be with him.

Her mind raced with the possibilities of their future together, of a life free from the constraints of her inheritance and her mother's expectations. She imagined herself as Mrs. Wickham, mistress of her own home, able to make her own choices and live life on her own terms.

But even as she allowed herself to be swept away by the intoxicating promise of a different future, a small voice in the back of her mind whispered a warning. Was she truly ready to turn her back on everything she had ever known, to risk her reputation and her family's disapproval for the sake of love?

As Anne looked into Mr. Wickham's eyes, she saw the answer reflected back at her. Yes, she was ready. For him, she would risk everything.

"We must act quickly, my love," Mr. Wickham murmured, his breath warm against her ear. "Your mother will never approve of our union, and your cousin Mr. Darcy would surely try to stop us. We must elope, as soon as possible."

Anne's heart raced at the thought of such a daring plan. She had always been the dutiful daughter, the obedient ward, but now, with Mr. Wickham by her side, she felt a new sense of courage and determination.

"Yes," she breathed, her eyes shining with excitement. "Yes, let us elope. I cannot bear the thought of being parted from you, not even for a moment."

Mr. Wickham smiled, his hand tightening around hers. "Then it is settled. We shall leave at dawn, before anyone else is awake. I will arrange for a carriage and meet you at the edge of Netherfield's park."

Anne nodded, her mind already whirling with the practicalities of their escape. She would need to pack a small bag, to leave a note for her mother explaining her decision. But even as she planned, a flicker of doubt crossed her mind.

"But what of my inheritance?" she asked, her brow furrowing. "Mr. Darcy and Colonel Fitzwilliam have control over it until I marry. How will we live without it?"

Mr. Wickham's smile only widened, his eyes glinting with a hint of mischief. "Do not worry, my love. We shall head for Gretna Green and be married long before they know of our plans. Trust me, and all will be well."

Anne did trust him, with all her heart. She knew that Mr. Wickham would take care of her, that he would provide for her in ways that her family never could. And so, with a final squeeze of his hand, she sealed her fate.

"I will be ready at dawn," she promised, her voice steady with resolve. "And then, we shall begin our new life together, free from the constraints of our past."

Chapter Fourteen

Elizabeth found Georgiana in the music room at Netherfield, her delicate fingers trailing listlessly over the piano keys. The young girl's face was pale and drawn, her eyes distant. Elizabeth's heart ached at the sight. She had become quite attached to Georgiana in the last few days, finding her to be a sweet girl, eager to please and not at all proud.

"Georgiana, are you quite well?" Elizabeth asked softly, settling herself on the piano bench beside the younger girl. "You seem out of spirits today."

Georgiana started, as if pulled from a reverie. "Oh! Forgive me, Elizabeth. I was wool-gathering." She attempted a smile, but it did not reach her eyes.

"You know you can confide in me, Georgiana," Elizabeth said gently, placing a hand over the girl's. "I hope you will consider me a friend."

Georgiana's lower lip trembled. "I do, Elizabeth. Truly."

"But you do not wish to attend the soirée at Lucas Lodge with us, and your cousin Anne, tonight?" Elizabeth pressed.

"No." Georgiana shook her head. "Thank you. I would rather not."

Elizabeth considered this, studying the lines of strain around Georgiana's eyes, the tautness in her shoulders. Clearly, more weighed on the girl's mind than a simple aversion to social events. An uneasy suspicion began to form.

"Georgiana," Elizabeth began carefully, "is there someone who is likely to be in attendance tonight, whom you might wish to avoid?"

Georgiana's eyes flew to Elizabeth's face, shock blooming in her expression. "How did you... did my brother say something?"

"He did not," Elizabeth refuted that suggestion quickly. "But Lydia mentioned that when she and Kitty took you into Meryton, Mr. Wickham paid you some attention. Has Mr. Wickham...has he done something to distress you? Something beyond his general disagreeableness? I know he and your brother are not on particularly good terms, and I hope Mr. Wickham has not taken his displeasure with Mr. Darcy out on you."

Georgiana flinched as if struck. For a long moment, she was silent, her breath coming faster. Then, in a voice scarcely above a whisper: "He tried to convince me to elope with him last summer."

Elizabeth inhaled sharply. Mr. Darcy had hinted that Wickham was not a man of good character, but to think he would prey upon a trusting young girl, to think of the pain Georgiana must have endured...rage and fierce protectiveness bloomed in her chest.

"Oh, my dear girl," Elizabeth breathed, drawing Georgiana into an embrace as the first tears began to fall. "You have nothing to be ashamed of, do you hear me? The shame is entirely Wickham's. He took advantage of your kind heart."

Georgiana clung to her, small sobs wracking her frame. "I was so foolish, Elizabeth. So naïve. I truly believed he loved me. But he only wanted my fortune."

"You were not foolish," Elizabeth said fiercely, stroking Georgiana's hair. "You were an innocent, trusting a man who should have protected you, not betrayed you. No more tears for one so unworthy, my darling."

Gradually, Georgiana's sobs subsided into sniffles and shuddering breaths. She pulled back, wiping at her eyes. "Fitzwilliam ...my brother...he stopped us in time. He was so angry, Miss Elizabeth. Not with me, but with Wickham. I had never seen him in such a fury."

"As well he should be," Elizabeth said staunchly. "Your brother loves you dearly, Georgiana. As do I. We will keep you safe, I promise you."

A wobbly smile bloomed on Georgiana's face, and she squeezed Elizabeth's hands. "Thank you, Miss Elizabeth. Truly. I do not know what I would do without your friendship."

"Well, you shall never have to find out," Elizabeth declared. "Now, dry your eyes. I will make your excuses to the Lucases. You needn't stir from Netherfield tonight unless you wish it."

Georgiana's smile returned, stronger now, and genuine gratitude shone in her eyes. "I shall not leave Netherfield's grounds without my brother. I made a promise to him, once I knew Wickham was in Meryton."

As Elizabeth drew the girl back into her arms, she silently vowed that Wickham would never again be permitted to darken Georgiana's door, nor to shatter her fragile trust.

The party at Lucas Lodge was in full swing by the time the Bennets arrived, red-coated officers mingling with the local gentry in a bright, colourful display. Elizabeth stood for a moment in the entryway, allowing her eyes to adjust to the brightness and her ears to the cheerful din of conversation and laughter.

It did not take long, however, for the genteel noise to be pierced by a shrill giggle that set Elizabeth's teeth on edge. She turned to see Lydia and Kitty huddled in a corner with Maria Lucas, their heads bent close together as they whispered and tittered behind their hands.

Elizabeth's brow furrowed as she watched them, a sense of unease prickling at the back of her neck. Lydia and Kitty were always prone to silliness, but there was a furtive, almost feverish quality to their mirth that troubled her.

Catching Charlotte's eye across the room, Elizabeth tilted her head towards the girls, a silent question in her gaze. Charlotte frowned, then nodded, moving to join Elizabeth as she made her way towards the giggling trio.

"Lydia. Kitty. I would speak with you, please." Charlotte's tone brooked no argument. "And Maria... I daresay you may as well come too. It will save Mother from having to repeat what I am about to say." Her expression was implacable, and both her stepdaughters and her sister followed her meekly from the room.

Satisfied that Charlotte would have some sharp words with the younger girls about their behaviour, Elizabeth relaxed and began to look about. Mrs. Hurst passed her on the arm of one of the officers, barely inclining her head to Elizabeth's greeting, and Elizabeth smiled wryly, before looking for Anne de Bourgh. Mrs. Hurst had declared she was happy to bring Anne to the party, wishing to get out of Netherfield, but had apparently left the heiress to her own devices. Knowing Anne to be very nearly as shy as Georgiana, Elizabeth thought she had better see if Miss de Bourgh would like the company of a familiar face.

Elizabeth was shocked, as she entered another room, to see Anne de Bourgh on a sofa with a red-coated officer, sitting intimately close as he whispered in her ear. Elizabeth was utterly aghast when both looked up at her gasp, and Elizabeth saw that the officer was Mr. Wickham.

With Georgiana's dreadful tale fresh in her mind, all Elizabeth could think of was getting Anne away from Mr. Wickham as quickly as possible.

"If you will excuse me," she said, trying to keep her voice steady. "Miss de Bourgh? There is someone I should like to introduce to you."

Anne rose to her feet with obvious reluctance, a hint of rebelliousness crossing her expression, but she was too cowed by her mother's obnoxious bossiness to do more than think of arguing with someone who acted as though they had authority over her, Elizabeth suspected. *And thank goodness for that*, she thought, as she seized Anne's hand and led her hastily from the room.

"Do you know Mr. Wickham well?" she asked as they made their way through the crowded parlour. "From your visits to Pemberley in your childhood, I suppose?"

Anne looked at her oddly. "I beg your pardon? I have never met Mr. Wickham before this week. Why should I have met him at Pemberley?"

"He is the son of the former steward there, I understand. Certainly, Mr. and Miss Darcy are well acquainted with him, and neither of them approve of his company." Elizabeth hesitated, and then decided to share a little of what she knew. "Part of Miss Darcy's decision not to attend tonight was because of the likely presence of Mr. Wickham."

Anne blinked, but then she shrugged a little defiantly. "Who my cousins choose or do not choose to associate with is nothing to me, Miss Elizabeth. Now, who did you want to introduce to me?"

Having forgotten the excuse she had made to get Anne away from Mr. Wickham, Elizabeth cast about for a moment before her eye alighted on one of their neighbours. "Mrs. Goulding should like to meet you, I believe. She hails originally from Kent, though I have no idea if anywhere near Rosings; you shall have to determine the geography with her directly."

As the Bennet carriage rolled down the dark lanes back to Longbourn, Elizabeth's mind raced with the events of the evening. The laughter and chatter from the party at Lucas Lodge seemed a distant memory now, replaced by a growing sense of unease that settled heavily in the pit of her stomach.

On the opposite seat, Charlotte, Jane and Lydia were all dozing. Elizabeth had insisted on staying until Mrs. Hurst left with Anne de Bourgh, and consequently they were among the last to leave as Mrs. Hurst would not quit the card tables. It was very late, and Elizabeth hoped her father was not sitting up wondering where they all were.

Beside her, Kitty giggled and hiccupped, the effects of too much wine evident in her flushed cheeks and glassy eyes. "Isn't it romantic?" she slurred, leaning heavily against Elizabeth's shoulder. "Anne and Mr. Wickham, running away together like something out of a novel!"

Elizabeth stiffened, her heart pounding in her chest. "What do you mean, Kitty?" she asked, trying to keep her voice steady. "What have you heard?"

Kitty grinned, her words tumbling out in a drunken rush. "I overheard them talking at the party," she confided, her voice dropping to a conspiratorial whisper. "They're planning to elope, can you believe it? Anne's going to sneak out of Netherfield before dawn, and Mr. Wickham will be waiting for her with a carriage. They're going to run away to Gretna Green and get married!"

Elizabeth's blood ran cold, her mind reeling with the implications of Kitty's words. After her conversation with Georgiana, she knew all too well the kind of man Mr. Wickham truly was - a fortune hunter, a liar, a man who would stop at nothing to secure his own interests. And now, it seemed, he had set his sights on Anne de Bourgh and her considerable inheritance.

The thought of poor, naïve Anne falling victim to Wickham's blandishments made Elizabeth's stomach churn. Anne, with her sheltered upbringing, was even more vulnerable than most.

As the carriage rattled on through the darkness, Elizabeth's mind raced with possibilities. She had to find a way to stop the elopement, to save Anne from making a terrible mistake that would ruin her life forever. But how? Wickham was cunning and persuasive, and Anne was clearly infatuated with him. It would take more than mere words to convince her of the truth.

Beside her, Kitty had fallen asleep, her head lolling against the carriage window. Elizabeth envied her sister's blissful ignorance, the way she could so easily dismiss the gravity of the situation as nothing more than a romantic tale. But Elizabeth knew better.

She had seen the pain and suffering that came with misplaced trust, and she would not let Anne fall victim to the same fate.

As the carriage finally pulled up to Longbourn, Elizabeth's resolve hardened. She would find a way to stop the elopement, no matter what it took. Anne's happiness, her very future, depended on it. And Elizabeth would not rest until she had made things right.

"Stepmother." She grasped Charlotte's hand. "I must speak to you. Now."

It took Charlotte only one glance at her face to know that Elizabeth's urgency was not feigned.

"Take Kitty and Lydia inside, Jane," Charlotte said, her voice calm. "We'll join you shortly."

"We have to go to Netherfield," Elizabeth said, as soon as her sisters had quit the carriage. "Now. Miss de Bourgh is about to make a terrible mistake, eloping with Mr. Wickham."

Charlotte's eyes widened. "Are you sure?" was all she asked, however, and when Elizabeth nodded, Charlotte said "Very well. Wait here for five minutes, and I will come with you."

Charlotte stepped out of the carriage and called up to the coachman, presumably telling him his night was not yet done, before going briefly inside Longbourn. Elizabeth sat in the carriage, wringing her hands together, the only thought in her mind that she must get to Netherfield in time to avert disaster.

As the carriage rattled along the dark country lanes, Elizabeth's mind raced with the implications of what Kitty had told her. Anne de Bourgh, eloping with Mr. Wickham, a man Anne claimed she had only met this week? It seemed unthinkable, and yet...

"Lizzy, are you quite well?" Charlotte's concerned voice broke through her reverie. "You look as though you've seen a ghost."

Elizabeth shook her head, trying to gather her thoughts. "Charlotte, I fear we may be too late. If what Kitty said is true..."

"We must hope it is not," Charlotte said firmly. "And if it is, we must do whatever we can to stop it."

Elizabeth nodded, her jaw set with determination. She would not let Anne throw her life away on a man like Wickham, not if she could help it.

As the carriage drew up to Netherfield, Elizabeth leapt out almost before it had stopped moving, Charlotte close behind her. They hurried up the steps and into the house, startling the sleepy-eyed footman who opened the door.

"Miss de Bourgh," Elizabeth said urgently. "Is she here?"

The footman blinked, looking confused. "I believe she retired to her room some time ago, miss. Shall I-"

But Elizabeth was already moving past him, taking the stairs two at a time in her haste, Charlotte hard on her heels.

They found Anne in her bedchamber, a small valise open on the bed, half-filled with clothes and valuable little trinkets. Anne looked up from where she sat at her writing-desk as they entered, her eyes wide with surprise and a hint of fear. "Miss Elizabeth, Mrs. Bennet," she said, her voice trembling slightly. "What are you doing here?"

Elizabeth stepped forward, her expression gentle but firm. "Anne, we know about your plans to elope with Mr. Wickham. And we're here to stop you from making a terrible mistake."

Anne's face flushed, and she drew herself up haughtily. "I don't know what you're talking about. And even if I did, it's none of your concern."

Charlotte shook her head, her expression sad. "Oh, Anne," she said softly. "If only you knew the truth about Mr. Wickham. He's not the man you think he is."

Elizabeth nodded, her heart aching for the young woman before her. "Anne, please listen to us. Mr. Wickham is a liar and a scoundrel. He's only interested in your fortune, not in you. If you go through with this elopement, you'll be ruining your life forever."

Anne's eyes filled with tears, her lower lip trembling. "No," she whispered, shaking her head. "No, that can't be true. He loves me, I know he does."

Elizabeth reached out, taking Anne's hands in her own. "I know it's hard to believe," she said gently. "But we have proof, Anne. Proof that Mr. Wickham is not to be trusted." Elizabeth left the room briefly, to find the young maid who had shown them upstairs and was now loitering uncertainly in the hallway. "Please wake Miss Darcy at once. Tell her that her presence is urgently required."

The maid curtsied and hurried away, leaving Elizabeth and Charlotte alone with the distraught Anne. Elizabeth approached the heiress tentatively, her heart aching at the sight of Anne's tear-stained face.

"Anne," she said gently, "I know this is difficult, but we must speak the truth. Mr. Wickham is not the man you believe him to be."

Anne shook her head stubbornly, clutching her half-written note to her chest. "You don't understand. He loves me, and I love him. We are meant to be together."

Charlotte sat down on the edge of the bed, her warm brown eyes full of compassion. "Oh, my dear girl," she murmured, "I know it feels that way now. But sometimes, what we believe to be love is nothing more than a fleeting infatuation."

Before Anne could respond, there was a soft knock at the door. Elizabeth opened it to find Georgiana standing there, her face pale and anxious. "You sent for me?" she asked, her voice barely above a whisper.

Elizabeth nodded, ushering her into the room and closing the door behind her, to ensure the curious maid could not overhear them. "Yes, Georgiana. I'm afraid we need your help."

Georgiana's eyes widened as she took in the scene before her - Anne's packed bag, the crumpled note, the tears on her cheeks. "What has happened?" she asked, her voice trembling.

Elizabeth took a deep breath, choosing her words carefully. "Anne was planning to elope with Mr. Wickham," she said quietly. "But we believe you could perhaps explain to her that he may not be the honourable man she thinks he is."

Georgiana gasped, her hand flying to her mouth. For a moment, she seemed unable to speak. Then, in a voice choked with emotion, she began to tell her story.

She spoke of Wickham's charm and flattery, of how he had made her feel special and loved. She spoke of the secret meetings, the whispered promises, the plans to run away together. And she spoke of the devastating moment when she had learned the truth - that Wickham had only been interested in her fortune, that he had never truly cared for her at all.

As Georgiana spoke, Anne's face grew paler and paler. By the time Georgiana had finished her tale, Anne was openly weeping, her shoulders shaking with sobs.

"I'm such a fool," she cried, burying her face in her hands. "How could I have been so blind?"

Charlotte gathered her into a warm, motherly embrace, rocking her gently back and forth. "Hush now," she soothed, stroking Anne's hair. "You are not a fool. You are a young woman with a tender heart, and that is nothing to be ashamed of."

As Charlotte comforted Anne, Elizabeth turned to Georgiana, her own eyes brimming with tears. "Thank you," she whispered, taking the younger girl's hand in her own. "I know how difficult that must have been for you."

Georgiana managed a watery smile, squeezing Elizabeth's hand in return. "I only wish I had spoken sooner," she said softly. "Perhaps then, Anne would have been spared this pain."

Elizabeth shook her head firmly. "You mustn't blame yourself," she said. "The only one to blame is Mr. Wickham, for his deceit and his cruelty."

Anne's sobs had quieted to the occasional sniffle, and she raised her head from Charlotte's shoulder, her face blotchy and her eyes red-rimmed. "Please," she said, her voice hoarse and trembling, "you mustn't tell my mother about this. She would be so terribly disappointed in me."

Elizabeth exchanged a glance with Charlotte, seeing the same sympathy and understanding she felt reflected in her stepmother's eyes. "We won't tell her," Elizabeth assured Anne gently. "But you must promise us something in return."

Anne nodded eagerly, clearly willing to agree to anything if it meant keeping her secret safe. "Anything!" she exclaimed.

Elizabeth took a deep breath, steeling herself for what she knew she must say. "You must promise us that you will never speak to Mr. Wickham again," she said firmly. "Not a word, not even in passing. If you should happen to meet him in company, you must not acknowledge him in any way. You will give him the cut direct."

Anne's eyes widened, and for a moment, Elizabeth feared she would protest. But then, slowly, the younger girl nodded. "I promise," she whispered. "I never want to see him again, not after what he's done."

Relief washed over Elizabeth, and she felt a weight lift from her shoulders. It was a small victory, but a victory nonetheless. She knew that the road ahead would not be easy for Anne, but with the support of those who loved her, she would heal in time.

As the first light of dawn began to filter through the curtains, Elizabeth felt the exhaustion of the long night catching up with her. She stifled a yawn, blinking heavily as she tried to focus on the conversation around her.

Beside her, Georgiana seemed to be struggling with her own fatigue, her head nodding forward as she fought to keep her eyes open. Without thinking, Elizabeth reached out and drew the younger girl into her arms, offering what comfort she could.

Georgiana stiffened for a moment, clearly surprised by the gesture. But then, slowly, she relaxed into Elizabeth's embrace, her own arms coming up to encircle Elizabeth's waist.

"We must go," Charlotte said at last. "Will the two of you stay together? We will come back later today, and I promise we will not tell Lady Catherine anything, but we do need to know more of what Wickham said to you, Anne."

"We will stay together." Georgiana reached out and took her cousin's hand. "Won't we, Anne?"

"Yes." Anne nodded. "I promise. And... thank you. For stopping me from making a terrible mistake."

"We are glad to have been of assistance, Miss de Bourgh," Elizabeth said.

"I think we are past such formalities now, don't you?" Anne smiled weakly. "You must call me Anne."

The carriage jolted as it hit a particularly deep rut in the road, shaking Elizabeth from her drowsy reverie. She blinked, taking a moment to orient herself to her surroundings. Beside her, Charlotte shifted, her own eyes heavy with fatigue.

Through the window, Elizabeth could see the sun rising over the horizon, casting a golden glow across the countryside. It was a beautiful sight, but one that she found difficult to appreciate in her current state of exhaustion. All she wanted was to sink into her own bed at Longbourn and sleep.

At the edge of the park, beneath a blasted oak tree, a solitary carriage stood waiting, driver slouched in his seat. And there, pacing back and forth beside it like a caged animal, was the unmistakable figure of Mr. Wickham.

Elizabeth felt a surge of anger at the sight of him, his handsome face twisted into a scowl of frustration.

Beside her, Charlotte let out a soft snort of disgust. "Look at him," she muttered, her voice dripping with disdain. "Pacing about like a petulant child denied a sweet."

Despite her exhaustion, Elizabeth couldn't help but smile at her stepmother's words. It was true; there was something almost comical about the sight of the dashing Mr. Wickham reduced to such a state of impotent fury.

As their carriage drew closer, Wickham's head snapped up, his eyes narrowing as he caught sight of them. For a moment, Elizabeth thought he might try to approach them, demand to see if Anne was with them.

But then, as if thinking better of it, he turned on his heel and stalked back to his own carriage, yanking open the door and climbing inside.

Elizabeth let out a breath she hadn't realized she'd been holding, slumping back against the cushioned seat. It was over. Anne was safe, and Wickham had been thwarted in his schemes.

She turned to Charlotte, a weary smile tugging at the corners of her mouth. "We did it," she said softly.

Charlotte squeezed her fingers, her own smile tired but triumphant. "We did," she agreed. "And now, my dear Lizzy, I believe it is time for us to get some well-deserved rest."

Elizabeth nodded, already feeling the pull of sleep tugging at her eyelids. As the carriage rolled on towards Longbourn, she allowed herself to drift off, secure in the knowledge that, for now at least, all was well.

Chapter Fifteen

Hoofbeats clattered on the gravel as Darcy's carriage rolled to a stop in front of Netherfield. Darcy alighted first, followed closely by Bingley and Colonel Fitzwilliam.

"It's good to be back," Bingley declared, beaming as he surveyed the grand estate. "And to have you joining us, Fitzwilliam! The wedding wouldn't be complete without Darcy's favourite cousin in attendance."

Colonel Fitzwilliam chuckled. "A chance to see you leg-shackled at last, Bingley? I wouldn't miss it for the world."

Darcy allowed a small smile at their easy banter, but his mind was elsewhere, lingering on sparkling dark eyes and a brilliantly clever wit. He had thought of little else on the journey from town, equal parts anticipation and trepidation warring in his breast. To see her again, to speak with her... But what would he say? How could he convey the depth of his admiration, his regard, without overstepping the bounds of propriety?

As they made their way inside, a blur of muslin and ribbons nearly bowled him over. Georgiana. Her face was flushed, her eyes wide and anxious. Darcy's brotherly instincts surged to the fore.

"Georgiana? What is it, what's wrong?"

She clutched at his sleeve, drawing him aside. "Oh Fitzwilliam, I must speak with you at once. Something has happened..."

Darcy listened with increasing amazement and alarm as the tale poured out - Anne's near elopement, Wickham's perfidy, and Elizabeth, brilliant Elizabeth, unravelling the scheme and saving them all from calamity. "My God." He could scarcely take it in. The Herculean effort of will it took to master his features, to hide the staggering wave of relief and gratitude and admiration that threatened to engulf him.

Gently disentangling himself from Georgiana's grasp, Darcy managed a reassuring smile for his sister. "You were right to tell me at once. But all is well, and we have Miss Elizabeth to thank for it. Pray excuse me, I must speak to Bingley and Fitzwilliam."

He strode away, mind awhirl. One thought crystal clear amidst the confusion. He must see Elizabeth, must find a way to convey his appreciation for her actions, subtly and with the utmost delicacy.

First, though, he must apprise his cousin of what Georgiana had revealed. As for what would come after... Darcy hardly dared to hope.

Darcy found Bingley and Colonel Fitzwilliam in the billiards room, engaged in a spirited game. They both looked up as he entered, their smiles fading at the sight of his grave expression.

"Darcy, what is it?" Bingley asked, setting down his cue. "Has something happened?"

Darcy nodded, his jaw tight. "I have just spoken with Georgiana. It seems that during our absence, there was an incident involving Wickham and our cousin Anne."

Colonel Fitzwilliam's eyes narrowed. "What sort of incident?"

Taking a deep breath, Darcy first swore Bingley to secrecy regarding what he was about to reveal, before he relayed the tale as Georgiana had told it to him, his voice low and tense. The attempt at elopement, Elizabeth's timely intervention, Anne's distress when Georgiana revealed the truth about Wickham. By the time he had finished, both men wore expressions of mingled shock and fury.

"Good God," Bingley murmured, shaking his head. "To think of what might have happened, had Miss Elizabeth not intervened..."

"I shudder to contemplate it," Darcy said grimly. "We owe her a tremendous debt of gratitude."

Colonel Fitzwilliam nodded, his face set in hard lines. "Indeed we do. And as for Wickham..." His hand clenched into a fist at his side. "I would like nothing more than to call the blackguard out for this."

"Believe me, I share the sentiment," Darcy said. "But we must tread carefully. The last thing we want is to draw undue attention to the matter and risk scandal."

"You are right, of course," Colonel Fitzwilliam conceded with a sigh. "But something must be done about Wickham. He cannot be allowed to continue unchecked."

"I agree." Darcy's mind raced with possibilities, each more unsatisfactory than the last. "Let me think on it. In the meantime, we must focus on the wedding and supporting Bingley and Miss Bennet."

As the Bennets arrived at Netherfield that evening, invited for dinner as Bingley could not bear another moment without seeing Jane, Darcy's anticipation grew. He had been eagerly awaiting the opportunity to speak with Elizabeth, to convey his admiration for her quick thinking and bravery in the face of such a precarious situation.

He found her in the drawing room before dinner, standing near the window looking out into the rapidly darkening evening, her elegant figure illuminated by the soft glow of the candles.

She turned as he approached, her fine eyes widening slightly in surprise.

"Miss Elizabeth," he greeted her, bowing respectfully. "Might I have a moment of your time to speak on a matter of some delicacy?"

She curtsied in return, a curious expression on her face. "Of course, Mr. Darcy."

He led her to a quieter corner of the room, away from the chatter of the other guests. "I wanted to express my deepest gratitude for your actions regarding my cousin Anne and Mr. Wickham," he began, his voice low and earnest. "Your courage and quick thinking prevented what could have been a disastrous situation."

Elizabeth flushed at his praise, her eyes lowering modestly. "I only did what anyone would have done in such circumstances," she demurred.

"On the contrary," Darcy insisted, "I believe your actions were quite extraordinary. You showed great presence of mind and fortitude, qualities I have come to greatly admire in you."

Her eyes flew to his, surprise and something else he could not quite decipher flickering in their depths. "I... thank you, Mr. Darcy," she managed, her voice slightly breathless. "Your words are most kind."

He inclined his head, a small smile tugging at the corners of his mouth. "They are well-deserved, Miss Elizabeth. And I hope you know that you have earned not only my gratitude but also my deepest respect."

She held his gaze for a long moment, a myriad of emotions playing across her expressive face. "I am honoured, Mr. Darcy," she said finally. "Truly."

As the evening progressed, Darcy found himself unable to focus on anything but Elizabeth, his mind awhirl with thoughts of their shared experiences and the depth of her character. He had always admired her intelligence and wit, but now he found himself captivated by her strength, her compassion, and her unwavering sense of what was right.

He watched as she conversed with Georgiana, her gentle manner coaxing smiles and even laughter from his shy sister. The sight warmed his heart, and he could not help but imagine a future in which Elizabeth was a permanent fixture in their lives.

The thought startled him, and he quickly turned away, his heart pounding. *It is foolish to entertain such notions*, he told himself sternly. Elizabeth was a gentleman's daughter, yes, but her family's position in society was far beneath his own. And yet, as he stole another glance at her, he could not deny the powerful attraction he felt, the longing to know her more intimately, to share his life with her.

Shaking his head, Darcy sought out Colonel Fitzwilliam, drawing him aside. "I must speak with you," he murmured, his expression serious. "About what occurred with Anne and Wickham."

Fitzwilliam's brows rose, but he nodded, following Darcy to a quiet corner. "What is it, Darcy?" he asked, concern etched on his face.

Darcy hesitated, glancing around to ensure they were not overheard. "I believe it is best that Lady Catherine never learns of what almost transpired," he said quietly. "The scandal, the shame it would bring upon our family... it does not bear thinking about."

Fitzwilliam's eyes widened, but he nodded slowly. "I agree," he said, his voice grave. "For the same reasons you and I decided to keep what happened in Ramsgate between the two of us. But what of Wickham? Surely he must be held accountable for his actions."

Darcy's jaw tightened, a flash of anger sparking in his eyes. "He will be dealt with," he vowed. "But discreetly. I will not have Anne's reputation tarnished, nor Georgiana's. They have suffered enough at his hands."

His cousin's expression softened, and he clasped Darcy's shoulder. "You are a good man, Darcy," he said warmly. "And a true friend. I will keep this matter in the strictest confidence, you have my word."

Darcy nodded, a rush of gratitude filling him. "Thank you, Fitzwilliam," he said sincerely. "I knew I could count on your discretion and understanding."

Colonel Fitzwilliam, ever observant, had not failed to notice the change in his cousin's demeanour. As Darcy's gaze once again drifted to Elizabeth, the colonel leaned in towards Darcy with a mischievous glint in his eye.

"I must say, Darcy," he began, his tone light and teasing, "I have never seen you so captivated by a young lady before. Miss Elizabeth Bennet seems to have quite an effect on you."

Darcy felt a flush creep up his neck, his pulse quickening at the mention of her name. "I... I admire her greatly," he admitted, his voice low and earnest. "She is unlike any woman I have ever met."

Fitzwilliam chuckled, clapping Darcy on the back. "That much is obvious, my dear cousin," he said with a grin. "And if I may be so bold, I daresay the feeling is mutual. The way she looks at you... it is clear she holds you in high regard."

Darcy's heart leapt at his cousin's words, a flicker of hope igniting in his chest. Could it be true? Could Elizabeth truly return his affections? He hardly dared to believe it.

As the evening drew to a close and the Bennets prepared to take their leave, Darcy found himself lingering by Elizabeth's side, reluctant to say goodbye. "Miss Elizabeth," he said softly, his voice filled with warmth, "I cannot thank you enough for all that you have done. Your bravery and quick thinking have saved my family from scandal and heartache. I am forever in your debt."

Elizabeth smiled up at him, her eyes sparkling with an emotion he could not quite name. "There is no debt, Mr. Darcy," she replied gently. "I only did what was right. And I would do it again in a heartbeat."

Too filled with emotion to speak, he could only bow deeply before handing her up into the carriage. The touch of her hand seemed to burn, even through the gloves they both wore. Did he imagine it, or did she give his fingers the lightest squeeze before letting go?

Darcy returned to the drawing room after bidding the Bennets farewell, distracted by thoughts of Elizabeth. He was startled to find Colonel Fitzwilliam and Anne alone, locked in an intense, private conversation.

The colonel stood facing Anne, grasping her delicate hand gently between both of his own. The colonel's face was alight with emotion as he professed, "Anne, I have been silent too long. My feelings for you overwhelm me - I have loved you devotedly for longer than I can recall."

Anne's eyes widened, a rosy blush blooming on her pale cheeks. In a tremulous voice she replied, "Cousin, I had no notion you harboured such affection for me!" A radiant smile slowly spread across her face. "For I too have long admired you beyond mere familial fondness."

Darcy observed in astonishment as his cousin tenderly drew Anne into an embrace. Gazing into her eyes, the colonel earnestly asked, "My dearest Anne, will you do me the honour of becoming my wife?"

Anne joyfully whispered her consent before laying her head contentedly against the colonel's shoulder. Darcy was struck by the powerful love evident between the newly betrothed pair. Anne's eyes shone with adoration for her intended; the colonel regarded his future bride as though she were the most precious treasure.

Darcy attempted to beat a silent retreat, but a traitorous floorboard creaked beneath his foot and the colonel turned his head.

"Darcy." A broad grin spread across the colonel's face. "Will you be the first to wish us happy? My dearest Anne has done me the very great honour of consenting to be my wife."

"Of course I will, cousin," Darcy said heartily. He came over and shook hands with the colonel, bending to kiss Anne's cheek. "I could not imagine a better husband for you, dear one," he told a blushing Anne kindly.

"I should tell my mother." Anne looked from one to the other of them, her expression clouding slightly. "She... could not prevent it, could she?"

"No, she cannot," Darcy confirmed. "Fitzwilliam and I are your legal guardians, and Lady Catherine cannot gainsay our decision. I think, however, you will find her quite satisfied with your choice."

Anne's expression brightened, and she hurried from the room.

Darcy turned to Colonel Fitzwilliam, brows raised. "Well, this is a secret you have been rather good at keeping."

"Unlike you, Darcy," the colonel said serenely, "I am exceptional at not wearing my heart on my sleeve."

Darcy grimaced, acknowledging the hit. It had not taken long for his cousin to discern his admiration for Elizabeth Bennet; indeed, he suspected he had been obvious in his feelings almost from the first time he met her, considering how jealous Caroline Bingley had immediately become.

"Do you think Aunt Catherine will be happy?" The slight break in the colonel's voice told Darcy his cousin wasn't quite as confident as he was trying to appear.

"Indeed, I do," Darcy said firmly. "You are the son of an earl, after all, and it has always been your destiny to marry an heiress, has it not? Considering that Lady Catherine wanted me to marry Anne, she can hardly object to you." It occurred to him, then, that Colonel Fitzwilliam must have suffered agonies over the years, hearing Lady Catherine continually harp on about Darcy being meant to marry the woman he loved. Not to mention how he must have felt hearing that Anne had planned to elope with that blackguard Wickham!

Darcy clasped his cousin's shoulder warmly. "I could not be happier for you both. You are well-matched and will surely find great joy together."

Colonel Fitzwilliam smiled, visibly relieved by Darcy's wholehearted support. "Thank you, Darcy. Your blessing means the world."

As Darcy retired that night, his thoughts returned unbidden to Elizabeth. Witnessing the colonel and Anne's sincere love had reawakened his own yearning. He found sleep elusive as his mind replayed moments shared with Elizabeth. Her laughter echoed in his ears, her eyes haunted him in the darkness of his room. Darcy could no longer deny the depth of his feelings for her, nor could he suppress the burgeoning hope that maybe, just maybe, Elizabeth held a similar regard for him.

Chapter Sixteen

Elizabeth watched, her heart swelling with affection, as Jane stood poised on the threshold of the church on their father's arm. Jane's beauty was unparalleled, her countenance glowing with pure happiness as she prepared to wed her beloved Mr. Bingley. The bride's gown was a vision of elegance, the delicate lace and flowing silk accentuating her gentle grace. Elizabeth could not help but marvel at the love that emanated from Jane.

"Until I have her goodness, I shall never have her happiness," Elizabeth murmured to herself, before laughing under her breath and shaking her head with a wry smile. "I shall never equal it, so I must resign myself to mere mortal happiness, not the angelic transcendence I see on her face!"

As the ceremony commenced, Elizabeth's gaze drifted to Mr. Bingley, whose adoring eyes never left Jane's face. The groom's expression was one of pure devotion, his smile wide and his heart undoubtedly full of the deepest affection for his bride. The couple's hands entwined as they exchanged their sacred vows, their voices filled with emotion and sincerity.

"I, Charles Bingley, take thee, Jane Bennet, to be my wedded wife," Mr. Bingley declared, his voice steady and strong. "To have and to hold, from this day forward, for better, for worse, for richer, for poorer, in sickness and in health, to love and to cherish, till death us do part."

Jane's eyes glistened with unshed tears of joy as she repeated her own vows, her soft voice carrying the weight of her love for Mr. Bingley. Elizabeth's heart swelled with happiness for her sister, knowing that Jane had found a love so pure and true, a love that would endure through all of life's challenges.

The ceremony drew to a close, and the newly wedded couple turned to face their guests, their faces alight with the joy of their union. Elizabeth caught a glimpse of Caroline Bingley, her features marred by a sneer of jealousy and discontent. Yet even Caroline's sourness could not diminish the happiness that permeated the air, for on this day, love had triumphed, and two hearts had become one.

The wedding party at Netherfield was a lively affair, filled with the joyous laughter and merry chatter of the guests. Elizabeth found herself swept up in the festivities, her heart light and her spirits high as she watched Jane and Mr. Bingley dance their first dance as husband and wife. The newlyweds moved with effortless grace, their eyes locked on each other, their love palpable to all who witnessed their embrace.

As the music swelled, other couples joined the dance, and soon the room was alive with the swirling of skirts and the tapping of feet. Elizabeth found herself partnered with Colonel Fitzwilliam, who proved to be an amiable and skilled dancer. As they moved across the floor, the colonel regaled her with tales of his adventures in the military, his wit and charm drawing laughter from Elizabeth's lips.

"I must say, Miss Elizabeth," the colonel remarked, his eyes twinkling with mirth, "I have never seen a couple so well-suited as your sister and Mr. Bingley. Their happiness is heart-warming to witness."

Elizabeth smiled, her gaze drifting to where Jane and Mr. Bingley stood, surrounded by well-wishers. "Indeed, Colonel. I could not be more delighted for them. They have faced their share of trials, but their love has only grown stronger for it. And I hear you too are to be congratulated?"

Colonel Fitzwilliam was not a handsome man, Elizabeth thought, his face too square and his nose too strong for handsomeness, but when he smiled at her question, she revised her opinion. His smile lit up his whole face as he glanced across the room to where Anne de Bourgh sat with her mother.

"Thank you, Miss Elizabeth. Miss de Bourgh and I will be married from Rosings in the spring, and I could not be happier about it."

As the dance came to an end, Elizabeth found herself face to face with Mr. Darcy, who had been observing her from across the room. His expression was one of quiet intensity, his eyes filled with a warmth that made Elizabeth's heart flutter in her chest.

"Miss Elizabeth," he said, his voice low and earnest, "might I have the pleasure of the next dance?"

Elizabeth felt a blush rise to her cheeks, her pulse quickening at the thought of being in Mr. Darcy's arms. "I would be honoured, Mr. Darcy."

As they took their places on the dance floor, Elizabeth couldn't help but marvel at the change that had taken place in her feelings towards the man before her. Once, she had found him proud and aloof, but now, she saw the depth of his character, the strength of his convictions, and the tenderness of his heart.

As they moved in perfect harmony, Elizabeth felt a sense of rightness, a feeling that this was where she was meant to be. And though she knew that there were still obstacles to overcome, still uncertainties that lay ahead, she couldn't help but feel a glimmer of hope that perhaps, just perhaps, her own story might one day have a happy ending, just like Jane's.

The wedding celebrations continued late into the night, as the guests revelled in the joy of the occasion. The magnificent party at Netherfield was a sight to behold, with the grand rooms adorned in the finest decorations, the tables laden with the most sumptuous of feasts, and the air filled with the strains of music and joyous laughter.

As the evening wore on, Elizabeth found herself drawn into conversations with friends and acquaintances, laughing and reminiscing over shared memories. She couldn't help but feel a sense of bittersweet nostalgia, knowing that this chapter of their lives was coming to a close, that this was the beginning of Jane's new life with her husband, leaving Elizabeth and their other sisters behind.

Amidst the joyous throng, Elizabeth espied Lady Lucas and Sir William, their faces alight with genuine happiness for the newlyweds. Lady Lucas, resplendent in a gown of pale lavender silk, glided towards Jane and Bingley, her arms outstretched in a warm embrace. "My dear Jane, you make a most radiant bride," she exclaimed, clasping the young woman's hands in her own. "And Mr. Bingley, you are a lucky man indeed to have won the heart of such a treasure."

Sir William, his eyes twinkling with mirth, clapped Bingley on the back, his booming laughter echoing through the room. "Well done, my boy!" he cried, his voice filled with affection. "I have no doubt that you and Jane will find every happiness together."

As Elizabeth watched the exchange, her heart swelled with love for her sister and her new brother-in-law. She marvelled at the way Jane's face glowed with contentment, the way Bingley's eyes never left his bride's face. It was a love story for the ages, a tale of two hearts that had found their perfect match.

Nearby, Mr. Bennet stood with Charlotte, who had a proud smile on her face for her stepdaughter. Jane stopped to draw Charlotte into a close, loving embrace.

"Thank you, for everything," Jane said tenderly. "I do not know what would have become of us without you, but I do not believe

I could possibly have achieved my present happiness without your loving guidance."

"You would, my dear girl." Charlotte cupped Jane's cheeks between her hands. "You are too good, and your Mr. Bingley is an astute man who would have known you for the diamond you are in any setting."

As the toasts and speeches continued, Elizabeth found herself lost in thought, her mind wandering to the future that lay ahead. Though she was thrilled for Jane and Bingley, a part of her couldn't help but wonder what her own path might hold. Would she find a love as true and lasting as theirs? Or was she destined to remain a spinster, content with her books and her own company?

"To the happy couple!" Sir William Lucas declared, raising his glass high in the air. "May your love continue to grow and flourish with each passing day!"

A chorus of cheers echoed throughout the room, and Elizabeth joined in, her voice ringing out alongside the others. As she sipped her wine, she caught sight of Caroline Bingley, her face pinched and sour despite the festivities. No doubt she was displeased with the attention being lavished upon Jane, Elizabeth thought with a wry smile.

But even Caroline's dour expression couldn't dampen the joy of the occasion, and as the music began to play once more, Elizabeth found herself swept up in the merriment. She danced with her father and her sisters, laughing and twirling until her cheeks were flushed and her feet ached in their slippers.

At last, as the evening began to wind down, Jane and Bingley made their way to the centre of the room, their hands clasped tightly together. "My dear friends and family," Bingley began, his voice trembling slightly with emotion, "Jane and I cannot thank you enough for sharing in our happiness today. Your love and support mean the world to us, and we shall carry the memories of this day with us always."

Jane nodded, her eyes shining with tears of joy. "And we have one more bit of news to share," she added, her smile widening. "We are leaving for a wedding trip to Bath in a few days, and Elizabeth, my dearest sister, we would be honoured if you would join us. I cannot imagine celebrating this new chapter of our lives without you by my side."

Elizabeth's heart swelled with love and gratitude, and she rushed forward to embrace her sister tightly. "Of course," she whispered, her voice thick with emotion. "I would be delighted to join you."

As Elizabeth stood talking with Sir William and Lady Lucas, she noted Mr. Darcy loitering awkwardly nearby, his gaze fixed on her. With a slight smile, she excused herself from the conversation and drifted over to stand near him.

"Miss Elizabeth," he said, bowing slightly. "I hope I am not intruding. I did not mean to interrupt your conversation."

Elizabeth smiled up at him archly. "No, but you did want to speak to me, did you not?"

"Indeed." He inclined his head. "I wished to bid you farewell before your departure," he said, his voice low and earnest. "We are both leaving Hertfordshire, it seems, though I am to accompany Georgiana to London to meet with the Earl and Countess of Matlock for Twelfth Night celebrations."

Elizabeth felt a pang of disappointment at his words, though she couldn't quite explain why. "I see," she said, hoping her voice did not betray her feelings. "Well, I hope you and Miss Darcy have a pleasant time in London."

Mr. Darcy bowed slightly, his gaze lingering on her face for a moment longer than necessary. "I have matters to settle in London before I make any decisions about the future," he said, his words heavy with meaning.

"No doubt you will make wise and considered decisions, Mr. Darcy," she said, a little confused as to what exactly he was trying to communicate to her.

"I shall miss your company, Miss Elizabeth," he said softly, his voice barely above a whisper.

Elizabeth's breath caught in her throat at his words, and she found herself at a loss for how to respond. Before she could formulate a reply to that startling statement, however, Mr. Darcy had bowed once more and taken his leave, leaving Elizabeth alone with her thoughts and the growing realization that her own feelings for the man were far more complex than she had previously believed.

Elizabeth watched as Mr. Darcy walked away, his tall figure disappearing into the crowd of well-wishers gathered to bid farewell to the newlyweds. She couldn't shake the feeling that something significant had just transpired between them, though she was at a loss to explain precisely what it was.

Had Mr. Darcy been trying to tell her something with his cryptic words about matters to settle before making any decisions? And if so, what could those matters be? Elizabeth's mind raced with possibilities, each more thrilling and terrifying than the last.

She thought back to the way Mr. Darcy had looked at her as he spoke, his eyes intense and full of some unnamed emotion. It was a look that had sent shivers down her spine and made her heart beat faster in her chest. Could it be that he was struggling with his own feelings for her, just as she was struggling with hers for him?

Elizabeth shook her head, trying to clear her mind of such fanciful thoughts. It would do no good to dwell on what might or might not be, especially when she had a journey ahead of her and a new adventure to embark upon.

Still, as she climbed into the carriage beside Jane and Bingley two days later, Elizabeth couldn't help but feel a pang of regret at the thought of leaving Longbourn and all that was familiar to her. She knew that the trip to Bath would be a welcome distraction from the tumultuous emotions swirling within her, but a part of her couldn't help but wish that Mr. Darcy was coming with them.

"I cannot wait to see Bath," Jane said, her voice trembling with eagerness. "I have heard such wonderful things about the city, about the grand assembly rooms and the elegant promenades."

"And the fashionable society," Bingley added, his eyes twinkling with mischief. "I daresay we shall be quite the talk of the town, arriving as newlyweds."

Elizabeth laughed, her heart swelling with affection for her sister and new brother-in-law. "I have no doubt that you will be the toast of Bath," she said, "and that every eligible gentleman will be vying for a chance to dance with the beautiful Mrs. Bingley."

Jane blushed, her eyes dropping demurely to her lap. "Oh, Lizzy," she chided, "you know that I have eyes only for my dear husband. 'Tis you who will be in demand as a dance partner!"

As the carriage rolled through the outskirts of Meryton, Elizabeth found herself lost in thought, her mind drifting back to the events of the past few weeks. The joy of Jane and Bingley's wedding, the bittersweet farewell to her family, and the strange, unsettling encounter with Mr. Darcy before her departure.

What did he mean, she wondered, *when he spoke of matters to settle before making any decisions? Could he truly have feelings for me, as I am beginning to suspect?*

Suddenly, a movement caught her eye, and Elizabeth turned to see a familiar figure standing at the edge of the road, watching the carriage pass by. It was Mr. Wickham, his handsome face twisted into a scowl as he met her gaze.

Elizabeth felt a chill run down her spine, a sense of unease settling in the pit of her stomach. *What is he doing here?* she thought, her mind racing with possibilities. *And why does he look at me with such barely concealed hostility?*

She glanced away quickly, her heart pounding in her chest as she tried to shake off the unsettling feeling. *It is nothing*, she told herself firmly, *merely a trick of the light, a figment of my overactive imagination.*

But even as she tried to convince herself, Elizabeth could not shake the sense that something was amiss, that Mr. Wickham's presence boded ill for the future. *I must be on my guard,* she thought, her jaw set with determination. *I will not let him ruin the happiness that Jane and Bingley so richly deserve.*

With a deep breath, Elizabeth turned her attention back to the conversation within the carriage, determined to put Mr. Wickham and his unsettling behaviour out of her mind. *Bath awaits,* she thought, a smile tugging at the corners of her mouth, *and with it, the promise of new adventures and the chance to explore the depths of my own heart.*

Chapter Seventeen

George Wickham stood seething, his eyes narrowed as he watched the Bingley carriage rumble away from Meryton. Through the window, he caught a glimpse of Elizabeth Bennet, her delicate features marred by a frown as she regarded him. He raised a hand in farewell, a disingenuous smile plastered across his handsome face, but Elizabeth had already turned away.

The carriage rounded the bend and disappeared from sight. Wickham's false smile instantly vanished, replaced by a scowl. That insufferable, meddlesome girl! He paced back and forth, his boots squelching in the muddy road.

"Thinks herself so very clever," he muttered under his breath. "Always poking her pert little nose where it doesn't belong."

His schemes had come to naught, his careful plans turned to ash and cinder. And there was no one to blame but Elizabeth Bennet. Her and her blasted family had upended everything!

Wickham kicked at a pebble, sending it skittering across the road. Anne de Bourgh, that sickly, simple-minded creature - she would have been an easy enough conquest, if not for Elizabeth's interference, and Wickham would have been rich beyond even his wildest dreams, the master of Rosings Park.

"Fool," Wickham spat. "Bloody, buggering fool."

He thrust his hands into his pockets, his fingers brushing against a few meagre coins - all that remained of the money he had bilked from his latest mark. It would not last long, not with his expensive tastes and mounting debts.

He needed a new plan, and quickly. But who? Wickham's mind turned to another prospect - Caroline Bingley. With her dowry of twenty thousand pounds, she would make a fine catch indeed, and with her brother away on his wedding trip, she was protected at Netherfield only by that drunken sot Hurst.

But even as he considered it, Wickham dismissed the idea with a frown. Miss Bingley was no fool. She had made her disdain for him quite clear during their brief acquaintance, her sharp eyes seeming to pierce right through his charming façade. She had very nearly given him the cut direct the one time he had asked her for a dance, at Lucas Lodge.

No, he would have to look elsewhere. Perhaps among the shop girls in Meryton...

Wickham shook his head, disgusted with himself. What was he thinking? Dallying with servant girls when he had a chance at something so much better?

A giggle made him turn his head, and a slow smile dawned on his face. Yes. Yes, that one would be perfect. Young, naïve, and utterly infatuated with him. It would be child's play to seduce her, to convince her to throw herself into his arms and beg him to elope. With her eldest sister married to Bingley, there was money to be had. Even if she technically had little dowry herself, Bingley would pay well to save his wife's sister from disgrace.

And if the chit proved too tiresome, well...there were ways to be rid of an unwanted wife.

A cold smile curved Wickham's lips as he contemplated his scheme. Yes, Lydia Bennet would do very nicely indeed. And if it just so happened to crush Elizabeth's tender heart in the process, so much the better.

She had rejected him, scorned his advances and thwarted his plans. Now she would pay the price for her folly. One way or another, George Wickham always got what he wanted.

With renewed determination, Wickham set about orchestrating supposedly chance encounters with Lydia in Meryton. At her aunt's, the milliner's, even on her daily walks - he always seemed to materialize at her side, ready with a charming quip or a roguish wink that never failed to set the girl giggling.

"Why, Mr. Wickham!" Lydia exclaimed in delight as he appeared beside her on the path one morning. "What a pleasant surprise! I had no idea you frequented this path."

"Indeed, I do not usually," he replied smoothly, taking her gloved hand and brushing a gallant kiss across her knuckles. "But I confess, the temptation to see your lovely face again drew me here as if by magnetic force. I simply could not stay away."

Lydia blushed and tittered, clearly thrilled by his bold flattery. "Oh, Mr. Wickham, you do say the most charming things! I declare, you shall quite turn my head with your silver tongue."

"Ah, but it is you who have turned mine," Wickham murmured, gazing deep into her eyes with feigned adoration. "From the moment I first beheld you, I knew my heart would never be free again. You have bewitched me, body and soul, sweet Lydia."

Her eyes widened, her breath quickening at his passionate words. "I... I hardly know what to say! No one has ever spoken to me thus. Do you truly mean it?"

"With every fibre of my being," he vowed, lying through his teeth with expert ease. "I know I have no right, that I am far beneath you in every way. But I cannot help how I feel. You are the only woman I could ever love, my dearest, loveliest Lydia."

Overwhelmed, she swayed towards him, and he caught her in his arms, pulling her close. She melted against him, putty in his hands, just as he'd known she would be.

Wickham hid his triumphant smirk in her hair, already envisioning the delights that awaited him - both sensual and financial. Lydia Bennet was his, and through her, he would have his vengeance on Elizabeth at last.

As the days passed, Wickham drew Lydia further into his web, meeting her in secret as often as he dared. With honeyed words and ardent looks, he worked to make himself the centre of her world, the sole recipient of her confidences and affections.

"Oh Wickham, you are the only one who truly understands me," Lydia sighed one afternoon as they strolled arm-in-arm along a secluded path, well away from prying eyes. "My sisters think me silly and frivolous. They do not see me as you do."

"Fret not, my darling," he soothed, patting her hand. "They are blind to your charms, your vivacity, your singular loveliness. In truth, I pity them their ignorance. But their loss is my gain, for it means I have you all to myself." He bestowed upon her a heated look.

Lydia flushed prettily, leaning into his side. "You say the most wonderful things. I hardly know how I shall bear to be parted from you, even for a day!"

"It is a wrench to my very soul each time we must say adieu," Wickham declared feelingly, though inwardly he chafed at the clinging neediness that was already beginning to grate. Still, he knew he must string her along until his plans came to fruition. "If only there was a way we could be together always, with no one to censure or interfere..."

He gazed at her with fabricated longing, and she quivered like an arrow questing for its target, ready to be loosed into flight. "Oh Wickham..."

"Shhh, do not fret, sweetling. I will find a way for us, I swear it. No matter the obstacles, our love will conquer all in the end. Trust in me..."

A rustle in the bushes startled them from their intimate exchange. Wickham's head snapped toward the sound, eyes narrowing. "Who's there? Show yourself!"

Sheepishly, Kitty emerged, twigs snagging in her hair. "Lydia? I'm sorry, I didn't mean to..."

"Kitty!" Lydia shrieked. "Have you been spying on us? How dare you!"

Wickham placed a soothing hand on Lydia's arm. "Peace, my dear. I'm sure your sister meant no harm." He fixed Kitty with a warning look. "But I trust she will keep our private conversations just that—private."

Kitty nodded vigorously. "Of course! I swear, I shan't breathe a word!"

Lydia huffed. "You had better not, or I shall never confide in you again!" She turned imploring eyes on Wickham. "Fear not, my love. Kitty may be a frightful snoop, but she knows better than to cross me."

"I'm sure that's true," Wickham agreed, though suspicion still lurked in his gaze as he watched Kitty's retreat. Once she had gone, he drew Lydia close again, his voice dropping to a seductive purr. "Now, where were we? Ah yes, I was just about to suggest something delightfully scandalous..."

Lydia shivered in anticipation. "Yes? Tell me!"

A wicked smile curved his lips. "What if we didn't wait for anyone's approval? What if we simply... eloped?"

Lydia gasped. "Elope? Truly? But... wouldn't that be terribly wicked?"

"More like terribly romantic," he countered smoothly. "Think of it, Lydia! Stealing away into the night, just the two of us... A secret ceremony at Gretna Green and a cosy honeymoon cottage, with no one to criticize or chaperone. Only our love to keep us warm."

Lydia's eyes glazed over dreamily. "Oh my... it does sound frightfully tempting..." She bit her lip, then launched herself at him. "Yes, Wickham, yes! Let's do it, let's elope! I cannot bear another moment apart from you!"

Wickham caught her, chuckling at her enthusiasm. "That's my girl," he praised, mind racing ahead. He would have to plan this carefully, but his trap had been set now. Lydia would soon be his, and through her, the Bennet family's respectability and whatever fortune he could gouge from Bingley. All that remained was to play his part convincingly.

He sealed his triumph with a kiss, as Lydia giggled giddily against his mouth, already lost in visions of their future, unaware that he plotted her downfall even as he held her in his arms.

Charlotte Bennet sat at her writing-desk, reading over again her latest letters, and smiling. Mary had returned to London with the Gardiners after the wedding, and had found, much to her surprise, that a young doctor in the circle of their acquaintance had missed her a good deal while she was away. Charlotte suspected a visit from the young man to Mr. Bennet, to ask his permission to court Mary, might be imminent, and she could not be happier. What a good thing Mary had decided to decline Mr. Collins!

The second letter, lying beside Mary's, was from Elizabeth. Although Elizabeth was enjoying Bath in Jane and Mr. Bingley's company - and reading between the lines, had found herself very popular among the eligible bachelors - there were hints in the letter that Elizabeth was feeling restless, finding something missing in her life. Thinking of the way that Mr. Darcy had stared at Elizabeth during the wedding, and indeed the way Elizabeth had constantly sneaked glances back at him, Charlotte suspected she knew what the problem was.

With a sigh, Charlotte set the letters aside. It was too late to begin her replies tonight; she would write back to both stepdaughters tomorrow. Closing her writing-desk, she popped her head into Mr. Bennet's study to bid her husband a good night before proceeding above stairs to her bedroom.

As she prepared for bed, Charlotte could not shake the feeling that something was amiss.

Lydia had been acting strangely of late, giggling and whispering with Kitty in corners, falling silent whenever Charlotte entered the room. At first she had dismissed it as mere high spirits, but now a sense of unease pricked at her. The sooner those two went back to school, the better, Charlotte thought to herself. She had done her best with them, but Lydia was difficult and stubborn, and frankly quite stupid. No matter what Charlotte tried to teach her, Lydia seemed determined to do whatever she pleased, heedless to the consequences to herself or others.

A knock sounded at the door, startling Charlotte. "Come in," she called, hastily composing her features.

Kitty poked her head in, eyes wide and worried. "Stepmama, I must speak with you urgently," she said in a rush. "It's about Lydia."

Charlotte's heart sank as Kitty spilled out the whole sordid tale - the secret meetings, the love letters, the whispered endearments. How Wickham had charmed Lydia with flattery and kisses, filling her head with romantic notions.

"I tried to stop her, truly I did!" Kitty wrung her hands. "But she wouldn't listen. And now..." She swallowed hard. "Now I fear she means to do something foolish. I overheard her telling Maria that she planned to elope!"

"Elope?" Charlotte echoed, aghast. "Is the girl mad? He'll ruin her!"

"Oh Stepmama, what do we do?" Kitty looked on the verge of tears. "I couldn't bear it if any harm came to her!"

Charlotte rose from her vanity, a determined set to her jaw. "Kitty, I need you to tell me everything you know about their plans. Where are they meeting? What time?"

Kitty scrunched her face, trying to recall the details. "I believe she said something about the old oak tree near Netherfield. And she is already gone... she slipped out through the French doors in the parlour just minutes ago. I came straight to find you."

"She would have to walk the whole way. We have time." Charlotte glanced at the clock on her mantel, thinking furiously.

That old oak was exactly where Wickham had waited for Anne de Bourgh… the man was nothing if not predictable.

"But what will you do?" Kitty asked anxiously.

"We will stop this foolishness before it goes any further." Charlotte's tone brooked no argument. "Now run downstairs and go find John Coachman. Tell him to get the carriage ready, as quick as he can."

Kitty nodded before running from the room, obviously eager to be of use. Charlotte could have wished Kitty had come to her sooner, before the situation got this far, but she would not reproach Kitty now. At least, not if they were in time to stop Lydia and Wickham.

Charlotte allowed herself one brief moment to close her eyes and gather her courage. Then she straightened her spine and went to fetch her husband. She would need his help, loath though she was to involve him.

In no time at all, the carriage had been readied and Charlotte clutched her pelisse tightly around her as they rattled along the moonlit lanes towards Netherfield. Kitty sat beside her, trembling in every limb. Charlotte had told her to go to bed, but Kitty begged to come, and in the end Charlotte relented.

Mr. Bennet sat opposite them, grim-faced and silent. He had said but little as Charlotte hastily explained the situation, only nodding in agreement to her plan.

Charlotte's mind raced as she stared unseeingly out the window. How could Lydia be so foolish, so headstrong? Did she not realize the ruin she courted in running off with the likes of Wickham? The damage to her reputation would be irreparable.

"I cannot believe Lydia would be so reckless," she murmured, wringing her gloved hands in agitation. "What can she be thinking?"

Mr. Bennet sighed heavily. "She is not thinking at all, my dear."

"We must stop her," Charlotte said firmly. "She is too young, too naïve to comprehend the gravity of her actions."

"And if we cannot? If she refuses to listen to reason and has already thrown her lot in with that blackguard Wickham?"

Charlotte heard the unspoken fear in her husband's voice. The spectre of a forced marriage loomed, of Lydia shackled for life to a dissolute wastrel. The scandal and gossip that would ensue did not bear thinking on.

She reached over to clasp his hand. "We will make her listen," she vowed. "Whatever it takes. I will not see Lydia ruined. Not while there is breath in my body."

Mr. Bennet lifted her hand to his lips and Charlotte felt the warmth of his love and gratitude flow through her. She knew he blamed himself for not keeping a closer watch on Lydia, for not curtailing her wild behaviour before it had come to this. She longed to reassure him, to ease the burden of guilt weighing so heavily upon his shoulders, but the words stuck in her throat.

The silence stretched between them, thick with unspoken fears and recriminations. Charlotte forced herself to take a deep breath, to focus on the task at hand. They must find Lydia, must stop her from making a mistake that would haunt her for the rest of her days.

Chapter Eighteen

George Wickham's boots trampled a muddy path beside the hired carriage as he paced in the darkness. The full moon peeked through wisps of clouds, casting a faint glow upon the lonely road. He pulled his pocket watch from his waistcoat pocket and scowled at the delicate hands ticking past the appointed hour. Lydia should have arrived by now.

A flicker of movement in the distance caught his eye. At last, a cloaked female figure emerged from the shadows, hurrying towards him with light footsteps. Wickham allowed himself a satisfied smirk. His charming words and secret smiles had worked their magic on the naïve girl, enticing her to throw propriety to the wind and run away with him. It had almost been too easy.

As the figure drew nearer, Wickham put on his most winsome smile. "There you are, my darling Lydia. I was beginning to fear you had thought better of our plan." He stepped forward and extended a gloved hand to help her into the carriage, eager to be on their way. The sooner they reached London, the sooner he could implement the next phase of his scheme. Lydia's ridiculous infatuation would deliver him from his debts and grant him his long-awaited revenge on that insufferable Darcy. With the Bennet family's reputation in tatters, Darcy could not possibly marry Elizabeth Bennet, delivering heartbreak to them both.

But as he grasped the woman's small hand, Wickham felt a flicker of unease. Something was amiss. The woman hesitated before the carriage door. Then slowly, deliberately, she reached up with her free hand and pushed back the hood of her cloak.

Wickham's heart seized in his chest as the woman's face was revealed in the moonlight. It was not Lydia who stood before him, but her stepmother, Charlotte Bennet. Her dark eyes glinted with a hard, knowing light, and her mouth was set in a grim line.

"Mrs. Bennet," Wickham stammered, dropping her hand as if it had burned him. His mind raced as he tried to conjure a plausible explanation for his presence on this deserted road in the middle of the night. "I... I was just..."

"Expecting someone else, perhaps?" Charlotte asked, her tone dripping with sarcasm. She arched one delicate eyebrow, surveying him with an expression of profound disapproval. "A certain foolish, impressionable girl, who you thought would be easy prey for your charming lies and empty promises?"

Wickham flinched at the accusation, but quickly recovered his composure. He forced a chuckle and spread his hands in a gesture of innocent confusion. "My dear Mrs. Bennet, I'm afraid I have no idea what you mean. I was merely out for a late-night stroll, enjoying the beauty of the moonlight."

Charlotte snorted in a most unladylike manner. "Please, Mr. Wickham. Spare me your practiced deceptions. You are nothing if not predictable." She took a step closer, her gaze boring into his. "Did you really think no one would notice your sly glances and whispered conversations with Lydia? That we would all turn a blind eye to your blatant attempts to seduce her away from her family and her honour?"

Wickham felt a bead of sweat trickle down his spine, despite the chill of the night air. He had underestimated Charlotte Bennet. She was far more perceptive and formidable than he had given her credit for.

"And in the very spot from where you attempted to elope with Anne de Bourgh?" Charlotte continued, gesturing to the blasted oak leaning precariously over the road. "Your arrogance knows no bounds, Mr. Wickham, but your scheme ends here."

Frozen in place, Wickham's heart pounded in his chest as the sound of approaching hooves and carriage wheels filled the air. The clatter grew louder, echoing in his ears like the tolling of a bell, until a carriage emerged from the shadows. It rolled to a stop beside them, the horses snorting and pawing at the ground.

The carriage door swung open, and Mr. Bennet stepped out. His face was set in a mask of cold fury, his eyes blazing with barely contained rage.

As if summoned by some unspoken command, a group of horsemen rode up behind the carriage. With a sinking feeling, Wickham recognized the familiar faces of his fellow militia officers. At their head, his commanding officer, Colonel Forster, regarded him with a stony expression that promised severe consequences.

Wickham's mouth went dry as he realized the true extent of his predicament.

"Well, well, Mr. Wickham," Mr. Bennet said, his voice dripping with sarcasm. "What an unexpected pleasure to find you here, in the company of my wife, no less." He stepped closer, his gaze sharp and penetrating. "I do hope you have a compelling explanation for this clandestine meeting."

Wickham's mind raced, desperately searching for a plausible lie to spin. He had always been able to talk his way out of difficult situations, but faced with the combined wrath of Mr. Bennet and Colonel Forster, he found himself uncharacteristically tongue-tied.

"Mr. Bennet, I assure you, this is not what it appears," Wickham began, his voice strained. "Mrs. Bennet and I were merely discussing... a matter of mutual interest."

"Is that so?" Mr. Bennet arched an eyebrow. "And what matter would that be, pray tell? The art of deception? The finer points of ruining a young girl's reputation?"

Wickham flinched at the accusation, his mind frantically grasping for a way to salvage the situation. But before he could utter another word, Colonel Forster dismounted his horse and strode forward, his face a thundercloud of anger.

"Lieutenant Wickham," he barked, his voice sharp and commanding. "You will explain yourself this instant. What is the meaning of this disgraceful behaviour?"

Wickham's gaze darted towards the carriage, where he saw Lydia's tear-streaked face pressed against the window, her eyes wide with fear and confusion. Beside her, Kitty sat rigidly, her expression a mixture of guilt and determination. In that moment, the bitter realization struck him like a physical blow: Kitty had betrayed their plans, and now he was left to face the consequences alone.

Desperation clawed at his throat as he turned back to face the men before him. He had to find a way out of this predicament, and quickly. Drawing upon his considerable charm and silver tongue, Wickham attempted to spin a tale that might salvage his reputation, if not his original scheme.

"Mr. Bennet, I understand how this must appear," he began smoothly, trying to look contrite. "But I assure you, my intentions were honourable. I was overcome by my emotions, by my deep affection for your daughter, Lydia. In a moment of passion, I proposed that we elope to Gretna Green and marry immediately."

The words tasted bitter on his tongue, but Wickham forced himself to continue, his expression one of earnest sincerity. "I realize now that it was rash and impulsive of me, and I deeply regret any distress I may have caused to your family. But please, believe me when I say that my love for Lydia is true and unwavering."

He held his breath, hoping against hope that his carefully crafted lie would be enough to sway the men before him. But even as the words left his lips, Wickham could see the scepticism and anger etched upon their faces.

A harsh bark of laughter shattered the tense silence that followed Wickham's declaration. All eyes turned to the driver of the hired carriage, who leaned forward with a smirk on his weathered face.

"Gretna Green, eh?" the man drawled, his tone dripping with scorn. "That's a fine tale, sir, but it ain't the truth. You hired me to take you to London, not Scotland. And you ain't paid me yet!"

Wickham felt the blood drain from his face as the driver's words sank in. His carefully constructed façade crumbled, leaving him exposed and vulnerable before the accusing glares of Mr. Bennet and Colonel Forster.

"London?" Mr. Bennet repeated, his voice low and dangerous. "And what, pray tell, did you intend to do with my daughter in London, Mr. Wickham?"

Wickham opened his mouth to reply, but no words came. His silver tongue, usually so quick and clever, had turned to lead in his mouth. He could feel the weight of his lies pressing down upon him, suffocating him with their enormity.

But it was the look on Denny's face that truly undid him. His erstwhile friend, who had stood by him through thick and thin, now regarded him with a mixture of fury and disgust. As Mr.

Bennet's accusation hung in the air, Denny's hand flew to his sword, his eyes blazing with barely contained rage.

"You never meant to marry her at all, did you?" Denny growled, his voice trembling with emotion. "You were going to ruin her, to use her and cast her aside!"

Wickham flinched, the truth of Denny's words striking him like a physical blow. As he stood there, the weight of his sins bearing down upon him, Wickham could not help but wonder how it had all gone so wrong. He had thought himself invincible, untouchable by the petty morals and conventions that bound other men. But now, as he faced the wrath of those he had wronged, he realized the folly of his ways.

And yet, even in that moment of reckoning, a part of him still clung to the hope that he might find a way out, that his silver tongue might yet save him from the fate that awaited him. But as he looked into the unforgiving eyes of Mr. Bennet and Colonel Forster, Wickham feared that this time, there would be no escape.

Colonel Forster's icy gaze bore into Wickham, his voice dripping with contempt as he spoke. "And what of your duties, Wickham? Did you plan to abandon your post, to desert the regiment without so much as a word of explanation?"

Wickham's stomach churned, a sickening realization dawning upon him. In his haste to secure Lydia, he had given no thought to the possible negative consequences of his actions.

"I... I had not thought..." Wickham stammered, his usually facile tongue deserting him in the face of his superior's wrath.

There was nothing he could say, no lie he could spin that would extricate him from this predicament.

Colonel Forster's eyes narrowed, his expression cold and unforgiving. "That much is clear, Wickham. You have brought shame upon yourself and upon this regiment. I have no choice but to place you under arrest, pending a formal investigation into your conduct."

Wickham's heart sank, a wave of nausea washing over him as the reality of his situation set in. He had gambled everything on this scheme, had risked his very future for the chance at a fortune. And now, it had all come crashing down around him, leaving him with nothing but the bitter taste of regret.

As his former friends stepped forward to take him into custody, Wickham could not help but wonder what fate awaited him. Would he be court-martialled, stripped of his rank and commission? Might they even hang him, for being caught in the act of desertion?

But even as these thoughts raced through his mind, Wickham knew that he had no one to blame but himself. He had sown the seeds of his own downfall, had let his greed and his ego blind him to the consequences of his actions, and now not even those he had gulled into thinking themselves his friends would step forward to say a word in his defence.

Elizabeth had just returned from a delightful evening at the theatre in Bath with her beloved sister Jane and Mr. Bingley when the express letter arrived, shattering the tranquil atmosphere with its distressing contents. The elegant script, instantly recognizable as Charlotte's hand, seemed to dance before Elizabeth's eyes as she read the alarming news.

Wickham attempted to elope with Lydia, the letter proclaimed, each word a dagger to Elizabeth's heart. She gasped, her fingers trembling as she clutched the paper, her mind reeling with the implications of such a scandalous act.

Jane, ever attuned to her sister's distress, rushed to Elizabeth's side, her brow furrowed with concern. "Lizzy, what is it? What has happened?"

Elizabeth, her voice quavering, relayed the shocking revelation. "It's Lydia... and Mr. Wickham. They tried to elope, Jane. Stepmother says he attempted to take her away."

Bingley, his usual jovial demeanour replaced by a grave expression, joined them, his eyes widening as he absorbed the news. "Good heavens! This is most distressing indeed. We must return to Longbourn at once. I'll order the carriage to depart first thing in the morning."

As they hastily prepared for their journey back to Hertfordshire, Elizabeth's thoughts raced, her mind conjuring a myriad of scenarios, each more troubling than the last. What had possessed Lydia to agree to such a reckless scheme? And Wickham... Elizabeth shuddered at the thought of his duplicitous nature, his charming façade concealing a heart devoid of true honour.

"Oh, Jane," Elizabeth lamented, her eyes brimming with tears, "how could Lydia be so foolish? To risk her reputation, her very future, for a man like Wickham..."

Jane, ever the soul of compassion, drew her sister into a comforting embrace. "We must have faith, Lizzy. Perhaps the situation is not as dire as it seems. Stepmama's letter did say that the elopement was only attempted, not accomplished."

Elizabeth nodded, drawing strength from her sister's unwavering optimism. Yet, even as they boarded the carriage bound for Longbourn, a sense of foreboding lingered in her heart, a silent prayer that they might arrive in time to mitigate the damage wrought by Wickham's deplorable actions.

"Before we depart, I shall write to Darcy," Bingley announced. "He will want to know."

Bingley's countenance, though troubled, held a determined air as he penned the letter to Darcy.

"I apologize for the brevity of this missive, Darcy," Bingley murmured as he wrote, his quill scratching against the paper, "but time is of the essence. Wickham has once again proven himself a scoundrel, attempting to elope with Mrs. Bingley's youngest sister, Miss Lydia. We hasten back to Longbourn, but I fear the damage may already be done."

He sealed the letter and handed it to a waiting servant, his eyes meeting Elizabeth's as he did so. In that moment, a silent understanding passed between them, a shared acknowledgment of the trials that lay ahead.

As the carriage rattled along the road that would lead them home to Hertfordshire, Elizabeth gazed out the window, her thoughts consumed by the unfolding drama. She could only imagine the turmoil that must have descended upon Longbourn, the whispers and speculation that would surely follow in the wake of such a scandal.

And amidst it all, one name echoed in her mind, a name that had once filled her with such conflicting emotions: *Mr. Darcy.* How would he react to this news, knowing that the man who had sought to destroy first his own sister and then his cousin, had now set his sights on Elizabeth's family?

When they arrived at Longbourn, the atmosphere was one of barely contained chaos. Servants scurried about, their whispers filling the halls, while the family were gathered in the parlour, their faces etched with worry and consternation.

Mr. Bennet, his usually sardonic demeanour replaced by a weary resignation, greeted them with a nod. "Ah, Elizabeth, Jane, Mr. Bingley. I'm afraid you've returned to a house in turmoil."

Elizabeth stepped forward, her voice steady despite the trepidation that gripped her heart. "Father, what has been done? Is Lydia...?"

"Safe, for now," Mr. Bennet replied. "And with a reputation that will remain mostly intact, thanks to the intervention of Mr. Denny, a most honourable young man. He came to me, after the attempted elopement, and offered for Lydia's hand."

Elizabeth's eyes widened, surprise mingling with a glimmer of hope. "Lieutenant Denny? But I thought…"

"That Lydia's affections lay elsewhere?" Mr. Bennet shook his head. "It seems that Mr. Denny's regard for her is genuine, and in light of recent events, he felt compelled to act."

Charlotte spoke up. "Silly though Lydia has been, she understands that Mr. Denny's is the only offer which will allow her to retain some semblance of reputation and permit her to continue to be recognised by the family. She has accepted him."

Bingley stepped forward, his voice filled with quiet determination. "Mr. Bennet, if there is anything I can do to assist in this matter…"

Mr. Bennet managed a wry smile, his eyes flickering with gratitude. "Your support is much appreciated, Mr. Bingley. For now, we must focus on salvaging what remains of Lydia's reputation and securing her future. Mr. Denny will marry her, and though he is from a good family, he has few prospects at the present time. We must do something for him. Come to my study, and let us speak on the matter."

Colonel Forster regarded Wickham with a mixture of disappointment and disdain, his lips pressed into a thin line as he surveyed the disgraced officer. The once-charming façade had crumbled, revealing the true nature of the man beneath, craven and contemptible.

"Mr. Wickham," Colonel Forster began, his voice dripping with contempt, "it appears that your past misdeeds have finally caught up with you. I fear that your actions have left me with little choice but to take drastic measures."

Wickham's face paled, his eyes darting nervously between the Colonel and Mr. Darcy, who stood silently by, his expression unreadable. "Colonel Forster, I assure you, this has all been a terrible misunderstanding. If you would only allow me to explain..."

"Enough!" Colonel Forster shouted, silencing Wickham's protests. "Your silver tongue will do you no good here, sir. Your actions have brought shame upon the regiment, and I will not allow such behaviour to go unpunished."

He turned to Mr. Darcy, a look of grim determination etched upon his features. "Mr. Darcy, I believe it is time we put an end to this sordid affair. Mr. Wickham will be stripped of his commission, effective immediately, and transferred to a regiment soon to be dispatched to the war front. Perhaps there, he will learn the true meaning of duty and honour."

Mr. Darcy nodded, his eyes never leaving Wickham's face. "I concur, Colonel. It is high time that Mr. Wickham faced the consequences of his actions. I only regret that it has taken so long for justice to be served."

Wickham's face contorted with rage, his fists clenched at his sides. "You cannot do this to me! I am a gentleman, and I demand to be treated as such!"

Colonel Forster's eyes narrowed, his voice low and dangerous. "You, sir, are no gentleman. You are a scoundrel and a disgrace to the uniform you wear. Be grateful that I do not see fit to have you flogged for your crimes."

"You are done, Wickham," Darcy said softly as the colonel turned on his heel and stalked out of the small room which Wickham had been confined to ever since being dragged back to Meryton in disgrace the night of the attempted elopement. "And allow me to assure you that if I ever so much as hear your name mentioned in my hearing again, I will hunt you down like the dog you are."

Wickham knew this was his last, his very last chance. "Your father would not have wanted..." he began, and realised just how far he had overstepped as Darcy's face flushed red.

"My father would be ashamed to see what you have become," Darcy said, his voice shaking with rage. "You have repaid his generosity with greed and his kindness with cruelty. Look at yourself, Wickham! You were provided a gentleman's education, given a livelihood which should have seen you comfortable for the rest of your days, and look where you have ended! In debt to the tune of hundreds, if not thousands of pounds - oh, I know all about your gambling debts to your fellow officers, not to mention what you owe the tradesmen of Meryton - desperately attempting to marry your fortune by seducing naïve young girls, and a scant step away from having your neck stretched for desertion! If God put a greater fool on this earth, I hope never to meet him."

As Darcy too turned and walked out, leaving him alone, Wickham sank to sit down on the bed, putting his face in his hands. Vain and arrogant, all his self-absorption could not allow him to deny that every scorching word Darcy had just thrown at him was the absolute truth.

Now, he supposed, the best he could hope for was not to die an ignominious death facing the French.

Chapter Nineteen

ELIZABETH WATCHED AS LYDIA, resplendent in a new gown, walked down the aisle on Mr. Bennet's arm to meet her groom at the altar. Lieutenant Denny's adoring gaze did not waver from Lydia's smiling face throughout the simple ceremony, his devotion palpable to all in attendance.

Afterwards, as the newlyweds received well-wishes from the assembled guests in the small church, Elizabeth observed the joyful scene with a mix of relief and trepidation. Lydia's impulsive nature had nearly led to ruin, yet somehow, a respectable match had been made despite it all. She could only hope that her youngest sister would find contentment and stability in her new life as a married woman.

"I must say, I had not expected to see Lydia wed before you," Mr. Bennet remarked wryly, coming to stand beside Elizabeth. "Though perhaps it is for the best. Denny seems a decent sort, and his fondness for our silly girl is evident."

Elizabeth nodded, a small smile playing on her lips. "Indeed, Father. Let us hope that Lydia's lively spirit will be tempered by the responsibilities of marriage, and that she will find happiness with her husband." She truly hoped that it might be so. The combined efforts of Lydia's family and friends had seen a captaincy purchased for Mr. Denny, which he would shortly be taking up, in the regiment of Colonel Fitzwilliam, who had promised to keep a close eye on them both. Considering what might have transpired, it was a far better outcome than Lydia deserved, though Elizabeth would keep that thought strictly to herself.

A few days later, Lydia and her new husband departed to join his new regiment, taking the genuine well-wishes of all at Longbourn with them. Kitty returned to school, and with Jane now mistress at Netherfield and Mary in London with the Gardiners, Elizabeth found herself the only Bennet daughter remaining at home.

Though it was pleasant to spend uninterrupted time with Charlotte, and with her father, Elizabeth found herself curiously restless. Jane encouraged Elizabeth to come to Netherfield as often as possible, but Elizabeth thought it would be best if she was not too much underfoot. Jane needed time to settle into her new role as mistress of the house.

"Are you going over to Netherfield this morning, Lizzy?" Charlotte asked, coming into the morning-room where Elizabeth was sitting by the window.

"Not today." Elizabeth glanced up from her book with a smile. "It is raining far too heavily to walk, I fear, and one of the carriage horses was not quite sound yesterday, John was going to walk him to Meryton to the farrier today. Miss Bingley and Mrs. Hurst planned to go to Hatfield shopping, so the Bingley carriage will not be available for Jane to send for me."

"I see." Charlotte gave her a knowing glance, before holding out a letter. "Well, John returned just a few minutes ago, and brought the post with him. A letter for you."

Elizabeth took the letter, her curiosity piqued by the unfamiliar seal and the expensive paper. As she opened it, the delicate scent of lavender wafted up from the pages. The letter was from none other than Anne de Bourgh, inviting Elizabeth to visit her in Kent until her upcoming wedding to Colonel Fitzwilliam.

Dear Elizabeth, Anne had written, *I find myself in a state of such joy and anticipation as my wedding day approaches. Your presence would bring me immeasurable comfort and delight during this time. I implore you to come and stay with me at Rosings until the ceremony. Your wit and companionship would be a balm to my nerves and a source of great pleasure.*

Elizabeth could not help but smile at the warmth and sincerity of Anne's words. The once reserved and sickly young woman had blossomed with happiness, and Elizabeth felt a surge of affection for her friend.

"An invitation from Miss de Bourgh, I presume?" Charlotte said with a warm smile.

"Indeed," Elizabeth replied, offering the letter for Charlotte to read. "She has asked me to visit her in Kent until her wedding day."

Charlotte raised an eyebrow, a smile playing at the corners of her mouth. "And will you accept?"

Elizabeth paused, considering the prospect of leaving her family for an extended period. Yet, the thought of being there for Anne during such a momentous time in her life was too tempting to resist. "I should very much like to," she said at last. "But it is fifty miles or more to Rosings; how shall I get there?"

"As to that, yours is not the only letter we have received today." Mr. Bennet entered the room to join them, waving another letter, this one with the seal already broken. "I have just received this, from Mr. Darcy. He is aware that Miss de Bourgh has asked you to attend her wedding, and has offered to escort you there when he goes to Kent with Miss Darcy, in a few days' time. I shall take you to London myself, to meet them."

Elizabeth looked from Charlotte to her father, unsure of what to say, and quite shocked by Mr. Darcy's offer.

"Well, Lizzy," her father said when she remained speechless, his tone laced with amusement, "it seems you have acquired quite the champion in Mr. Darcy. First, he secures a commission for our dear Mr. Denny, and now he offers to escort you to Kent. One might almost think he had a particular interest in your welfare."

Elizabeth's heart skipped a beat at her father's words, the realization of Mr. Darcy's role in Mr. Denny's good fortune hitting her like a thunderbolt. "Mr. Darcy... *he* obtained the commission for Mr. Denny?" she asked, her voice trembling with emotion.

Mr. Bennet chuckled, patting her hand affectionately. "Indeed, he did. Though I suspect he would prefer that knowledge to remain between us. The man has a remarkable talent for discretion, it seems."

As her father walked away, leaving her to her thoughts, Elizabeth felt a rush of gratitude and admiration for Mr. Darcy. That he would go to such lengths to ensure the happiness of her family, even after all that had transpired... it spoke volumes about his character and the depth of his feelings for her.

With a smile playing at her lips, Elizabeth looked out of the window again at the falling rain, her heart filled with anticipation for the journey that lay ahead. Perhaps, she thought, there was hope for her and Mr. Darcy after all.

The journey to Kent was a pleasant one, with Mr. Darcy and Georgiana proving to be delightful travelling companions. Elizabeth found herself engaging in lively conversations with both siblings, her heart warming at the sight of the usually reserved Mr. Darcy's tender interactions with his sister.

As they arrived at Rosings Park, Elizabeth was greeted by a sight that took her breath away. Anne de Bourgh, who had previously appeared a pale, sickly creature, now stood before her with rosy cheeks and a radiant smile, her happiness evident in every aspect of her demeanour.

"Elizabeth!" Anne exclaimed, rushing forward to embrace her. "Oh, how I have missed you! I am so glad you could come."

Elizabeth returned the embrace warmly, marvelling at the transformation in her friend. "My dear Anne, you look positively radiant. It is wonderful to see you so happy."

Anne laughed, a musical sound that filled the air with joy. "I have never felt so happy, Elizabeth. My dearest Colonel Fitzwilliam has brought such light into my life, and even Mother seems to have softened in his presence."

As if on cue, Lady Catherine emerged from the house, her usually stern features softened by a smile. "Miss Bennet, welcome to Rosings Park," she said, her tone lacking its usual haughtiness. "I trust your journey was pleasant?"

Elizabeth curtsied, hiding her surprise at the change in Lady Catherine's demeanour. "It was indeed, Lady Catherine. I cannot thank you enough for your kind invitation."

As they made their way into the house, Elizabeth found herself walking alongside Mr. Darcy, her heart racing at his proximity. Gathering her courage, she turned to him, her eyes shining with gratitude.

"Mr. Darcy, I must thank you for your role in securing Mr. Denny's captaincy," she said softly, her voice filled with emotion. "It was an incredibly generous act, and one that has brought great happiness to my family."

Mr. Darcy's eyes widened in surprise, a faint blush colouring his cheeks. "It was nothing, Miss Bennet," he said, his voice low and earnest. "I should have dealt with Wickham after his attempted elopement with Anne, but I foolishly believed that your sister would be safe from his machinations, given her lack of fortune. It was a mistake on my part, and one that I deeply regret."

Elizabeth shook her head, her heart swelling with admiration for the man before her. "You have nothing to regret, Mr. Darcy. Your actions have shown the true depth of your character, and for that, I am eternally grateful."

As they entered the house, Elizabeth felt a sense of hope and anticipation washing over her. Perhaps, she thought, this visit to Kent would prove to be the beginning of something truly wonderful.

In the days that followed, Elizabeth found herself spending more and more time with Georgiana, the two young women forging a deep and lasting bond. They spent long hours walking through the gardens of Rosings Park, talking and laughing as if they had known each other for years.

"I must confess, Miss Bennet," Georgiana said one afternoon, her voice tinged with shyness, "I have always been a bit intimidated by my brother's friends. But with you, I feel as though I can truly be myself."

Elizabeth smiled warmly, squeezing Georgiana's hand in reassurance. "And I feel the same way about you, Georgiana. You have become like another sister to me, and I am so grateful for your friendship."

As the days passed, Elizabeth couldn't help but notice the way Mr. Darcy watched her interactions with Georgiana, his eyes filled with a mixture of pride and longing. She felt her heart flutter every time their gazes met, and she found herself wondering if perhaps, just perhaps, he might be harbouring feelings for her as well.

But just as Elizabeth was beginning to allow herself to hope, the arrival of the Earl and Countess of Matlock brought a new sense of unease. From the moment they stepped into Rosings Park, Elizabeth felt as though she was being scrutinized, her every move and word analysed for some hidden meaning.

"Tell me, Miss Bennet," the Countess said one evening, her voice dripping with false sweetness, "what are your thoughts on the importance of family connections in securing a suitable match?"

Elizabeth felt her cheeks burn with indignation, but she forced herself to remain calm. "I believe, Lady Matlock," she said, her voice steady and clear, "that true happiness in marriage comes not from wealth or status, but from mutual respect, admiration, and love."

The Countess raised an eyebrow, her lips curling into a smirk. "An idealistic notion, to be sure. But one that is rarely borne out in reality, I'm afraid."

As the days wore on, Elizabeth couldn't shake the feeling that she was being tested, her worthiness as a potential match for Mr. Darcy being weighed and measured by the disapproving eyes of his relatives. She felt a sense of despair washing over her, wondering if perhaps her hopes for a future with the man she loved were nothing more than a foolish dream.

It was in this state of melancholy that Elizabeth received a letter from Jane. She had eagerly anticipated news from home, hoping for some distraction from her troubled thoughts. However, as she read her sister's words, her heart sank even further.

Jane wrote of the increasing difficulties she faced at Netherfield, with Caroline Bingley's subtle but relentless cruelty wearing away at her confidence and joy. *She questions my every decision*, Jane confided, *and undermines me at every turn. Charles remains blind to her machinations, and I fear that our happiness is slipping away.*

Elizabeth felt torn, her love for her sister warring with her own growing feelings for Mr. Darcy. She longed to rush to Jane's side, to offer comfort and support, but she knew that her place, for now, was in Kent. She could not abandon Anne in the days leading up to her wedding, nor could she bear the thought of leaving without some resolution to the unspoken tension between herself and Mr. Darcy.

As she sat in the drawing room, the letter clutched in her hand, Elizabeth was startled by the sound of footsteps behind her. She turned to see Mr. Darcy himself, his eyes filled with concern as he took in her troubled expression.

"Miss Bennet," he said softly, "forgive me for intruding, but I couldn't help but notice your distress. Is there anything I can do to help?"

Elizabeth hesitated, torn between her desire to confide in him and her fear of revealing too much. "It's my sister, Jane," she said at last, her voice barely above a whisper. "She writes of difficulties at Netherfield, with Miss Bingley, I'm afraid."

Mr. Darcy's face darkened, and he let out a heavy sigh. "I am sorry to hear that," he said, his voice filled with genuine regret. "I had hoped that my friend's marriage would bring happiness to all involved, but Miss Bingley has clearly not reconciled herself to the match."

Elizabeth nodded, feeling tears pricking at the corners of her eyes. "I feel so helpless," she confessed. "I want to be there for her, to offer her my support and advice, but I cannot leave here until after the wedding."

Mr. Darcy was silent for a moment, his expression thoughtful. "Perhaps there is a way to lend support to your sister without your having to leave Rosings," he said at last. "I could write to Bingley, and remind him of his duties as a husband and a gentleman. And perhaps Georgiana and I could accompany you on a visit to Netherfield, once the wedding is over. I would be glad to offer my support and friendship to your sister."

Elizabeth felt a rush of gratitude towards him, and a warmth spreading through her chest at the thought of his kindness. "Thank you, Mr. Darcy," she said, her voice filled with emotion. "I cannot tell you how much your support means to me, and to my family."

Mr. Darcy smiled, a rare and precious sight that made Elizabeth's heart skip a beat. "You are welcome, Miss Bennet," he said, his voice low and sincere. "I would do anything to ensure your happiness, and that of those you love."

The words seem to hang in the air between them, and Elizabeth found herself holding her breath. Would he speak now, tell her of the feelings she was beginning to be sure he harboured, and which she now believed she reciprocated?

But loud voices in the hall heralded Lord and Lady Matlock coming to join them, and Darcy looked away, the moment broken.

Chapter Twenty

Elizabeth gazed upwards at the vaulted ceiling of the chapel at Rosings, marvelling at the intricate frescoes depicting angelic choirs in rapturous song. The melodious strains of the wedding march filled the air as Anne de Bourgh, resplendent in a gown of jonquil silk overlaid with delicate Chantilly lace, glided down the aisle on the arm of her uncle, the Earl of Matlock.

Colonel Fitzwilliam awaited his bride at the altar, his scarlet regimentals striking against the dark wood of the pews. He stood tall and erect, a slight smile twitching at the corners of his mouth as he watched Anne approach. Mr. Collins, officiating in his capacity as clergyman, puffed out his chest with an air of immense self-importance.

As the bridal couple took their vows, Elizabeth found her eyes drawn to Mr. Darcy where he stood beside his cousin. How well he looked, so tall and proud of bearing! Their eyes met for the briefest of moments and Elizabeth felt a curious fluttering in her breast before she quickly lowered her gaze.

The ceremony concluded and the guests began to file out of the chapel to repair to the sumptuous wedding breakfast Lady Catherine had arranged. "The ceremony was a credit to you, Mr. Collins," Elizabeth overheard Lady Catherine remark to the obsequious vicar. "You comported yourself with admirable gravity. I confess I had some reservations about your... provincial background, but you have exceeded all my expectations."

"Your ladyship is too kind," simpered Mr. Collins, bowing so low he nearly toppled forward. "To have secured your esteem is the crowning glory of my life."

Elizabeth bit back a laugh at the tableau, hastening her steps to escape the chapel before her mirth could betray her. *What an idiot,* she thought. *Thank goodness I refused him. I should never have been able to restrain myself from rudely laughing in his face when he made such nonsensical remarks.*

As Elizabeth made her way about the room, politely mingling with the wedding guests, she found herself waylaid by none other than Mr. Collins. The obsequious clergyman had managed to disentangle himself from Lady Catherine's side and now stood before her, his face a mask of barely concealed disdain.

"Cousin Elizabeth," he said, his nasal voice dripping with condescension. "I trust you have found the ceremony to your liking? Though I dare say it is far grander than the nuptials I had once envisioned for you and I."

Elizabeth felt her cheeks flush with anger at his presumption. How dare he bring up his ill-fated proposal now, after all this time? "I assure you, Mr. Collins," she replied coolly, "I have no regrets about the path I have chosen."

Mr. Collins sniffed, his small eyes narrowing behind his spectacles. Before he could speak again, Elizabeth cut him off.

"And I understand my sister Mary feels the same," she added. "She is residing in London with our Gardiner relations and we are led to understand that a Dr. Watley is soon to be paying my father a visit."

Elizabeth felt no small amount of satisfaction in the way Mr. Collins' nostrils flared in obvious fury, his cheeks flushing an even darker red. He opened his mouth, probably to shout at her if the way his chest inflated was any guide, but before he could commence, a commanding voice cut through the air. "Mr. Collins! My brother would like a word, if you please." It was Lady Catherine, her imperious gaze fixed upon the clergyman.

Mr. Collins blanched, his bravado wilting under the force of her ladyship's stare. "Of course, Lady Catherine," he stammered, bowing deeply. "I am at your service, as always."

As he scurried away to find the Earl of Matlock, Elizabeth found herself face to face with Lady Catherine. The grande dame regarded her with a calculating look, her lips pursed in disapproval.

"Miss Bennet," she said, her voice as cold as the marble statues that adorned Rosings Park. "You may have refused Mr. Collins' offer of marriage, but I believe the opportunity has not yet passed. He is still a most eligible bachelor, and I would be willing to overlook your previous... indiscretion... if you were to reconsider."

Elizabeth felt a wave of shock and revulsion wash over her. The very idea of marrying Mr. Collins, of subjecting herself to a lifetime of his pompous lectures and empty flattery, was enough to make her stomach turn. How could Lady Catherine even suggest such a thing?

"I thank you for your... generous offer, Lady Catherine," she managed to say, her voice tight with barely suppressed anger. "But I am afraid I must decline. My feelings on the matter have not changed, and I have no intention of accepting Mr. Collins' hand, now or ever."

"Do you have any idea what you are throwing away? The chance to secure your family's future, to rise above your station?" Lady Catherine's gaze slid away from Elizabeth's even as she spoke, and Elizabeth could not help but glance to see what caught her ladyship's attention.

Ah, Elizabeth thought, as she spied Mr. Darcy standing with Colonel Fitzwilliam and Anne. *Lady Catherine is making one last bid to remove me from the field.*

But aloud, she merely inclined her head, a small, tight smile playing about her lips. "I appreciate your concern, Lady

Catherine," she said, her voice as smooth as silk. "But I am quite content with my decision. Now, if you will excuse me, I see Georgiana looking for me. We are to play a duet on the pianoforte to amuse your guests, and I believe it is time for us to begin."

And with that, she turned on her heel and walked away, her head held high, leaving a sputtering Lady Catherine in her wake.

The duet was well received by the guests, but afterwards, Georgiana, overcome by all the attention, begged Elizabeth to slip outside with her for a walk in the garden.

"Of course, dear one." Elizabeth squeezed the younger girl's hand. "Let us escape this noisy crowd a little while."

They did not go outside alone, however. Mr. Darcy joined them as they slipped out into the gardens, moving in between them and taking one of them on each of his arms.

"No escaping without me," he said, his tone almost playful.

Elizabeth laughed, and teased him back. "Did you need an escape so badly, sir?"

"I think you know me well enough by now to understand that a room so full of people as that one is difficult for me to navigate, Miss Bennet," he said, his tone full of warmth. "I am not at my best in a crowd, even one comprised of those with whom I am familiar."

Georgiana giggled. "And in a crowd of those with whom you are unfamiliar you are positively horrid!"

"Oh, indeed," Elizabeth agreed. "Did you ever hear what he said of me at the first assembly he attended in Meryton? He said that I was tolerable, but not handsome enough to tempt him."

Georgiana let out a little shriek, and Darcy's mouth fell open.

"Dear Lord," he said. "You *did* hear that?"

"I did, I'm afraid."

"I must offer you my most fervent apologies, then! I was..."

"Deeply uncomfortable and desperate to avoid being introduced to yet more strangers? I forgave you long ago, Mr. Darcy."

"I hope you understand that my opinion of you is very far from that I espoused then." He looked deeply into her eyes. "I have long known you to be one of the most handsome women I have ever had the pleasure of looking upon."

A red flush rose uncontrollably through Elizabeth's cheeks, and she dropped her gaze, unable to bear the intensity in his eyes.

There was a brief moment of silence before it was broken by, surprisingly, Georgiana. "We couldn't help but overhear what Lady Catherine said to you earlier," she said softly. "About Mr. Collins, I mean. Are you quite all right?"

Elizabeth felt a rush of warmth towards the younger girl. *Dear, sweet Georgiana*, she thought fondly.

"I am perfectly well, Georgiana," she assured her. "Lady Catherine's words were hardly a surprise to me. She has made her feelings on the matter quite clear in the past."

Mr. Darcy frowned, his brow furrowing. "It was most improper of her to speak to you in such a manner," he said, his voice low and intense. "Especially on a day that should be a joyous occasion for our family."

Elizabeth shrugged, trying to appear nonchalant. "I have grown accustomed to Lady Catherine's meddling ways," she said. "And in truth, I find the idea of marrying Mr. Collins rather amusing. Can you imagine the sort of life we would have together?"

She affected a high, nasal voice, mimicking Mr. Collins' pompous tones. "'My dear Mrs. Collins, I must insist that you join me in paying our daily respects to Lady Catherine. It is, after all, our duty as her most humble and obedient servants.'"

Georgiana giggled, covering her mouth with her hand, and even Mr. Darcy's lips twitched in amusement. Elizabeth felt a rush of pleasure at having made him smile, however briefly.

"It would have been a most laughable mismatch. Your wit and intelligence would have been entirely wasted on a man like Mr. Collins," Darcy said quietly, his expression sobering again.

"You are too kind, Mr. Darcy. But I assure you, I have no regrets about refusing Mr. Collins' proposal. I could never marry a man I did not love and respect, no matter how advantageous the match might be."

Georgiana nodded, her eyes wide with understanding. "I am so glad you refused him, Elizabeth! You deserve so much better than that."

Elizabeth smiled at the younger girl, touched by her sincere concern. "Thank you, Georgiana. That means a great deal to me."

Mr. Darcy cleared his throat, looking slightly uncomfortable with the turn the conversation had taken. "Yes, well... I hope you know that you have our full support, Miss Bennet. If there is anything we can do to make your stay at Rosings more pleasant, please do not hesitate to ask."

Elizabeth met his gaze, her heart swelling with gratitude and something else, something deeper and more profound. "I appreciate that, Mr. Darcy. Truly."

For a moment, they simply stood there, lost in each other's eyes, the rest of the world falling away. And though no words were spoken, Elizabeth felt a new understanding pass between them, a sense of kinship and shared purpose that filled her with hope for the future.

A few days later, after bidding a fond farewell to a blissfully happy Colonel and Mrs. Fitzwilliam, the carriage bearing Elizabeth, Mr. Darcy, and Georgiana rumbled up to Longbourn. Elizabeth's heart swelled with a mixture of relief and trepidation as she caught sight of the familiar house, its homely weathered bricks and ivy-covered walls a welcome sight after the grandeur and formality of Rosings.

As the carriage rolled to a stop, Elizabeth stepped down with the assistance of Mr. Darcy's strong hand. She turned to him with a grateful smile. "Thank you, Mr. Darcy, for seeing me safely home. Your kindness and generosity throughout our stay at Rosings have been greatly appreciated."

Mr. Darcy inclined his head, his dark eyes intense as they met hers. "It was my pleasure, Miss Bennet. I hope you know that you have become a dear friend to both Georgiana and myself. We shall miss your company greatly."

Elizabeth felt a flush rise to her cheeks at his words, her heart fluttering in her chest. She opened her mouth to reply, but before she could speak, the front door of Longbourn was flung open and Charlotte emerged, a warm smile on her face.

"Lizzy, my dear! Welcome home!" Charlotte exclaimed, hurrying forward to embrace her stepdaughter. She turned to Mr. Darcy and Georgiana with a courteous nod. "Mr. Darcy, Miss Darcy, thank you for bringing Elizabeth safely back to us. Won't you come in and join us for tea?"

Mr. Darcy and Georgiana exchanged a glance, and Elizabeth felt a sudden pang of disappointment at the thought of their departure. But to her surprise and delight, Mr. Darcy nodded, a small smile tugging at the corner of his mouth. "We would be honoured, Mrs. Bennet. Thank you for your kind invitation."

As they made their way into the house, Elizabeth couldn't help but marvel at the change in Mr. Darcy's demeanour. Gone was the proud, aloof gentleman she had first met at the Meryton assembly. In his place was a man who was kind, attentive, and genuinely interested in the well-being of those around him. *He is so very different among those he knows well,* she thought.

Over tea, Mr. Darcy and Georgiana were the very picture of graciousness, engaging Mr. Bennet and Charlotte in lively conversation about the latest news from London and the goings-on at Rosings. Elizabeth watched with a sense of pride and affection, her heart swelling with each passing moment.

After a leisurely and delightful conversation, Mr. Darcy and Georgiana departed for Netherfield with gracious thanks, expressing hopes they would see Elizabeth again soon.

"You certainly shall," Elizabeth said with a laugh, "for I will be at Netherfield tomorrow morning to see my sister."

"We shall look forward to seeing you then," Mr. Darcy said, and added for Elizabeth's ears alone, "I have something particular I would like to talk to you about."

Stunned, Elizabeth watched as Mr. Darcy handed Georgiana up into the carriage. It had long since rolled out of sight and still she stood there, staring at where it had been.

Did he mean what I suspect?

What shall I say when he asks me?

A smile came to her lips, but still she stood there, until Charlotte came out to find her and call her inside, wanting to hear more of Anne and Colonel Fitzwilliam's wedding.

But the next day, Elizabeth's happiness was shattered by the arrival of Jane, who burst into the breakfast parlour at Longbourn in a flood of tears, before Elizabeth could even think of setting off for Netherfield. Elizabeth leapt to her feet, spilling her tea in her haste, her heart constricting at the sight of her beloved sister's distress.

"Jane, my dear, what is it? What has happened?" Elizabeth cried, gathering Jane into her arms and guiding her to the settee.

Through her sobs, Jane managed to choke out the words that sent a chill down Elizabeth's spine. "It's Caroline. She's been simply awful to me, Lizzy. I don't know what to do!"

As Jane collapsed against her, her body shaking with the force of her tears, Elizabeth felt a fierce protectiveness rise up within her. She would not stand by and watch her sister suffer at the hands of that spiteful, manipulative woman.

Elizabeth stroked Jane's hair, her brow furrowed with concern. "Tell me everything, dearest. What has that wretched woman done to you?"

Jane sniffled, dabbing at her eyes with a lace-trimmed handkerchief. "She's so cold, so dismissive. Nothing I do seems to please her. She criticizes my every move, from the way I pour tea to the way I arrange the flowers. It's as if she's determined to make my life a misery."

A hot flush of anger suffused Elizabeth's cheeks. How dare Caroline treat her sweet, gentle sister with such disdain? "This cannot be allowed to continue, Jane. You must speak to Mr. Bingley about his sister's behaviour."

Jane's eyes widened, a look of alarm crossing her face. "Oh, no, Lizzy. I couldn't possibly. I don't want to cause any trouble between them."

"Trouble?" Elizabeth scoffed. "The only trouble is what Caroline is causing with her spiteful ways. Mr. Bingley needs to be made aware of the situation. He would want to know if his sister was mistreating his wife."

Charlotte, who had been listening quietly, spoke up. "Elizabeth is right, Jane. You must stand up for yourself. Show Caroline that you will not be cowed by her petty cruelties."

Jane bit her lip, uncertainty etched across her delicate features. "I don't know if I have the strength, Stepmother! I've never been one for confrontation."

Mr. Bennet, who had been observing the scene with a wry expression, chuckled. "Perhaps we should have sent Lydia to stay at Netherfield for a time. That would surely teach Caroline a lesson."

Despite the seriousness of the situation, Elizabeth couldn't help but smile at her father's jest. "I fear that would only make matters worse, Papa. Lydia's exuberance might well drive Caroline to even greater heights of unpleasantness."

Sobering, Elizabeth turned back to Jane, taking her sister's hands in her own. "You must find the courage within yourself, Jane. You are stronger than you know. And remember, you have all of us here to support you."

As they stepped into Netherfield's drawing room, Caroline Bingley's icy gaze fell upon them, her lips curling into a brittle smile. "Miss Eliza! How lovely to see you back in Hertfordshire," she said, her tone dripping with insincerity.

Elizabeth narrowed her eyes, her suspicions confirmed by Caroline's overly polite demeanour.

Georgiana, who had been sitting quietly by the window, rose to greet them, her gentle presence a balm to the tension in the room. "It's wonderful to have you here," she said, her voice warm and genuine.

As they settled into the room, Elizabeth couldn't help but notice the way Caroline's gaze flickered between Jane and Georgiana, a calculating gleam in her eye. She leaned closer to Jane, whispering, "Stay strong, dear sister. Remember, you are mistress of this house now, not her."

Jane nodded, her delicate features set in a determined expression. She turned to Caroline, her voice steady as she spoke. "Caroline, I must speak with you about a matter of some importance. I fear there has been a misunderstanding between us."

Caroline's eyes widened in mock surprise, her hand fluttering to her throat. "A misunderstanding? I can't imagine what you mean, Jane."

Elizabeth fought the urge to roll her eyes at Caroline's theatrics. She glanced at Georgiana, who met her gaze with a knowing look. In that moment, an idea began to form in Elizabeth's mind, a way to expose Caroline's true nature.

Leaning close to Georgiana, Elizabeth whispered, "I have a plan, but I shall need your help. Can I count on you?"

Georgiana nodded, her eyes shining with determination. "Of course, Elizabeth. Anything for Jane."

As the two young women put their heads together, Elizabeth felt a thrill of anticipation coursing through her veins. With Georgiana's aid and Jane's newfound strength, they would surely find a way to outmanoeuvre Caroline and secure Jane's rightful place at Netherfield. For the love of her sister, Elizabeth would stop at nothing to ensure her happiness.

Chapter Twenty-One

"What a lovely day for a turn in the gardens!" said Elizabeth brightly. "The fresh air would do you good, Jane." She well knew that Jane would never resist an opportunity to spend time among the flowers and herb beds of Netherfield's lovely gardens.

"That sounds delightful," Jane replied, rising from her chair.

Caroline Bingley sighed, tossing aside the book she had not been reading. "I suppose we might as well. Heaven knows there is little entertainment to be found in here."

Elizabeth shot a covert glance at Georgiana, who gave an almost imperceptible nod. Their plan was in motion. Mr. Darcy had promised to ensure he and Mr. Bingley would be in the library. Little used as it was, the open windows would mean anyone in the room would clearly overhear conversations in the flower garden immediately outside, and Caroline Bingley would never think anyone might be in there.

As the ladies stepped outside, Jane took a deep breath, closing her eyes contentedly. "You were right, Lizzy. It is so pleasant out here among the flowers."

She leaned down to clip some rosemary, inhaling its aromatic scent. Georgiana drifted away from them deliberately, aware that Caroline would not unleash the full force of her venom in Miss Darcy's presence.

"Foraging for herbs *again*, Jane?" Caroline remarked in a honeyed tone. "How... quaint. I suppose such simple pleasures must seem quite novel to those unaccustomed to the finer things in life."

Elizabeth bristled at the thinly veiled insult, but Jane merely smiled and nodded. "Oh yes, I find such joy in the beauty of nature. It is a balm to the soul, don't you think?"

"Really, Jane," Caroline drawled, her voice dripping with disdain. "I know you come from a... shall we say, humble background, but surely you realize that a woman of your new station has more important concerns than playing in the dirt like a common labourer."

Elizabeth's eyes flashed with anger, her hands clenching into fists at her sides. She opened her mouth to deliver a scathing retort, but Jane, ever the peacemaker, laid a gentle hand on her arm.

"Caroline," she said softly, her voice filled with quiet dignity. "I understand that we may have different interests and pursuits, but surely there is room for us both to find joy in our own ways. I would never presume to judge your choices, and I would hope that you could extend me the same courtesy."

"You?" Caroline let out a little laugh. "Judge *me*? By what measure could you possibly presume to judge me? You, with no education and little pretence to intelligence or accomplishments?"

With every cruel word, Jane shrank further into herself, until Elizabeth had absolutely had enough. Never, in the whole course of her life, had she resorted to violence, but she was so angry that a red mist descended before her eyes. Her arm swung in a wide arc, and her palm cracked against Caroline Bingley's cheek.

Caroline staggered back, her mouth opening and closing with shock, scarlet blooming on her cheek in the imprint of Elizabeth's fingers. "You... you *hit* me," she said in disbelief.

"Someone should have spanked your bottom long ago," Elizabeth snapped back at her. "Perhaps then you would have learned to behave in a more ladylike manner!"

"Elizabeth," Jane was gaping with horror. "You should not have..."

They were interrupted by the sound of running feet, and a moment later Darcy and Bingley were upon them. Caroline lost no time in pointing at Elizabeth and screeching "She *struck* me! Brother, I demand she be removed from Netherfield this instant!"

"Caroline," Bingley said, striding straight past his sister to Jane, and gathering his wife in his arms, "shut up before I slap you myself."

Astonished, Caroline stopped mid-screech. She looked from her brother to Mr. Darcy, obviously unsure as to why they were not immediately sympathetic to her plight.

"I am afraid, Miss Bingley," Darcy said in icy tones, "that your brother and I were just in conversation in the library." He pointed to the open windows just a few feet above their heads. "Mr. Bingley was extremely upset to hear you speaking to his wife in such a way."

"I..." Caroline took an uncertain step back. "I... she..."

"Is this why you have been so quiet and sad, since we have returned home from Bath?" Mr. Bingley asked Jane, his tone gentle.

Jane hesitated, looking into his eyes, then slowly, she nodded. "I am sorry," she whispered, twisting her hands together. "I have tried everything..."

"This is not in the slightest your fault, dear angel." Mr. Bingley pressed his lips to Jane's brow, and then he looked over the top of her head at his sister and said "Get out."

"I beg your pardon!" Caroline drew herself up straight and looked down her nose at him.

"Get. Out," Mr. Bingley enunciated clearly. "Pack your bags and leave my house. Today."

"Charles, I am your sister!" Caroline's voice rose again. "Where am I supposed to go?" She was almost shrieking.

"I do not care. You have twenty thousand pounds, Caroline; it is entirely within your control. Take it and begone. I am done with your tantrums and your demands. I have weathered it without objection, for the sake of our family, but I will not subject my wife to your petty cruelties, not for one minute longer."

Elizabeth had never imagined that quietly-spoken, mild-mannered, charming Mr. Bingley could look so fierce. His voice remained calm and even, but his eyes were deadly cold, and she could not doubt that he meant every word he said.

"You will never again spend a single night beneath the same roof as my wife," Bingley said steadily. "If you are not out of this house by nightfall, I will have you removed, and you can sleep in the hedgerow for all I care. Now get out of my sight, before I decide that Miss Elizabeth's suggestion has a great deal of merit, and have you spanked thoroughly before you leave to teach you some manners!"

Caroline stared in stunned silence for a moment, and then her whole face flushed red. She stamped her foot, clenched her fists, and started forward, her mouth opening in a wordless scream before she began to hurl invective at Elizabeth. Some of the words she used, Elizabeth had never even heard before.

Bingley covered Jane's ears, and Mr. Darcy stepped in between Elizabeth and Caroline, grasping the latter's arm firmly.

"Control yourself, Miss Bingley," he said sharply. "Let us go inside and find your sister, and set your maids to packing." He glanced over his shoulder at Bingley, who nodded at him gratefully.

The silence which fell as Mr. Darcy led Caroline away was broken only by Jane's soft sobs against her husband's chest.

"I daresay I should not have slapped her, and I apologise, Mr. Bingley," Elizabeth said, feeling her anger drain away now that Miss Bingley was no longer present. "But when I heard her saying those things to Jane..."

"You were quite right to slap her, Miss Elizabeth, and perfectly correct when you said she should probably have been spanked long ago." Bingley stroked Jane's hair as he spoke. "Caroline has ever been spoiled and wilful, but I never imagined she could be so cruel."

There was little Elizabeth could say. Bingley took a still-crying Jane inside the house, and Elizabeth was left alone in the gardens. She walked quietly for a while, trying to find serenity amid nature, and was somehow not surprised when Mr. Darcy fell into step beside her.

"I imagine you are relieved to escape the hysterics upstairs," Elizabeth said, flashing a quick smile at him.

Darcy grimaced. "I confess I strategically removed myself from the scene once the packing commenced. I thought it best to leave Miss Bingley to her sister."

"I must thank you, for what you did for Jane. It was most kind of you," Elizabeth said.

He inclined his head, a faint smile tugging at the corners of his mouth. "It was nothing. Your sister deserves all the happiness in the world, and Bingley is lucky to have her."

"As she is lucky to have him," Elizabeth agreed, her gaze drifting back to the path where the couple had disappeared. "I only hope that one day, I might be so fortunate as to find a love like theirs."

The words were out before she could stop them, and she felt her cheeks heat with embarrassment. What must he think of her, to hear her speak so plainly of such things?

But when she dared to meet his eyes once more, she found no judgment there, only a curious intensity that made her heart race. "I have no doubt, Miss Bennet," he said softly, "that you will find a love that surpasses even theirs. For who could know you, and not love you?"

Elizabeth's breath caught in her throat at his words, scarcely daring to believe what she had heard. "Mr. Darcy," she whispered, "what are you saying?"

He took a step closer, his gaze never leaving hers. "I am saying that you are the most remarkable woman I have ever known. Your wit, your intelligence, your fierce loyalty to those you love - all of these things have captivated me from the moment we met. And today, seeing you willing to go to such extraordinary lengths for your sister, even in the face of such unpleasantness… it only confirmed what I have long believed."

He reached out, taking her hand in his, and Elizabeth marvelled at the warmth of his touch. "Miss Bennet - Elizabeth - I have struggled with my feelings for you, fearing that my attentions would not be welcomed, after my ghastly misstep insulting you on our very first meeting. But I can remain silent no longer. You must allow me to tell you how ardently I admire and love you."

For Elizabeth, for a long moment, the entire world seemed to hold its breath. She could hear nothing over the roaring in her ears; her vision narrowed to Darcy's face, no longer proud but intensely vulnerable as he laid bare his heart to her.

Chapter Twenty-Two

DARCY'S HEART DRUMMED A staccato rhythm in his chest as he awaited Elizabeth's response, her wide, expressive eyes holding his own. The breeze whispered through the towering oaks framing Netherfield's gardens, ruffling tendrils of Elizabeth's hair. After what felt an interminable moment, her lips parted, and Darcy felt suspended on the precipice between elation and despair.

"Mr. Darcy, I..." Elizabeth hesitated, glancing down at their joined hands. Her gentle fingers trembled in his grasp. "I confess I am quite overwhelmed."

"Forgive me," Darcy said quickly, silently berating himself. "I have been too abrupt in my declaration. But Miss Bennet - Elizabeth - surely you must know the depth of my regard, the fervency of my admiration these many months. Not a day has passed that my thoughts have not been consumed by you."

Elizabeth raised her eyes to his once more, and in their depths Darcy perceived the warring of emotion - a glimmer of reciprocated affection vying against a shadow of uncertainty. Her brow furrowed slightly.

"I am deeply honoured by your words, Mr. Darcy. Truly. I had not dared to hope..." She trailed off, worrying her bottom lip between her teeth.

Darcy's pulse hammered in his ears as he awaited her to continue, to put him out of his exquisite misery one way or the other. He knew not how he would bear it if she rejected him, and yet, the hesitation in her manner gave him cause to fear it might be so.

"Please," Darcy whispered, unable to keep the note of pleading from his voice. "Tell me what it is you hesitate to say, Elizabeth. Have I misunderstood your feelings? Is your heart already promised to another?"

He scarce knew how he uttered the words, so painful was the thought of Elizabeth in the arms of another man, smiling up at him as a lover, as a wife. His grip on her hands involuntarily tightened.

"No, no," she hastened to assure him, shaking her head vehemently. "You have not misunderstood. My heart is entirely my own." She paused, gathering her resolve. "That is, it was. Until you captured it so completely."

Darcy's breath escaped him in a ragged exhalation, his shoulders sagging with palpable relief. But Elizabeth was not finished.

"In your character, and in my feelings for you, I have not the slightest reservation," she continued, her voice growing stronger, surer. "Nor in my welcome from certain of your family, namely dear Georgiana, Anne, and your cousin Colonel Fitzwilliam. But I confess... I harbour doubts about my suitability in the eyes of Lady Catherine and Lord and Lady Matlock. I fear they do not consider me a worthy match for one of your consequence, and I know that you respect and honour their opinions."

Darcy's finger beneath her chin gently tilted her face upward, compelling her to meet his earnest gaze. "Elizabeth," he said firmly, willing her to absorb the conviction in his tone, "in this, I assure you, you are mistaken."

A frown creased Elizabeth's brow, confusion and disbelief warring in her expressive eyes. "Mistaken?" she echoed. "But Lady Catherine, at least, has made her disapproval abundantly clear."

Darcy's lips curved into a rueful smile. "Indeed, my aunt's initial reservations were not easily overcome," he acknowledged. "But Elizabeth, you must know - the grace and strength of character you displayed during your time at Rosings did not go unnoticed. You won them over, one and all."

He paused, his fingers tightening around hers as he willed her to understand. "Before I took my leave, each of them - Lady Catherine, Lord and Lady Matlock - expressed to me their wholehearted approval of you as the future mistress of Pemberley. If you were to be my choice."

Elizabeth's heart swelled with incandescent joy as the full import of Darcy's words sank in. The approval of his distinguished relations, the promise of a shared future as man and wife - it was almost too wonderful to be believed.

"Truly?" she breathed, her voice trembling with emotion. "Lady Catherine, Lord and Lady Matlock... they would accept me as your bride? As the mistress of Pemberley?"

Darcy's smile was tender, his eyes brimming with adoration as he gazed down at her. "Most assuredly, my love. They have seen, as I have, the rare gem that you are. Your grace, your keen mind, your generous spirit - you would be an adornment to any family."

He lifted her hands to his lips, brushing reverent kisses across her knuckles. "But most especially to mine. Our union would bring me untold pride and felicity."

Tears of happiness blurred Elizabeth's vision as the last lingering doubts fell away, replaced by a burgeoning sense of belonging, of rightness. This man, this love... it was everything she had scarcely let herself dream of.

"Well then," she managed, her lips curving in a radiant smile even as a crystalline drop spilled onto her cheek. "In that case, my answer can only be yes. Yes, Mr. Darcy, I will marry you. I will be your wife, now and always."

A whoosh of breath left him, his eyes drifting closed as if the weight of the world had lifted from his shoulders. When he opened them again, they glowed with wonder and purest elation.

"My Elizabeth," he rasped. "My dearest, loveliest Elizabeth. You have made me the happiest of men."

With that, he drew her to him, capturing her lips in a searing kiss that left her breathless and weak-kneed, clinging to his shoulders. He poured every ounce of his passion, his devotion into the caress, and she returned it measure for measure, sealing their pledge with the mingling of breath and pulse and all-consuming love.

In that perfect, shining moment, the future unfurled before them, ripe with promise and possibility. Whatever challenges lay ahead, they would face them together, steadfast in the unshakable bond they had forged.

Elizabeth's soul sang with quiet triumph and bone-deep contentment as she lost herself in her beloved's embrace. This, she knew, was a love for the ages - a love that would shelter and sustain them all the days of their lives.

And oh, what a glorious life it would be.

A surprised gasp pierced their blissful interlude, wrenching the lovers back to the present. They broke apart hastily, flushed and flustered, to find Georgiana gaping at them from the garden path, her eyes round as saucers.

"Oh! I do beg your pardon," she stammered, a furious blush staining her cheeks. "I did not mean to intrude. I had no idea..." She trailed off, clearly mortified by her untimely interruption.

Darcy cleared his throat, attempting to regain some semblance of composure. "It is quite all right, Georgiana," he assured her, his voice still rough with emotion. "You have nothing to apologize for." He glanced at Elizabeth, his eyes dancing with barely suppressed mirth. "In fact, your timing could not be more perfect."

Elizabeth bit her lip to contain a giddy laugh, her heart so full it felt fit to burst. "Indeed, Georgiana, we have the most wonderful news to share with you." She reached for Darcy's hand, twining their fingers together in a gesture of unity. "Your brother has asked me to be his wife, and I have accepted."

Georgiana's mouth fell open in a silent "oh" of astonishment, her gaze darting between them as if searching for confirmation. Finding it in their radiant smiles and joined hands, she let out a squeal of pure delight. "Truly? Oh, this is the most marvellous news! I am so very, very happy for you both!"

She flung herself at them, embracing first her brother, then Elizabeth, with unbridled enthusiasm. "I could not have wished for a more perfect sister," she declared, her eyes shining with happy tears. "And Fitzwilliam, I have never seen you so content. It is all I have ever wanted for you."

Darcy's throat worked as he struggled to master his emotions. "Thank you, dearest," he murmured, pressing a tender kiss to his sister's forehead. "Your blessing means the world to us."

Elizabeth's heart swelled with affection for this sweet, guileless girl who would soon be her family. "We are so grateful for your support, Georgiana," she said warmly, squeezing her hand. "I hope you know how much I already love you, and how eagerly I anticipate being your sister in truth."

Georgiana beamed at her, all traces of shyness forgotten in the face of her overwhelming joy. "I feel exactly the same, Elizabeth. We shall be the happiest of families, I just know it."

As the three of them stood together in the sunlit garden, basking in the glow of this momentous occasion, Elizabeth marvelled at the twists of fate that had brought her to this point. Who could have imagined, during those early days of misunderstanding and prejudice, that she would find such profound love and acceptance with the proud, enigmatic Mr. Darcy?

But now, Elizabeth knew beyond a shadow of a doubt that this was where she belonged. With Fitzwilliam by her side and Georgiana's unwavering affection, she could face whatever challenges the future might hold, secure in the knowledge that she was loved, valued, and understood in a way she had never dared to dream possible.

The fading light of day had begun to paint the sky in hues of amber and rose as Darcy and Elizabeth approached the familiar gates of Longbourn. Hand in hand, they walked up the path, their steps in perfect unison, a testament to the deep connection they shared.

As they entered the house, Elizabeth couldn't help but marvel at the surreal nature of the moment. The very walls that had witnessed her growth from a precocious child to a discerning young woman now seemed to pulse with the energy of this new chapter in her life. She squeezed Darcy's hand, drawing strength from his steady presence as they made their way to her father's study.

Mr. Bennet looked up from his book as the couple entered, a knowing smile tugging at the corners of his mouth. "Well, well, what have we here?" he mused, his eyes twinkling with mirth. "I must say, Mr. Darcy, I had begun to wonder if you would ever muster the courage to ask for my Lizzy's hand."

Darcy chuckled, his shoulders relaxing as he realized that Mr. Bennet's words were spoken in jest. "I assure you, sir, it was not a lack of courage that delayed me, but rather a desire to ensure that my affections were truly reciprocated."

Elizabeth, her cheeks flushed with happiness, interjected, "And they are, Papa, most ardently."

Mr. Bennet's gaze softened as he looked upon his beloved daughter. "I have no doubt of that, my dear. I have watched you both these past months, and I can say with certainty that I have never seen two people more perfectly suited to one another." Rising from his chair, he extended his hand to Darcy. "You have my blessing, and my deepest gratitude for making my Lizzy so happy."

As Darcy and Mr. Bennet shook hands, Elizabeth felt a wave of emotion wash over her. In this moment, surrounded by the love and approval of the two most important men in her life, she knew that all the trials and tribulations of the past had been worth it, for they had led her to this perfect, shining moment.

Later, as Darcy took his leave, Elizabeth found herself in the company of her beloved stepmother, Charlotte. The older woman's face was alight with joy as she embraced Elizabeth tightly. "Oh, my dear girl," she exclaimed, "I am so incredibly happy for you. I must confess, I had always hoped that you would find a love match, but never in my wildest dreams did I imagine a match as grand as this."

Elizabeth laughed, her heart full to bursting. "I can scarcely believe it myself! But I know in my heart that Mr. Darcy is the only man for me, and I am so grateful that fate has brought us together."

Charlotte smiled, her eyes shining with pride and affection. "You are more than worthy of this match, Elizabeth. Your intelligence, your strength of character, and your unwavering compassion have always set you apart. Mr. Darcy is a lucky man indeed to have won your heart."

Epilogue

THE PIANOFORTE NOTES FLOATED merrily through the grand drawing room of Pemberley as Georgiana's fingers danced across the keys. Garlands of holly and evergreen boughs adorned the mantelpiece and windows, filling the air with the crisp, earthy scent of the season. A crackling fire cast a warm glow across the smiling faces of family gathered together once more.

Charlotte allowed herself a small, secret smile as she observed her assembled family. Mary, recently wed to the kind and bookish Dr. Watley, had blossomed under his attentions, her serene countenance reflecting the joy of a contented heart. Even flighty

Lydia appeared more settled since her marriage to Captain Denny, her laughter now born of genuine mirth rather than empty frivolity.

But it was Kitty who drew Charlotte's discerning eye. The once directionless girl now carried herself with a quiet dignity, her gaze frequently straying to the tall, handsome gentleman at Mr. Darcy's side. Mr. Tom Bertram, Charlotte had learned, was not only a particular friend of Mr. Darcy's but also stood to inherit a baronetcy and a considerable estate in Northamptonshire. The admiration in his eyes as he regarded Kitty spoke volumes.

"Well, well," Mr. Bennet murmured, following Charlotte's gaze. "It appears our Kitty may soon have an announcement of her own to make. A baronet, no less!"

Charlotte chuckled softly. "Indeed, my dear. Though I suspect Kitty's affections are engaged by more than mere titles and estates."

"As they should be," Mr. Bennet agreed, a wry smile tugging at his lips. "We Bennets have a talent for securing spouses far above our station. I credit you with setting the example, Mrs. Bennet."

Charlotte's gaze drifted to where Mr. Darcy stood, his normally stern countenance softened by obvious pride and contentment as he surveyed the domestic scene before him. He never strayed far from Elizabeth's side, Charlotte had noted, standing now where he could watch her sitting between Jane and Kitty, all three of them laughing as they listened to Lydia telling a humorous anecdote.

"What a joyous occasion it is to have all my daughters under one roof again," Mr. Bennet remarked. "I daresay Pemberley has never seen such liveliness!"

Charlotte smiled. "It does my heart good to see them so happy. Our girls have grown into fine young women."

"Indeed they have, my dear. And it is in no small part thanks to you." Mr. Bennet patted her hand fondly. "You have been a true mother to them in every way that matters."

Warmth blossomed in Charlotte's chest at his words, and she drew a steadying breath, preparing to tell her husband the secret she had been holding close to her heart for some weeks now. Before she could begin, however, he spoke again.

"I suppose it shan't be long now before we are overrun with a veritable army of grandchildren!"

Charlotte smiled, a slight nervousness fluttering in her belly as she met her husband's gaze. She knew the moment had come to share her news, yet a part of her hesitated, savouring these last few seconds before their world would change forever. Her hand drifted unconsciously to her midsection, a gesture that did not go unnoticed by the observant Mr. Bennet.

"Charlotte?" he queried, a note of concern creeping into his voice. "Is everything quite all right?"

She took a deep breath, steeling herself for the revelation to come. "Indeed, Mr. Bennet, everything is more than all right. It's just that I…" She trailed off, suddenly at a loss for words.

Mr. Bennet's brow furrowed. "You what, my dear? Come now, out with it. You know you can tell me anything."

Charlotte felt a rush of love for this man who had become her partner in every sense of the word. She reached out, taking his hand in hers and giving it a gentle squeeze. "I'm afraid you may have to wait a bit longer for those grandchildren, Mr. Bennet. It seems that before you are to be a grandfather, you shall first be a father again."

For a long moment, Mr. Bennet simply stared at her, his expression unreadable. Then, to Charlotte's immense relief, he let out a great crack of laughter. "Well, well! It appears that even in my dotage, I am not yet past my prime. Mr. Collins will be most displeased to learn of this development, I daresay."

Charlotte couldn't help but laugh at her husband's jest, feeling a weight lift from her shoulders at his obvious delight. "I'm sure he will find a way to bear the disappointment," she replied wryly. "After all, he has Lady Catherine to console him. And there is, of course, no guarantee I will give you a son to carry on Longbourn's legacy."

Mr. Bennet's eyes softened as he drew Charlotte closer, his hand coming to rest gently upon her still-flat belly. "A legacy that you, Mrs. Bennet, have played no small part in securing. I could not ask for a more excellent wife or mother to my children, and I care not if you give me a son or another five daughters."

Tears pricked at Charlotte's eyes as she leaned into her husband's embrace, the love and contentment that filled the room enveloping them both. In this moment, surrounded by the laughter and joy of their family, the future had never seemed so bright nor so full of promise.

~ The End ~

If you enjoyed this book, why not try another of my Austen variations? Read on for a free sample chapter of *A Loss at Longbourn*!

A Loss at Longbourn – sample chapter

THE NETHERFIELD BALL

"Those girls are an embarrassment," Caroline Bingley declared to Mrs Hurst, glaring as Lydia and Kitty Bennet ran by, shrieking. "Why they are out in society I cannot conceive." She spoke loudly, obviously uncaring that Elizabeth stood close by with Charlotte Lucas, well within hearing range.

"Don't say anything, Lizzy!" Charlotte caught at Elizabeth's sleeve. "She is our hostess, remember!"

"I know." Elizabeth, like Charlotte, kept her voice soft so that Caroline Bingley would not overhear. "And, Charlotte, for once I am in agreement with Miss Bingley. Lydia and Kitty should not be Out."

Charlotte made no response, and Elizabeth, at that moment spying both her father passing by and Mr. Collins heading determinedly in her direction, decided to escape the one in the company of the other. Hurrying to her father's side, she tucked her hand into his arm.

"And how are you enjoying yourself, Lizzy?" Mr. Bennet enquired genially, smiling fondly down at her. "Sitting out this one? I saw you dancing with Mr. Darcy, a fine pair you make."

"It pleases you to jest with me, Papa." Elizabeth smiled up at him, then sighed as Lydia and Kitty squealed past again. "Papa..."

"I know full well what you want to say, Lizzy, and I regret that my answer is still No. Your mother would make my life not worth living if I sent Kitty and Lydia back to the schoolroom, no matter how much they would benefit from it."

"Perhaps not back to the schoolroom, Papa, but a firmer hand from you... Surely you must see that their behaviour casts our whole family in a most unfortunate light!" Elizabeth caught sight of Mr. Darcy at that moment, frowning deeply as one of the officers pursuing Lydia almost barged into him. The young man pulled up as though shot as Mr. Darcy's fearsome glare landed upon him, backing hastily away.

"We'll see, Lizzy." Mr. Bennet brought his free hand up to rub at his chest. "I for one shall be glad when the evening is over."

The dance ended just then and they found themselves close to Jane and Mr. Bingley, who came over to speak with them.

"Are you feeling quite well, Mr. Bennet?" Mr. Bingley enquired solicitously. "You look somewhat wearied. Perhaps you would care to peruse Netherfield's library, meagre though it is compared to your own."

Mr. Bennet brightened considerably, though he continued to rub at his chest. "I should be delighted, Bingley."

"Let me summon Peters to conduct you there."

Elizabeth watched her father go, pleased he would find at least some entertainment to his liking in the evening. Jane caught at her hand and the two shared a smile before Elizabeth spotted Mr. Collins again.

"Oh, no," she said under her breath, but Jane heard her, and in one quick glance understood the situation.

"Mr. Bingley, you have not danced yet with my dearest sister," she said sweetly, placed Elizabeth's hand in his and moved elegantly away to intercept Mr. Collins. "Why, cousin, are you not having a wonderful time tonight? I declare I could dance all night, if there were but partners enough!"

"She is too good to me," Elizabeth could not help but say.

"Your sister is an angel," Mr. Bingley said quietly, and Elizabeth looked up at him. They smiled at each other in perfect accord.

The following morning, Darcy and Caroline did their best to persuade Bingley to London. He agreed, but said that they would go the following day. One more day would make little difference, after all, and he intended to go to Longbourn to bid Jane farewell in person. A letter from Caroline would be too impersonal, he insisted, and Darcy eventually sighed and acquiesced. And thought to himself that just one more look at Miss Elizabeth, one more gaze into those beautiful eyes, before he farewelled her for the last time, would make no difference. It would be hard enough to forget her as it was.

The two gentlemen rode over to Longbourn after nuncheon, suspecting correctly that there would be many late risers at Longbourn that morning. They were admitted at the front door by Hill, who bobbed a curtsy and led them towards the parlour. But before they got there, the door to Mr. Bennet's study suddenly crashed open and Jane came stumbling out.

"Hill – oh, Hill, my father is not well... MAMA!" And then she saw the two men and, white-faced, clutched at Bingley's arm, all that serenity and reserve stripped away in an instant and her true emotions clear for them to see. "Charles, oh Charles, help me, I don't know what to do!" She stared up at him, her eyes terrified but trusting that somehow he would make everything all right.

Darcy didn't hesitate. He pushed straight past Jane and the frozen Mrs Hill and into the study. Mr. Bennet was slumped over in his favourite reading chair, grey-faced. And not breathing. A cup of tea had been placed on the table by his elbow, obviously put there by Jane before she actually looked at her father.

One touch of the man's hand and Darcy knew they were too late. Bennet's skin was already cold. He'd been dead for several hours, at least. Whirling, he moved back to the door to try and block entry, but Elizabeth, the first to respond to Jane's screams, was already passing the doorway.

"Don't look..." he tried his best to protect her, but one glance and she knew.

"Papa..." her voice was a scant whisper, and she went to her father, ducking under Darcy's outstretched arm. Falling to her knees at Mr. Bennet's feet, she took one cold hand in hers and pressed her brow to it. "Oh, Papa, what shall I do now?"

Judging that Elizabeth was not about to go into hysterics, Darcy headed back into the hall, where Bingley was doing his best to comfort a distraught Jane. Darcy met Bingley's enquiring look with a shake of his head.

"We must send for the doctor..." Jane said then, and Darcy sighed.

"Miss Bennet – we shall. But it is too late, I fear."

Mrs Bennet arrived then, entering immediately into quite the wildest fit of hysterics Darcy had ever seen, screaming about them all being tossed from their home to starve in the hedgerows. Collins came down the stairs and Mrs Bennet promptly fainted, which at least reduced the noise level.

The house was thrown into uproar. Jane and Elizabeth, while distraught, were at least calm. Both Darcy and Bingley found their dislike for Collins massively increased, as he walked about pontificating smugly, saying that of course, his dear cousins should not leave Longbourn, they should all stay there together and once their mourning period was over, they should all be sisters to him anyway once Miss Elizabeth became his wife.

"Miss Elizabeth?" Darcy turned in astonishment. The three men were waiting in the front parlour for the arrival of the vicar, since Collins did not seem desirous of performing any clerical offices for his cousin. "*You* are engaged to Miss Elizabeth?"

"Well," Collins hedged, "there is an understanding. Your esteemed aunt, Lady Catherine de Bourgh, sent me here for the express purpose of selecting a wife from among my cousins, and while Miss Bennet would naturally have been my first choice, it appears that her heart is already bestowed elsewhere." He gave a slight bow to Mr. Bingley, who looked absolutely astonished.

As well he might, Darcy thought bleakly, for had not Caroline and he been doing their best to convince Bingley that Jane was indifferent to him, pushed on him by her insufferable mother? Not that Bingley would ever believe that now, not considering the way Jane had looked at him in the hallway. Darcy had not the slightest notion the cool and collected Miss Bennet was even capable of such depth of emotion until that moment.

Collins was blathering again, but Darcy no longer heard. Bennet would not have been such a fool as to bestow his daughter on this twittering idiot, even if Elizabeth herself had been agreeable, he thought. But Bennet was dead, and the pressure on Elizabeth would be incredible. What choice would she have, really? Her family was about to be sequestered in mourning, and when they came out of it, her choices would be limited to marrying Mr. Collins, or seeing her family homeless. Darcy did not doubt that the fawning lickspittle would turn nasty if thwarted.

"I fear you are mistaken, Mr. Collins," Darcy found himself saying. "For only last night at the ball, when Mr. Bennet and I spoke privately together in the library, I asked him for permission to formally court Miss Elizabeth." From the corner of his eye he saw Bingley turning to look at him, mouth agape, but he ploughed on. "Mr. Bennet was in agreement. I am quite certain he would have mentioned to me any *understanding* between yourself and Miss Elizabeth." He'd been in there for no more than a minute or two with Bennet, and the pair of them had not exchanged more than half a dozen words, but there were no witnesses to say otherwise.

Collins spluttered to an astonished halt. "What – but..." was all he managed to get out for two full minutes, and then he gathered himself. "But, Mr. Darcy, you are engaged to Miss Anne de Bourgh!"

"I most certainly am not," Darcy responded, his eyebrows lifting disdainfully.

"But Lady Catherine said that you had an understanding..."

"My cousin and I are both quite clear that we shall not marry. The understanding you speak of, Mr. Collins, exists solely in the mind of the one person who desires that union – Lady Catherine herself. Rather as I suspect the understanding between yourself and Miss Elizabeth to be."

"Certainly not – Mrs Bennet..."

"Mrs Bennet rightly feared that her husband might die and leave them all dependent on your mercy," Bingley interrupted. "She did as any mother who loves her daughters would do, her very best to see them all comfortably settled."

Collins just stood, blinking, staring between the two of them. But Darcy could already see that furtive little mind working, calculating how he could still have Elizabeth.

"Collins, you are of course from this day forward no longer dependent on my aunt's goodwill," he said, doing his best to be kind. "But allow me to tell you that she would never have approved Miss Elizabeth as a match for you. Miss Elizabeth is too independent, too inclined to speak her mind. She would not be at all suitable for the wife of a clergyman." As soon as he had spoken, Darcy realised he should have left out the last part of the statement.

"But she will not be the wife of a clergyman – she will be mistress of Longbourn," Collins said triumphantly. "A post for which you cannot deny she is eminently suited."

"I do not deny, sir, that she is well suited for a position as mistress of an estate. I had in mind Pemberley for her, though."

To that, there was no viable response that Collins could possibly make. Darcy turned, avoiding Bingley's eye, and moved to the door. He had spied through the window the vicar walking briskly up the drive.

Want to find out what happens next? Read A Loss At Longbourn- now!

Also By Catherine Bilson

The Blushing Brides Series

An Earl For Ellen

A Marquis For Marianne

A Duke For Diana

A Captain For Clarissa

The Bookshop Belles series (co-written with Ebony Oaten)

Estelle's Ardent Admirer

Marie's Merry Gentleman

Louise's Christmas Champion

Bernadette's Dashing Doctor

Matthew's Willing Widow

The Brides of Belle Haven series

A Bride For Belle Haven (prequel novella)

Good Golly, Miss Molly

Miss Clara and the Marquess

Miss Anna's Mistake

Miss Eliza Takes Charge

Miss Charlotte Makes A Mess

Miss Laura In Love

Miss Louise Meddles

Regency Novels

His Darling Duchess

Phoebe And The Pea

Kidnapping Lord Blaymire

The Captain's Runaway Bride

The Wassail Wager

The Bride Said No

St. George and the River Horse

Christmas Courting (collection of novellas)

American Pioneer Romance

Coming From California

Returning From Rhode Island

Pride & Prejudice Variations

The Best Of Relations

Infamous Relations

Mr Bingley's Bride
A Christmas Miracle At Longbourn

Grief and Grievances

The Second Mrs. Bennet

A Loss At Longbourn

The Meddling Matlocks

Lydia and the Colonel (forthcoming)

The Secret Diary of Anne de Bourgh (forthcoming)

The Crime & Consequences Trilogy

Malice and Misfortune

Rivalry and Ruination

Intrigue and Inheritance

<u>Sign up to the Shenanigans Press newsletter to find out about our latest new releases!</u>

Made in the USA
Monee, IL
28 April 2026

49136208R00184